D1032207

POSTMARK
BAYOU CHENE

POSTMARK BAYOU CHENE

A NOVEL

GWEN ROLAND

LOUISIANA STATE UNIVERSITY PRESS
BATON ROUGE

Published with the assistance of the Borne Fund

Published by Louisiana State University Press
Copyright © 2015 by Gwen Roland
All rights reserved
Manufactured in the United States of America
First printing

Designer: Laura Roubique Gleason
Typefaces: Whitman, text; Brandon Printed, display
Printer and binder: Maple Press

Library of Congress Cataloging-in-Publication Data

Roland, Gwen, 1948–
    Postmark Bayou Chene : a novel / Gwen Roland.
        pages ; cm
    ISBN 978-0-8071-6144-9 (hardcover : acid-free paper) — ISBN 978-0-8071-6145-6 (pdf) — ISBN 978-0-8071-6146-3 (epub) — ISBN 978-0-8071-6147-0 (mobi) 1. Atchafalaya River Valley (La.) —Social life and customs—Fiction. 2. Atchafalaya River Delta (La.) —Social life and customs—Fiction. 3. Louisiana—Social life and customs—Fiction I. Title.
    PS3618.O5375P67 2016
    813'.6—dc23

2015006258

The paper in this book meets the guidelines for permanence and durability of the Committee on Production Guidelines for Book Longevity of the Council on Library Resources. ∞

In memory of Maggie,
the lab-beagle whose courage and loyalty inspired
the character Drifter.

And for the old Bayou Cheners,
who knew that we never die as long as someone,
somewhere, is telling our stories.

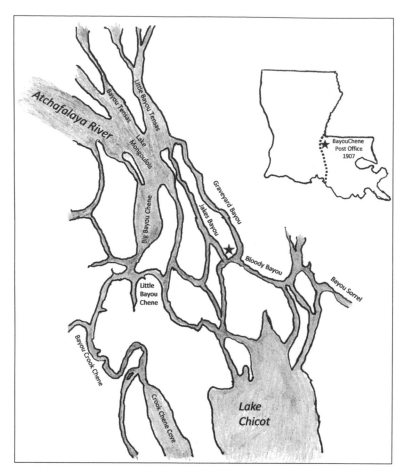

Ancient network of bayous around Bayou Chene, based on Abbot map (1863).
Inset showing approximate channel of Atchafalaya River today. Illustration by
Preston Roland.

AUTHOR'S NOTE

Bayou Chene (pronounced *Shane*) means "Oak Bayou" in French. Named for the live oaks that once lined its banks, Bayou Chene is a natural distributary of the Atchafalaya River in South Louisiana. The name also refers to a village site located along the network of bayous in that area and inhabited from ancient times until the mid-twentieth century.

The people of Bayou Chene didn't tell stories to transfer information so much as to expand themselves, capture their listeners, take the floor, pass the time of day, give themselves to their audience. They most often found that audience at the Bayou Chene Post Office, which doubled as a general store (or saloon, depending on who's telling the story), located at different homesteads through the generations.

While its characters and events are loosely based on anecdotes, rumors, myths, gossip, outright lies, and a few facts handed down through proud descendants of Bayou Chene, this book is a work of fiction meant to celebrate the independent spirit and resourcefulness of what has been called the last frontier community in the United States.

POSTMARK
BAYOU CHENE

— 1 —

April 3, 1907, kicked off a fracas around Bayou Chene. They all agreed on that much. What they never could agree on was what started it all in the first place.

Fate Landry said:

It all started with that empty skiff, if you ask me. Oh, I'd a noticed it right off because of the colors, even if it hadn't come floating around the bend empty. Unless, of course, you counted the dog, which I did. Wasn't in the skiff so much as floating alongside, towed by the bowline around its neck.

Wasn't good daylight yet. April mornings take their time waking up in South Louisiana. You know how it is. Come August, now, it's a different story. That summer sun rouses up so quick and strong, it's like it never went to bed at all but just stepped behind the trees and come out on the other side.

But back to that empty skiff. I was bailing rainwater out of my boat when here it comes looking like an alligator gone blind. It bumped into Ron Theriot's log dock like it was looking for something and then poked its nose into a mat of willow roots on the bank. That's when the current caught the stern around, the willows let go of the bow, and that dog's body swung out just as graceful as a cast net. That's when I saw it was a skiff not built around here. Blue and black, at that!

Out here on the Chene our skiffs flare out on the sides so they float high like an acorn cap; it makes them quick to steer with an extra push on one oar or the other. This skiff floated deep and straight like a water trough or a coffin.

It was big in every way—longer, wider, and higher than anything we use around here. How it didn't get hung up coming around some of those tight bends, I couldn't tell. Wouldn't have made it in low water, that's for sure. The more I studied that setup, the dog seemed the most normal-looking thing about it.

It didn't take nothing for me to snag that blue and black oddity with my paddle as it went past. I always keep a knife handy for the day a line's gonna wrap around my leg just when I toss a net or anchor overboard. It happens to every fisherman at least once, and I know my time's coming. Could be what happened to the owner of that skiff.

That morning I used it to saw through the line towing that dog. Then I lifted her out of the water and laid her on my seat. All four legs still there, a miracle considering the number of gators paddling these waters. That meant the body hadn't been overboard long, probably just a few hours.

Black and stocky she was, with a square, broad head. Her muzzle was white and freckled like a bird dog, and there was bayou water puddled in the flap. Sharp white teeth, so she was young. Patch of white fur run across the chest and down her stomach. Sturdy black legs ending in white feet, kind of webbed between the toes. Never saw such before. She would've been a strong swimmer, probably kept up with the boat longer than most dogs.

A wedge of ear flopped down over one eye. Don't ask me why, but I moved it. That very second her eyelid quivered like the tail of a squirrel trying to decide whether to run or not. I pushed my hand flat against her chest, right under the front leg. It was cold as death and dripping, but way down deep I felt the faintest beat tapping against my hand.

"Lafayette Landry, what you got down there!"

It was my cousin Loyce Snellgrove on the porch of the Bayou Chene Post Office and General Store. I could smell coffee and wood smoke drifting down with her voice. She uses my whole name when she's feeling testy, which is most of the time if you ask me. I was named for my daddy, but he went by Lauf, and they call me Fate.

"A dog, Loyce, a drowned dog, or just about anyway," I grunted and kept on rubbing at that dog's chest. Then I pushed hard right under her rib cage, making water dribble from her mouth.

"What do you mean just about? Is it dead or not?"

"It's a she and more dead than alive."

I pushed harder. More water poured out, and she roused up enough to cough.

"That sounds more alive than dead to me—bring her on up here," Loyce bossed, just like always when I'm about to do something anyway. She thinks she's got to be the one to come up with what I aim to do next just because she's four months older than me.

I took my time tying that skiff to the dock, and, sure enough, I heard Loyce slap her leg with her hand. That's what she does when she gets testy and I'm out of reach. When I picked up the dog, water dripped from both ends of her onto the plank walk for the twenty steps it took me to get to the porch. It still takes Loyce more than thirty, like when we were little.

"Hey, what you got there, Fate? Baiting with dog now?"

I swiveled my eyes over and saw Valzine Broussard standing at the edge of the woods path coming from the docks. Val's part Irish, which might explain all that yellow hair and a leaning toward clothes you don't see around here much.

"Not exactly, but dog might work better'n some bait I've used," I said. "She drifted up just now tied to that blue skiff over yonder."

Val squinted toward the dock. He's part Cajun, too, and talks sort of Frenchified sometimes.

"I seen plenty boats on the river," he said. "Don't hardly see no blue and black 'tween here and Morgan City. That's for true."

Like I didn't know that. Here on the Chene we use red and green. Maybe the old Cheners made a good trade with a steamboat for some red and green paint—I don't know. If there's a better reason, no one old enough to remember it ever told me. All me or anyone else knew was that our boats had always been red and green.

"And high sides like that usually mean a boat come off the Mississippi, not out in the swamps like this," Val went on.

3

He was just showing off for Loyce now, in my opinion. He's been sweet on her all his life. Seeing as he's first mate on the *Golden Era*, Val thinks he knows more than anyone else about what kinds of boats come from where. Just because he's been on boats since he was so little he had to tie hisself to the deck to keep from blowing overboard. I know all that about him, and more, because we been best friends forever. Like I knew he was gonna right then give that silky red scarf a twirl around his neck. It's one of the things he does when he's thinking hard.

He was right about them high sides, I'll give him that. It don't get rough enough for high sides, even out on the 'Chafalaya, unless there's an uncommon high water or a bad storm. That skiff had to come from up the Mississippi.

"That's right, would've come down through Lake Mongoulois," I said, beating him to it. "Some poor upriver person done lost his boat, his dog, and everything else, probably dead to boot."

"Well, either keep standing there talking, and we'll bury her later, or bring her on up here and see if we can save her," Loyce said.

She had the door open, so all I had to do was duck through and carry that sad little bundle to the back of the stove, where there's always a box of rags. It was warm back there and felt good when I crouched down to make a little nest with my free hand. I moved the pup to the crook of my elbow and rubbed her with the towel Loyce had ready. Then I laid her down to see what would happen next. Nothing.

When I stood up, Loyce was pouring scalded milk halfway up a cup for Val. Two more cups already had milk in them for me and her, like usual. She put the milk pan back on the stove and picked up the coffeepot with her right hand, using her left to steer the spout over the cups. When it was aimed just right over each one, she moved her hand down where she could feel the temperature of the cup change as the hot coffee eased up the side of it. She always clangs the pot when she sets it back down on the warming eye. She likes being in charge of such a loud sound.

"Let's give her time to warm up," she said, handing me and Val our cups.

We followed Loyce through the doorway and along the dogtrot that divides the post office side from the house side. The porch runs across the whole front of the building, giving a fine view up Jakes Bayou toward Lake Mongoulois and, if you turn the other way, downstream toward Bloody Bayou. I had the habit of sitting out there watching everything wake up since my houseboat faces the wrong way for sunrise.

It's always been my favorite time of day, just before everyone else starts stirring in the houses and houseboats along the banks. In an hour or so skiffs and pirogues would be tying up at the dock in front of the post office. People on foot and horseback, most of them kin to me one way or another and some more than once, would start turning onto the dirt road that runs along the bank, scaring late-leaving possums back into the woods for the day.

Then the steamboats that had laid over for the night would fire up. Loyce could always beat me at identifying their whistles. Some pitched so high they hurt your ears, others so low you felt them in your stomach more than heard them. A few were pure as the calliope on a showboat; others sounded like a boar hog with the croup. No matter how they sounded, they was all saying the same thing—it was time for deck hands to leave whatever pastime they had found and get ready to cut loose for Morgan City to the south or the Mississippi River and parts north. Smaller packet boats would be redding up for trips east through Bayou Plaquemine or west by way of Bayou Teche.

Railroads suck off a lot of the boat traffic now, but Bayou Chene draws more commerce than you might expect right smack here in the middle of the 'Chafalaya Swamp, and almost all of it ties in some way or another to the post office and general store, which has been run by different branches of my family going way back.

But for right then it was quiet in that time between the owls and roosters. The air was still night cool. I could tell by looking at Loyce she was waiting for the first rays of sunlight to fork through the tree trunks right at the waterline and play across her face. I'd watched her wait for that signal more mornings than I could count. It was her way of knowing that daylight had come again. She's been blind since before she could walk, much less remember.

Loyce tells it this way:

Oh, I knew something was up when I heard Fate's bailing change tunes while I was still at the top of the stairs. I'd stopped to hitch up the knot at the end of my braid. I listened awhile before starting down again. I like to slide my hand along the banister just to feel the smoothness. It's cypress, like the rest of the house built by Great-Grandpa Wash Landry for my Great-Grandma Viney, who was Viney Seneca back then. That was during the westward expansion frenzy of their day, after President Jefferson bought the Louisiana Territory from Napoleon. Most everyone back in civilization thought the president had slap lost his mind, but the people out here didn't care one way or the other.

Lots of people started coming through the Chene then, some on purpose and some just getting sidetracked on their way somewhere else. Men living in surveying camps or timber camps said a lot of things to Bayou Chene girls in those days, and Wash wasn't the first one who had taken a shine to Viney. She didn't pay his court much mind and barely noticed when his camp pulled up stakes and moved on. Then one cold winter night, more than a year later, Wash came knocking on her daddy's door, telling Viney his surveying stint was over and he was ready to settle down.

Not one to let romance turn her head so far as to get a crick in her neck, Viney agreed to marry Wash Landry if he built her a proper home. No little ol' slab and moss shack like some swamp families made do in but a two-story house of planed cypress like the ones rich people all over the country were building from 'Chafalaya cypress. They said termites didn't eat it and bees didn't drill it. I don't know about all that since termites would drown in a hurry out here, and I've felt sawdust drifting down from many a buzzing bee on my porch. But I *can* tell you it smells like fresh cypress needles no matter how old it gets.

Anyway, from what I gather, Viney wasn't setting outrageous standards for Wash. Timber made its first big boom around then so that more big houses were mixing in with the older shacks and houseboats lining the banks. A fair number of sugar plantations were taking hold by then, too, even some sugar mills. So, once Viney was solidly on board, so to speak, Grandpa figured it made good sense to go ahead and build their house big enough to run a store on one side. Being a surveyor, he was good with figures, so when the U.S. Postal Service thought Bayou Chene was big enough to have a post office, he got the contract. Our family has been right here ever since.

I never got to meet Great-Grandpa Wash or Great-Grandma Viney, but they say she once killed a wildcat under the steps with a broom. If you're only gonna pass down one thing about a person, that says a lot.

But that was then, and now was now. Wildcats didn't lurk under steps around the Chene anymore, and I had to start early on the net I was knitting for Alcide Verret. So, instead of waiting for the fresh milk Papa was probably squeezing out of the Jersey right about then, I just poured a slug from the day before into two cups—then three—when I heard Val's voice. He can show up most any time.

I can't say I miss being able to see since I can't even remember it. Papa said it started as an ear infection that got worse instead of better, and by the time that got me to a doctor in Morgan City, it was too late to save my eyes, but they did save my brain, which if I would've had to make the choice myself is exactly the way I would have gone. Like I say, you don't miss something you can't remember, but at times I do squirm under the pure inconvenience of it. I could tell from the rainwater Fate was pouring back into the bayou that our Grandma Mame wouldn't be watering the geraniums and hollyhocks in front of the porch that day. Then he stopped bailing.

Without even thinking about it, I was following his move-

7

ments out of habit and nothing better to do. The bailing can in mid-scoop plinking water onto the bottom of his boat. His paddle grabbing hollow wood. Something sizable being lifted, dripping, from the bayou. The cough. Then his boots coming heavier than usual up the plank walk. Only twenty steps, as he never lets me forget. Sighted people act impressed as all get out at how much I know about what's going on, but it's just a matter of paying attention, that's all. They could do the same if they just took time and paid attention.

Like right then. I just stood still and waited, knowing that whatever had interrupted Fate's morning was going to bust in on mine. That's what always happens with Fate.

"Well, either keep standing there talking, and we'll bury her later, or bring her on up here and see if we can save her," I said. "Val, you can put the mail over there for Papa; he's still in the cow lot."

"*Mais cher!* How you knew I had the mail?" Val asked, tossing the sack on the bench where I had pointed.

"Unless you've taken to wearing leather chaps and picked up a limp since the last time you were here, I figure you're toting something on one shoulder that smells like the mail bag," I told him.

I swear, sometimes sighted people are so simpleminded. It's as if being able to see with their eyes keeps them from using their other senses.

After we settled the dog behind the stove, we took our cups out to the porch, but there was no settling down for Fate. That's the way he is when something's on his mind. Before Val and I were half through with our coffee, he was back in the kitchen messing with that basket full of nearly dead dog. I heard him dragging her from behind the woodstove and figured I better go on and help before he worried her slap to death.

I took the towel from Fate, knelt down, and started rubbing from her ears all the way to her tail. She was cold and limp from one end to the other. Soon her coat was barely damp, but I still couldn't feel any sign of life. Had I imagined that cough down at the bayou bank?

"I don't know, Loyce, I done seen my share of drowned critters, and I'm thinking this is one of 'em," Val said. I was already thinking the same thing myself. No surprise. Val and I think alike uncommonly often. Fate says Val's sweet on me. I guess that could be so. I know he treats me better than my own cousin. Besides, we never hear stories floating back down the river about Val being shot at or chased by some father or jealous husband. Those rumors been drifting back from Fate's tomcatting since he should've been too little to know what it was all about.

Right then, Fate fetched another towel he had put in the warming oven. I edged away so he could wrap it around the dog. Just like him to drag this thing in, stir everyone up, and then we have a mess on our hands. We squatted there together, him breathing uselessly on my neck while I rubbed her chest some more under the warm towel. Suddenly I felt a quiver run through the body, right before Fate and Val started yammering, "Look her eyes are opening," and elbowing each other like they were responsible for breathing life back into her all on their own without any help from God or me and my hard-rubbing hands.

"Hey, is this some new kind of laying on of hands?" Papa's voice came from the back door, followed by the thump of the milk bucket on the table. The smell of the cow came with him, along with the peppermint his feet had crushed at the back steps and the morning scent of the woods out back.

"Hmmm, that one might be a lost cause," he said.

"Just a drifter—showed up with that skiff," Fate said, and I could feel him nodding toward the dock.

Papa sloshed some milk from the bucket into a bowl, while Fate told him the story, embellishing his part way beyond good taste in my opinion. I rolled her so that she rested on her belly and Fate could hold the bowl in front of her nose. I didn't have to say anything—we always could work together that way.

I felt her ribs rise in short little spurts while she breathed in the smell of that sweet, warm milk. I even felt the little blink when she opened her eyes. Then the tap, tap, tap when her tongue reached out, touched the milk, and drew back with a little slurpy sound. Again and again, the sound picked up speed until it was a flutter. Then a smeary sound as she polished off the bottom of the bowl. Finally, she sighed and dropped her head back down on the towel.

"Put her basket behind the stove; she can stay here long enough to see if she's going to pull through," I told Fate, who had started moving in that direction before I'd even made up my mind. He's like that. "But it's up to you to figure out what to do with her, since you're the one who brought her here," I added, just so he'd know I was still in charge of what goes on behind the stove in my kitchen.

"Well, I figured you could use a good dog," Fate said. I could hear him tucking the towel closer around her before standing up, putting off having to face me.

"What? And have one more thing to stumble over?" I slapped my thigh, a habit I'm prone to when agitated, something that happens a lot when Fate's around. "You keep me bruised enough, leaving things setting about all over the place. More's the wonder I don't just stay head over heels!"

"Well, she could be protection," he went right on, like my opinions on what lived in my house wasn't any more than the sound of the frogs outside harping on last night's rain.

"And what do I need protecting from other than your schemes?" I shot right back. "I know everybody who's likely to walk in here, kin to most of them, and I'm never alone anyway."

"Well, what about when you go outside, *enh?*" Val broke in. "Maybe she could learn to take you different places. Me, I done heard of dogs doing that."

"If she could do that, we could make some money showing her off," Fate said, and I could hear him start pacing.

Thinking, talking, and moving are all of a piece for him. I cocked my ear to catch how his feet and his tongue would outrun his brain this time.

His voice drifted down from about a head taller than most men who come around here. I remember the summer a few years back when he started growing past me until finally my feet were off the ground when he lifted me to his level, something he does regularly, no matter how much I slap his hands and tell him not to. That was around the time his voice started to break until he sounded like a honking *gros bec* flying to roost on a spring evening. After a while it came back deeper, taking me by surprise when I came home from the Blind School for good last year. That's what everyone calls it—the Blind School, like a building can see or not—but the real name is the Louisiana School for the Deaf and Blind. I went all the way through the eleventh grade and graduated—making me the most educated girl from the Chene so far. Truth be told, I have more schooling than most girls anywhere in the state, thanks to being blind.

Those years I was gone, everything about Fate grew, even his laugh. These days it rumbles from somewhere deep in his belly. Even the smell of him grew stronger, but I don't mind that, considering all the powerful smells that float around here on a hot day. In fact, I always liked his smell better than anyone else I know, even when he's being a torment, which is most of the time. Take his highfalutin' plans to make easy money.

"Make some money, hmmmmph? Just like you did with that goat-powered butter churn that left the porch ceiling smelling like sour milk for months?" I asked, even though we all knew there was no question to it.

"Well, that one came close. Wambly said it would have worked if that goat had been more tractable. I swear, Loyce, I could have had her churning her own milk into butter in no time and with no effort on our part."

"Our part! When was the last time you spent any effort trying to do anything except listening to that no-good Wambly Cracker and trying to get out of work."

Wambly Cracker is a peddler. Farm equipment mostly. When he makes rounds to that college in Baton Rouge, he picks up snatches of information from the researchers. He weaves all those snatches together into schemes to sell more equipment. He keeps things stirred up among the swampers, and it seems someone is always hot on his trail. Fate's the only person who constantly falls for the crazy ideas he comes peddling around here.

"You got it all wrong, Loyce," Fate pushed on ahead. "Those ain't just Wambly's ideas. They come right out of that college up there in Baton Rouge. They do research with real scientists. It ain't his fault if sometimes things don't work out here. They probably have a better class of goats up there at the research farm than we have out here in the swamp."

"Hmmph. Seems to me his research is all about ruining as many families as he can out here to make more time for sitting on his big butt inside the store."

"What would a blind girl know about the size of Wambly's butt?" Fate said, always quick to take the first rabbit trail off his shortcomings.

"I don't need eyes to feel the breeze from his coattails—they must be the size of a cast net. Or to hear the way a porch banister groans when he hauls himself up the steps. And his big feet flapping across the floor like shutters in a hurricane. Since his voice is on the same level as my ears when I'm sitting down, I figure he must be just about as wide as he is tall. Am I right?"

"You got 'im, *cher*, for true!" Val hooted. "Right down to the coattails. All you left out was the li'l derby hat perched on top his greasy hair like a cow patty."

Some images do make blindness a blessing.

I felt the breeze from Fate's arms beating the air, marking time with his words. "Go ahead and say what you want, but I know when I'm onto something."

"And you think a dog leading a blind girl around an island might be it?" I gave my thigh a good slap for emphasis—my way of puffing up, Fate says.

"It seems as much of a draw as that fuzzy little dog on the *Majestic* that walks on his front legs," he shot back.

"So, if we get this working right, do it mean Loyce she'll have to go on the showboat with the dog?" Val broke in. He's always had a way of translating what Fate is really getting at.

"Now you're onto something," I said, warming up to this fight. "I'll travel around with my trick dog and live high on the hog. No more knitting nets or sitting on this porch all day!"

"But you'll need someone along to manage your affairs," said Fate.

"So this blind girl and her orphan dog will be working the rivers to pay for you?" Val supplied, sounding helpful but making fun. Fate never catches on, even though Val has been doing that since we were little.

"If I have a watch dog, what'll I need *him* for?" I waved my hand at his pacing across the porch. "Anyway he'll just be getting us in trouble with fathers and husbands all along the way. We'll be supplying alibis to cover his sorry ways from New Orleans to Natchez."

Val, as usual, had his own version:

Seems to me that letter was the start of it all. 'Bout the time Fate was pulling that skiff to the bank, I was pushing my chair back from breakfast in the galley, me. They had just blew the whistle, and being the mate, I had to get the crew up top for docking.

Tot was already peeling the potatoes that give him his Cajun name, Patot, because he was just about as round as one. When you worked on Tot's boat, you ate as good as the passengers up top. Me, I knowed those potatoes would end up full of hot peppers, onion, garlic, and ground-up garfish before dinnertime. And then, don't you know, he'd wait till we was milling around the galley table before he'd start dropping them garfish balls into hot lard. *Mais oui,* when that smell drift out over the water, other crews want to jump overboard and swim to whatever boat Tot was cooking on. It paid to stay on his good side, for true. I stopped before going out the door.

"Tot, you don't have no honey? It's a shame to pour that ol' cane syrup over biscuits good like yours," I said. "It's a li'l early in the year, but I'll get us some honey before we leave if nothing happens to keep me away from my hives."

"Ain't nothing likely to happen at this stop—outside you playing music too late to get back to the boat in time," he said. "Been plowing this river since before the war and ain't heard of nothing happening yet at Bayou Chene."

'Course Tot was right. Other than talk about that pirate Lafitte hiding around here a long, long time back and then some jayhawk doings during the war, not much ever happens here. If anything, people came to get away from happenings.

The Chene, giving up her channel to the 'Chafalaya like she does and then forking off into petite bayous, always seem to get herself found by people looking for a place to start over. Sometime they have a past they want to lose, but mostly they just young, hoping to get they start with nothing but a strong back and gumption. Shoot! You never know where they come from next, that's for true. They come from other countries right through New Orleans. Or Morgan City, my own hometown. Sometime they come from way out East, hearing about cheap land here in the big woods. Land that could grow anything, but if you had *enough* of that land, you put it into sugar.

White gold. That's what they call the sugar back before the war. The Chene, she was busy as a hive of bees in nectar season according to Grandpère, what with the plantations and the sugar mills and the syrup makings and the hauling of it all in and out. Then the Yankees done burnt what the Rebs didn't steal, and by the time it was all over, the planters had move out. Yassir, they just line up, one right next to another, along the Mississippi levee where the railroad track connect them with everywhere they was needing to be. No more toting everything into the swamp and back out again, *enh*?

Bayou Chene, she didn't really miss all that sugar doings, no. She seem happy to ease back down to the slow way she been used to since Injun times. These days most everybody farms a little and keeps some stock, at least some pigs and chickens, if nothing else. Once that big logjam was broke up by the government just before the war, more water come down this way. Then they broke up an even bigger jam after the war, in the seventies. More and more water come pouring in from that Red River, yas, and the Mississippi already too. *Mon père,* he can tell about that. He saw it happen. That was just in time for the big steamboats to start coming through. My boat, the *Golden Era,* she's not even the biggest that comes through the Chene, and she's 150 feets long.

With the 'Chafalaya bringing more and more water every year, that's when people start fishing and picking moss to sell instead of just using for themselves. They sell all kinds of stuff out of the swamps by riverboat, keeping them paddle wheels busy. Some people—York Bertram, he's one, with his sawmill and charcoal—could keep riverboats stopping here just for theyselves. What with the farming, the fishing, and the riverboats, you can't help but make a living on the Chene.

For true, the Yankees who come down here for the war, they saw how easy it could be in a good year. After the dodging and shooting stop, more than one Yank decide to stay, some even change they names and start over when it was easier to let people back home think they was dead. Not many out here even remember which side of the war they was suppose to be on. That's one of the things I like about the Chene—newcomers just pick up their life wherever it fits them, without lots of questions about what brought them here.

Me, that's just what I was thinking about that morning when I push through the galley door to the deck. I took me a good look around and say to myself, "*Mais oui,* it would be fine to have me a few hundred hives along these bayous and never have to get on a boat again except to sell a barrel or two of honey."

I'm with the third generation of Broussards to work on the river. These days it's the steamboats shoving off from Morgan City where the 'Chafalaya, she runs into the Gulf. Sometime we head down around the bottom of Louisiana to New Orleans, where Mama's family lives in the Irish Channel. But most often we go up the 'Chafalaya to the Mississippi River that carries us to Natchez and other places up north.

I got the music in my blood, don't you know, from both my families—the Irish and the Cajun. My favorite trips? *Mais oui, cher!* The ones that stop over in Bayou Chene. Mostly 'cause I can play music with Loyce and Fate. Me, I love they twin fiddles as good as any I play with down and up these rivers.

I was still in short pants when *mon père* first drop me off at the post office ever time his boat dock at the Chene. Mama's family, they own the boat, but *mon père*, he drive it. I can't count how many times I threw a line since the days when I was so short I had to stand on my toes and throw with both hands. Even now I'm not tall as most men old like me—and that's about twenty—but I got more muscle in my arms and shoulders than just about any of them.

That morning I made a easy throw to the dock man, who caught it just as easy. He pass the eye over a timberhead, while I wrap the loose end around a capstan, taking up all the slack. We toss three more lines and caught and tied 'em. After we put out the gangplank, I done cross over and turn left under the oak trees along the bank. The Injuns done start this path a long time before my people got here, probably a thousand years or more back. Injuns was here so long and ate so much shellfish their shell mounds raise the ground around Bayou Chene higher and higher. 'Course that made white people like the Chene even better, and they start finding their way out here in the 1600s. I learn that and more by passing time with all the kinds of people on the river. Not much for them to do but watch the bank pass by and talk to anyone who act like they listening.

Right then the 'Chafalaya, she was burdened down with snow melted from up north. We was docked where Bayou Tensas poured a load of that water down Jakes Bayou. That time of year *Golden Era* could easy fit down Jakes, but she wasn't headed that way this trip, so I took off walking. I had plenty time while the *Era* took on some bales of moss and who knows what else before going down Big Bayou Chene.

Jakes Bayou, she rummaged along on my right, while the oaks, they bent over the left side of me. It was easy to see why the oaks gave their name for the Chene. Leaves and moss thick as curtains. They shade out everything underneath, don't you know. Me, I could see all the way to houses and gardens on the other side of the island. It was a fine sight.

"Val! Val!" Perry Patin, our cabin boy, run up behind me. Dust flying, mail pouch flapping. "Captain says if you going to Miss Loyce's, drop this off at the post office."

Don't know why he had to ask. They all knew I'd be heading out to see her soon as my feets they hit the bank. I took the pouch and hung the strap over my own shoulder.

"Shore 'nuff, Patin, but don't you want to walk up there with me?"

"Naw, Captain says I gotta stay on his watch till noon, then I'm going berry picking. Tot's gonna pay me a dime a bucket."

He took off back the way he come, and me, I turn across the island toward the post office. The path cut through where York Bertram had his sawmill, a charcoal pit, a whiskey still, and a two-story house. York hisself was dozing by a big pile of wood that he was turning into charcoal. The steam, she go *pht, pht* in the cool air.

"Got anything for me?" he asked, not wasting a *bonjour* on me. "Save me the trip to the post office?"

York, him is all the time looking for a way to save some time or money, like he needs more of that stuff than most people. His eyes watered from watching the fire all night. You got to keep it from blazing up or smothering under that cover of dirt. Most people that sold charcoal hired boys to watch the fires, but not York. He probably sat there through the night, him counting the pennies he done saved in a year by doing it hisself.

I went through the mail sack.

"Well, let's see here," I says, "looks like something being sent back to Mary Ann is all."

York, he squinched up his eyes at the envelope. *M. A. Bertram, Bayou Chene, Louisiana,* the return address said. Then SOUTHERN LETTER UNPAID was stamped in blue over a name and address I didn't know: *M. Poussant, Hautes-Pyrénées, France.*

I guess York didn't know the name too. He was still squinching at it and didn't even notice when I told him *au revoir* and then yelled over to Fate carrying that dog across the clearing.

— 2 —

As postmaster, Adam had his own take on the situation:

Come right down to it, I'd have to side with Val and say it all commenced with the letter, but then again, I am partial to mail.

I do know Loyce and Fate are always gonna argue about something, and Val's always ready to egg 'em on. That morning I paid attention with one ear; you get used to that if you watch over as many people as I do. Sure enough, they settled down from yelling to plain old arguing before I finished straining the milk. I set the bowl in the icebox so Loyce could get to it when it was ready for skimming. Then I picked up the mailbag where Val had dropped it on the bench and went on across the hall to take up my official position as Bayou Chene postmaster. Most people think of me as just the storekeeper, but without the post office we wouldn't have a store or much of anything else here on the Chene.

I take care of the mail for about three hundred people. Everyone calls it the Chene, but we're scattered on islands all over this part of the swamp where the 'Chafalaya comes charging full force through Lake Mongoulois, bringing water down from the Red River and the Mississippi. The main river channel pours through Big Bayou Chene, where the largest paddle wheelers follow it down through Lake Chicot, then Grand Lake, and on to the Gulf. But a lot of that water branches off around Big Bayou Chene into a maze of quieter bayous all sizes and shapes.

Our houses and houseboats are settled in along these bayous.

Jakes Bayou, where I keep the post office, shoots off from the big river a little upstream of Big Bayou Chene, which is why we get quieter water. Oh yes, there's Big Bayou Chene, Little Bayou Chene, and even Bayou Crook Chene, where it makes whopping big loops.

There's plenty bayous like Jakes Bayou—named for people alive, dead, or just lost in history back there somewhere. Take your pick, there's Bayou Jean Louis, Bayou Cozine, Willie's Bayou, Murphy's Bayou, and more. There's a whole run of unlucky-sounding names like Bloody Bayou, Dead Man Bayou, Blind Bayou, and Graveyard Bayou. The one where some people look for buried treasure is Four Hundred Dollar Bayou.

There's more bayous out here than names for them; if you want to name one, go ahead. Somebody else might name it something else next year or the year after. Just let me know where you settle so I can send your mail out when someone goes that way. No matter if you don't come in for months, I'll hold your mail. That's my sworn duty, and I take pride in doing it right.

As for the mess in the store they all talk about? It's not nearly as bad as they put on. There's a path right through the fish traps and around the dry goods tables. Sure, you have to navigate a little around the salt blocks and the barrels of tar, sugar, or flour, but the coffee bean sacks are easy to see. What all that mess of goods amounts to is just about everything Cheners can't dip or wring from the swamp. You have to keep your eye on the clear spaces and even understand that sometimes the path moves around, depending on what's come in and gone out recently, but it's there. You just have to look for it.

That day, as usual, when I reached the post office side and set the mail sack on the counter, I took out the packages first—prescription medicine for Ida Mendoza's seizures and eyeglasses that Pie Richard had mailed off to be fixed more than a month past. Those seizures could make Ida fall down any time or place, and she got nervous when her medicine was low, started skipping pills. And Pie can't tell whether she's grabbing an egg or a chicken snake in the nest without her glasses. I set those two packages on the counter to remind me in case one of their neighbors came in. If no one came, I'd walk across the island before dark and deliver them myself. Just one more thing when you have a lot of people to watch out for. I picked up the first handful of letters and slid them into pigeonholes nailed to the wall behind the counter.

Of course, everybody goes on about how neat the post office corner is compared to the store. Well, that's the way my wife, Josie, set it up when she started sorting the mail right there in that corner after she finished third grade. Back then Josie's pa, Elder Landry, was the postmaster, and Mame Landry ran the store. Josie wasn't much more than a big kid when Elder died, but she took over the rest of the post office work as if he were still postmaster. She kept that corner neat as a pin until the night she died.

None of us will likely forget that night when we lost half our family—not just my dear Josie but her brother, Lauf, and his wife, Beatrice, as well. Fate and Loyce were around six years old. Josie and I had lost two babies before Loyce was born and had hoped for more to come.

Beatrice was supposed to have a few more weeks before her next baby came, but her labor started. There was nothing else to do but put Beatrice in the boat and set out across Lake Mongoulois in the dark. It would take twice as long to go over there and bring the midwife back. The last Mame and I saw of them, Lauf was standing up rowing, and Beatrice was sitting in the bottom. Josie was on the bow, holding a lantern, not so much to see but to be seen.

As anyone can tell you, even on a dark night the glint of water can guide you between the banks. So, the danger is not what you might run over but that a big boat could run over you and never even know it. That's what happened. No one heard them cry out, no paddle wheeler ever claimed to be the one that hit them. They just never made it across the lake.

When they didn't come back and we eventually faced up to what happened, Mame went daft. So, you might say I lost her too. She had been more than just a mother-in-law. My own mother signed up to be a census taker around the Chene while I was in college. During months of rowing around these bayous asking about other people's families, Mama and her partner took a notion to get married themselves. They moved back to his home in New Iberia and later to Chicago when he inherited a family business there. Mame looked after me, along with Lauf and Josie. Of course, we were mostly grown by then.

After the drownings I grieved for Mame just like I grieved for the dead ones. Her hair turned white overnight; if you don't believe it, ask anyone who knew her back then. Later years, when she let it down, you could see the black part hanging almost to her knees. There was a sharp line where the black stopped and then white went all the way up, no gray at all. In summer the white part would turn pink, green, and blue as her bonnets faded from her sweat.

Mame never was big, but after that she shrunk down to mostly bones, and she pretty much hid out under that bonnet. Tending the flowers and vegetable garden around the store was sort of her comfort. We all got used to seeing her crouched over the plants with her hatchet or butcher knife, chopping out the weeds. She looked like a bundle of rags that someone intended to put away but hadn't decided where. Her back started to curve from all that squatting so that she eventually had to sew her clothes in two pieces—a top and a bottom—that way she could make one side longer to cover the hump.

As years went by, she didn't seem unhappy, just sort of removed. These tuneless Latin-sounding hymns would come floating out from beneath her bonnet. It was a puzzle where she picked up that music, since back then we only had the Methodist church out here. I figured the musical memory must be from her childhood and brought escape from her loss. If you walked by, she'd break off humming and nod her head but mostly didn't bother to look up to see who spoke to her.

She stopped cooking and even stopped eating with us. Eating was the last thing on my own mind, but Fate and Loyce didn't have anyone else, so I started figuring out how to get plates to the table with something on them. As far as I could tell, Mame just passed through the kitchen now and then and picked up a piece of cornbread or a baked sweet potato. I'd see her eating out of hand while squatting on her haunches looking over her work in the yard.

Everybody handles grief their own way. For me reading and cooking became a comfort, just like pulling weeds seemed to comfort Mame. While she plunged into despair after the drownings, I suppose I just sort of waded in over my head. My own grief got buried under trying to raise a blind daughter alone, keep the store and post office open for the rest of them, and halfway looking after Fate and Mame.

It seemed like all those details started to cover me up like moss in a grove of oaks. I gave up fishing but still couldn't get ahead of all there was to do. Deliveries came to the store, and I just stashed them in any vacant spot. Customers got used to searching for things they wanted to buy or had ordered, so I just left out the pry bar and hammer for them to open the crates and barrels. It got to where layers of dust told me how long something had been part of the inventory.

Sometimes I just let everything go and lost myself in a book. At first it was *Little Women*, one of Josie's favorites as a child. A strange choice for a man, you might say, but all that domesticity was a comfort to me. Besides, it was about a parent trying to handle everything alone, like me. Mrs. March seemed a lot better at it than I was, but I noticed that the book didn't mention who did the washing of all those big skirts and petticoats.

Later I spent a lot of time in *The Innocents Abroad*, Mark Twain's story about traveling all over the world. He went just about everywhere and didn't back up from saying when he didn't approve of something. Before Josie drowned, we used to take turns reading that one aloud to the rest of the family. She'd get to laughing so hard, I had to take over from her most nights.

Come down to it, which book I read didn't matter. Mostly I just took comfort from handling the pages and breathing deep of the covers she treasured. It brought her close to me again.

I know some say I'm lazy, especially when they come in and see me sitting on a case of canned goods with my nose in a book, but that's not the whole story. As a U.S. postmaster, the mail is my sworn duty. Along with sorting what comes in, I help people get their packages and letters ready to go out of this swamp and into the world. Sometimes I write down the most personal kind of information for my customers who can't do it themselves—applications for war widow pensions, notes to relatives about births, letters telling the inside story of marriages, not to mention the death notices of every man, woman, and child who dies here with relatives off somewhere. I know the secrets of every family on the Chene, a privilege I don't take lightly.

And when it comes to the store, why, every baby still gets weighed on my dry goods scale until they pass the twenty-pound limit. That hasn't changed since the days of Elder Landry. And don't forget that letting people serve themselves when I'm busy doing something else is an advantage if a customer is short of cash; he just pays what he has in his pocket and writes what he owes in the account book. Some people say my way of doing business hasn't turned a profit since Josie died. Can't say whether that's true or not, but I know it's kept goods flowing through the Chene and helped more than one family during hard times. Still and all, I'm probably not as good at running the store as I am at being postmaster.

The morning that dog showed up, I was just about finished sorting the letters when the screen door opened and slammed shut again. I knew from all the commotion coming with her it was Mary Ann Bertram. She's married to Mame's nephew, York Bertram.

Mame's baby brother, Martin, settled in Plaquemine after the war. He never came back, even for a visit, but his son, York, moved here a few years ago, bringing his bride, Mary Ann. They've made a good run of the old homestead where Jakes Bayou splits off from Lake Mongoulois and takes its own winding way down to Lake Chicot. The Bertrams had a sugar mill on that point before the war. Now York's turned it into a place to make lumber, charcoal, whiskey, and I don't know what all.

York's plum crazy about machines—in fact, that's how he met Mary Ann. Her pa has a big machine shop in Plaquemine, and York was always fooling around in the shop with her brothers.

Mary Ann, now, it's critters she loves, especially those horses that pull her wagon. She does a handy business delivering goods from the Jakes Bayou dock all around our island, including to my store. That morning she brought a hunk of ice for my icebox. Mary Ann is as jolly as York is glum.

"Adam Snellgrove, I've seen pigpens cleaner than this! If there was another store around, I'd shop there." She always starts talking soon as she gets through the door, sometimes before.

I'm tall, and her blue eyes were even with mine as she pushed her way through the merchandise. Instead of a bonnet, she pulls a felt hat down over her hair and ties it with a leather cord. As usual, a man's flannel shirt was tucked into canvas work pants, which were tucked into tall rubber boots. She gets her rough-and-tumble ways from being the only girl in her family.

"Well, you'd be the expert there," I said. "How's that new litter coming along on those Dr. Legeare vitamins?"

"Eating like hogs, ever one of 'em. Never saw a turnaround so quick on a bunch of runts."

"I don't remember who ordered those vitamins or even what kind of livestock they were for, but I'm glad they came in handy," I said, and I meant it.

Mary Ann has helped all of us at one time or another with our animals. You'd never know she wasn't from the Chene—in fact, only been here a few years.

"Hmmph," she grunted with the effort of moving a crate. "There's no telling what's packed away in here. If you'd ever clean this place up we'd all know."

She swiped a cloud of dust off a pair of black rubber boots and checked the size on the bottom before placing them on the counter.

"That rooster spurred another hole in York's boot, the left one again. I told him not even you are going to sell me one boot, so tally up this pair. It's gonna aggravate the tar out of him to have those two extra right boots. Whatcha wanna bet he'll be dancing a jig trying to get the right one spurred next time. Any mail for us today?"

"Nope, I just got through sorting what Val brought in," I said.

Just then Alcide Verret pulled open the screen door. The old spring waited a bit before slamming closed behind him. I always listened for the time it just couldn't pull anymore. Then I'd change it out. That meant looking for my extra springs, and I hadn't gotten around to that yet.

Cide's suspenders were run up as short as they would go, but he still crossed them in the back, trying to take them up a little more. He might be short, but he's thick and strong. I've seen him pull a crosscut saw with two men on the other end, holding up his part and talking the whole time. Might be why people rarely notice how short he is. Or how old. He's foggy about when he was born, but no one on the Chene can remember a time when he wasn't here.

"What a rain last night! I had to kick my way through drowned frogs just to get to my pirogue this morning," he said.

Cide's always good for a colorful take on a situation. He also likes the ladies, and he winked up at Mary Ann, who snagged him right up in a headlock and ruffled his white hair. The ladies like him back.

"Speaking of drowned, Fate pulled a dog out of the bayou this morning," I said. "Don't know if she'll make it. Loyce has her over in the kitchen drying out."

"Couldn't she swim?" Mary Ann let go of Cide and looked back at me.

"Probably real good," I said, "But she was tied to an empty skiff. No telling how far she come. It's black with blue trim, not from anywhere close to here."

"Guess somebody'll be pulling up a body on their net anchor 'fore long." Cide shook his head in sympathy.

Mary Ann stomped to the other side of the breezeway to inspect the box and give us all advice for the dog's recovery. By noon the story of the mysterious skiff and its passenger had made the rounds, and the dog had officially picked up the name Drifter.

At that time none of us knew about the letter.

— 3 —

Two weeks later the little dog was still hanging on but was more mysterious than ever.

"Fate, how about scraping the leftovers into this, and I'll see if I can get Drifter to eat a bite," Loyce said, sliding a pie tin across the table.

Fate wasn't surprised when it stopped just short of the edge. They had been practicing such diversions for so long it was second nature.

"Half-inch, not bad," was all he said.

"It just beats everything; she's strong enough to eat but won't." Loyce's voice lifted above the rattle of utensils.

"Seems like she'd be glad to find a home, after what she's been through," Fate began, as he scraped another plate into Drifter's pan, adding a little extra gravy over the biscuits.

"Don't say she's found a home—she's not staying here!"

Loyce popped a wet dish towel near his ear for emphasis.

Fate charged around the table. Loyce sensed his feint and stepped in the opposite direction. He anticipated her guess, and she found herself nose to chest with her agile cousin. Fate grabbed the dish towel and stepped outside her reach. Second nature, he thought. Second nature.

Loyce pretended to ignore his victory and went back to the problem at hand.

"We just need to get her well enough to go somewhere else,"

she pondered. "What I set out for her last evening was covered in ants this morning. I don't think she ate any of it. Starting to look like she might not make it after all."

As soon as the black dog had gained enough strength to leave the porch, she had followed her nose to the skiff. Fate had upended the odd vessel on the bank to keep it from filling with rainwater. When she reached it, her tail wagged feebly for the first time. Her nose snuffled the ground from bow to stern. She circled the boat two more times before lifting her head to scan the bayou, upstream and down. Then she whimpered and crawled under the skiff, refusing to come out. Two days later Fate attempted to pull her out, but she only growled and backed farther into the gloom.

Sometimes early in the morning or late in the evening, if no one was near, she would creep out and sit on the upended boat, watching the water, ears up, tail moving back and forth hopefully. If another boat landed at the dock or if someone stepped off the porch, she scurried back under the shelter of the skiff.

Morning and evening Fate or Loyce brought a pan of food—leftover bread, gravy, deer ribs, or fish picked clean of bones. Most of the time it was still there at the next meal, minus what the ants toted off. Days passed, and her profile grew sharper as she sat watching the water. Fate described the outline of her ribs to Loyce whenever he saw the lonesome figure sitting on top the skiff.

At night Loyce's sensitive ears picked up soft whining. Barely audible so as not to draw attention to her grief, sadness seeped out of the starving dog. Loyce listened and remembered her first nights at the school for the blind when she was separated from every smell or sound that was familiar—from everyone she loved.

One night the whimpering was so pitiful, Loyce couldn't sleep. Swinging her legs over the edge of the bed, she felt for her cloth slippers with her feet. It was a warm night, so she didn't even cover the cotton gown but padded downstairs and across the porch to the steps. Touching the banister lightly for orientation, she reached down with one slippered foot until it was safely on a step, then set the other foot beside it. She descended in this halting manner until she reached the plank walk, one of three that Adam had built for her years ago. Most often she used only the planks that went out back to the privy and the rainwater cistern. She rarely took this front one toward the dock. There was no call for her to use it unless someone was taking her somewhere in a boat. That didn't happen often because everyone in the community came through the store and post office on a regular basis. Most days her world was no bigger than the porch.

Her feet shuffled eleven steps before she put a cautious foot out to the right, off of the raised wooden path. She had counted the distance the first time Fate had led her out to bring a pan of food. As usual, scuttling sounds told her the dog was backing under the skiff.

"Hey, you oughta know by now I'm not going to grab you. I can't see, remember?" she said more gently than usual. "I'll just sit here and keep you company for a while."

She brushed the ground in front of the skiff with her foot to make sure it was clear before settling down with her back against the side of the boat. Drifter stopped whining but other than that didn't seem to notice she had company.

Loyce took a deep breath. It was a good night to sit out; the breeze was cool and smelled like young leaves. An owl hooted. A fish rippled the water. Fate's little houseboat knocked against the dock; most likely, he had turned over in bed.

"You know, Drifter, there's a lot to listen to on a quiet night if you just pay attention," Loyce said, by way of conversation. "I used to be so lonesome missing home that I couldn't sleep. Then I found that I could busy my mind and figure out what was going on around me just by paying attention to the sounds. A boat's whistle on the river always meant something, and it wasn't long before I could tell whether they were coming in to the dock or leaving or passing another boat. I could tell from the milkman's step on the walk whether his feet were hurting that morning. The clang of the pans told me what we were having for breakfast just as if I'd asked the cook! I think that's when I noticed music—just lying there, listening, in the dark."

Not a sound came from beneath the skiff, but Loyce thought

she could feel the dog listening. It was a start, and it gave her an idea. She began humming "In the Good Old Summertime." The bouncy little tune was the most recent one Val had brought back to her from upriver. The second time through the song, she added the words to see how they would go over with Drifter. She thought she heard the slightest thump of a tail at the end.

"Well, if you liked that, here's one of my favorites because you can play it, sing it, or dance to it."

She jumped right into "It rained all night the day I left," tapping out the beat on her thigh as if she were center stage at a dance. The last *kneeeeeeee* hadn't faded from her lips when she heard Drifter breathing closer to the edge of the boat. Heartened, she kept going.

"Here's one you might have heard before, seeing as you came off the river. Val told me it's an old sailor's song. He knows lots of versions, but this here's my favorite."

She started out low.

> Oh Shenandoah, I long to hear you,
> Away, you rolling river.
> Oh Shenandoah, I long to hear you,
> Away, I'm bound away, 'cross the wide Missouri.

The pure loneliness of the song on the night air set up a longing in the young woman for something she couldn't name. Loyce sensed that Drifter recognized that longing but that, unlike herself, the little dog could name the person she was missing. Whatever the reason, as the mournful notes faded, she felt Drifter breathing softly on her hand.

In this manner the blind woman and the dog kept company until nearly daylight, when the roosters began to crow from their perches in trees or inside homemade coops. As with the boat whistles, Loyce knew their individual voices, which ranged from the rusty croak of an old gentleman whose sunrises were numbered to the competitive trumpeting of young cockerels.

There was a whole chorus of young cocks across the island that spring. Every morning she listened to them compete. It was as if they knew that only one would be kept as the service rooster. She parsed out each call, knowing ahead of time which one would crow next, getting her bearings for the tail end of the night as it eased into morning.

Sure enough, at the time she knew to expect it, the clang of the stove door told her Adam was awake and stirring up the fire for coffee. She stood and dusted off the back of her gown.

"Well, Drifter, I don't know about you, but I'm stiff as a poker from this damp ground. You can stay out here if you want, but I'm going in."

Not a sound from under the skiff.

"Just because we shared a song or two doesn't mean you're won over, does it? Have it your way then."

She listened a second more and then tapped a foot in the direction of the plank walk. One, two, three steps.

"Argguuu," rumbled from under the skiff.

She froze, puzzled, thinking it sounded like one of Val's beehives. Suddenly she was knocked off-balance. Loyce staggered, reaching out with her hands in hope of steadying herself, not knowing where to go. She couldn't step just any which way because she had lost track of the bayou. How close was the dock? She couldn't remember. She couldn't even remember which way she had turned when the sound startled her.

"Arggguuufff!" The sound was Drifter! Growling like a wild animal.

It had never occurred to her that the mysterious dog might attack. She had nothing for defense, not even that useless cane she'd brought home from school.

This was just the sort of thing that would make Fate fuss at her later on. She could already hear him saying a blind girl wasn't supposed to go walking around at night. But what difference did day or night make to her? It was just like Fate to break into her concentration when she was trying to flap her hands at the dog, grab the air for balance, and run away at the same time. She fumed, knowing that all of those efforts together were doing her as much good as trying to fly.

Suddenly the growling was interspersed with slapping and thumping on the plank walk. What was that? The violent sounds told Loyce she should jump but didn't give her a clue about the direction. When things couldn't get any worse, they did. The plank walk started bouncing from both directions. She felt empty space beneath her slippers as she flew into the air.

"What is it?" Adam's voice coming from the porch was interrupted by Fate from the bayou side, "Loyce? What the hell?"

Their pounding feet were turning her plank walk into a seesaw.

"Whoa! Are you bit? Where?"

One more bounce, higher than any before, sent her flying upward; her gown billowed out as she changed course and started down. Then she was clamped tight. Fate's long arms held her higher off the ground than usual.

"No, she didn't bite me, but she's fighting with something." Loyce squeezed out the words through his grip, which was cutting off her air. That's Fate, making things worse by trying to help, she thought.

"Not her! The snake! That *something* is a granddaddy of a cottonmouth!" Fate was still yelling, and Loyce pushed her ear into his shirt to soften the sound. "It must have been hunting for an easy meal around the fish traps. If it'd gotten tangled up in your gown, you'd be bit a dozen times by now. You got that black dog to thank."

Thank! Her face burnt hot, and she pushed against the solid wall of his chest.

"Well, if it wasn't for that black dog, I'd be safe in my bed right now," she retorted, feeling braver but not yet ready to put her feet down on the plank walk. "First thing in the morning you find her a home."

— 4 —

For days to come, more customers than usual crowded around the post office and propped themselves against the porch banister. They had rowed and walked considerable distances to hear about the fracas firsthand, and they were not disappointed.

Fate stretched the cottonmouth across the plank walk for everyone to admire. He also stretched his own part in the story way out of proportion for Loyce's taste. To counter his bragging, Loyce found herself taking Drifter's part, expounding on the little dog's courage. Loyce's declarations prompted Fate to jump in with even bigger plans for Drifter—teaching her to lead Loyce safely around the island.

That's just the way things get out of hand when Fate's around, she fumed, rocking harder and jabbing her shuttle in and out of the twine. Before she could figure out how to regain control of the situation, Mary Ann Bertram burst through the back door.

"Adam, do I have to wait till the holidays to find some pecans, or do you have some stashed in here somewhere?" the young woman yelled while striding to the middle of the room.

Loyce listened as Mary Ann's voice took on a distant quality. Had she pitched forward into one of the barrels? Sure enough, rummaging sounds ensued and then gave way to bundles crashing onto the floor. Next her sensitive ears followed the step of Adam's boots around the counter. When they stopped in front of

Mary Ann's ruckus, Loyce could almost hear him pondering on the whereabouts of pecans.

"Might be some over there, but they'd be last year's, not too good," he offered.

"Don't matter how good they are. I just need some for a bread pudding I'm making York," Mary Ann grunted.

"I thought York didn't like nuts—they hurt his teeth," Adam said, taking advantage of her help to unpack some of the things she had tossed out of the barrel. He began making little piles of like goods in vacant spaces—tins of spices, paper packets of sewing needles, jars of olives packed tight in salty vinegar.

"He hates 'em, but he loves my bread pudding more than just about anything," she grunted with the effort of lifting a bucket of sugarcane syrup out of her way. "Nothing will torment him more than to follow the smell of that pudding through the doorway, spoon up a big pile, and bite in to all those pecans." She stopped long enough to beam at the image.

"What'd he do to get on your bad side?" Adam asked.

The Bertrams were known for going out of their way to win an argument, entertaining everyone else as they tried to out-spite each other.

"Killing my rooster is the latest shenanigan, but he ain't been fit to live with for a month or so," she said. "Got broodier than an old setting hen for no reason I can make out. Don't talk, not that he ever contributed much to conversation before. But now he don't say a word for or against night or day. Just stays out at the sawmill or his still, working, but he don't forget to eat."

"How'd he kill your rooster?" asked Adam. "Not that I blame him—that varmint was gonna take someone's eye out sooner or later. Just look at your arms."

Mary Ann scratched thoughtfully at the scabs in various stages of healing but then drew up to her full height and huffed out.

"I was right over in the calf lot and saw it all, so there's no denying it, even if he cared enough to, which he don't. Won't answer me a bit about it. The rooster charged him from behind the sweet peas, which was one of his favorite hiding places, so it wasn't like York was surprised or anything. He picked up that piece of stove wood he keeps there and walloped him upside the head, knocking him stone cold like always."

Adam nodded, remembering the times he'd toted that same piece of stove wood in order to get from the boat dock to their door if the rooster happened to be out front.

Mary Ann continued. "That always took the fight out of him for a couple of days, and York knew that. But this time he went right on over and stomped that rooster in the head, over and over, until nothing but the comb was showing above the dirt."

"Maybe he was worried about you or someone else getting hurt bad," offered Adam. "Leastways, now you don't have to arm yourself to get in and out of your boat."

"He ain't worried about me or nobody else. Just himself and the price of rubber boots," said Mary Ann.

Then she triumphantly held up a tin of shelled pecans.

Out on the porch Loyce's fingers slipped the wooden shuttle methodically through the cotton thread of the net as she listened to Mary Ann's plan. Whenever Loyce visited the Bertrams, someone had to protect her from the rooster since she couldn't see to kick at him herself. That was another aggravation of being blind. She had to wait for someone to take her everywhere outside the house or the plank walks. Not that there was anywhere to go.

Getting out and about was what she missed the most about school. Finding her own way through the well-marked halls to classrooms and play areas had been easy; she didn't have to wait for someone to lead her. Then there were daily outings when teachers escorted groups of students along the sidewalks of Baton Rouge. They would stroll past a French bakery or a flower shop, inhaling the fragrances that sighted people couldn't fully appreciate. There were field trips, where they learned to swim and ride horses. The music students played concerts for the public and also attended professional musical performances in town.

Loyce worked at not complaining. She knew how lucky she was to have traveled more than most people born and raised on the

Chene. But her world had shrunk considerably in the past year, and it took some getting used to.

Mary Ann's long stride reached the screen door and kicked it open. She stepped through before the tired spring could pull it back. Loyce felt her stop and bend over, bringing the milky scent of barnyard to the porch. That was followed by the yeasty fragrance of Drifter's ears being ruffled.

"Well, you still got that little pup!" Mary Ann exclaimed. "I thought Fate was supposed to give her to Alcide?"

"After that snake fracas, she walked right up the steps like I'd called her, which I can tell you I didn't," Loyce laughed. "Brazen as anything, parked herself by my foot, and now she's set her mind to stay there. Been that way ever since she killed that cottonmouth. I sure don't need a dog, just something else to trip over."

"Well, whether you want a dog or not, it looks like she's here to stay," Mary Ann said. "She's so stubborn, I'm guessing her last name might be Bertram. If so, you might as well give up and keep her, or it'll wear you out trying to stay ahead of her. I know 'cause I'm married to a Bertram."

Loyce listened to Mary Ann's boots clomp through the breezeway and down the back steps to the woods path, free to walk wherever she pleased. Just then Drifter shifted position, and Loyce felt the comforting weight settle against her foot. She placed the shuttle in her lap and reached for the silky ears.

"Drifter, could Fate have a plan this time that will work? Do you think you could learn to take me a few places around the island?"

All she got was a tail thump, but she thought it sounded promising. The squeak of barrel wood being pried open told her that Adam was still putting away stock on the momentum Mary Ann's search had started.

— 5 —

"Take it easy there, little fella," Adam murmured as he slipped a hand into the fish cart hanging alongside the dock. The afternoon was hot for late April and made the water feel cold. His fingers closed behind the fins of a small blue catfish. Sure, it took practice to keep from getting finned, but he knew the right mind-set was just as important. Talking to them helped too.

"You have potential to live up to, and you can be sure I won't let you slack off," he said to this one.

It had been years since Adam could go out—away from the store and post office—to fish. There was just too much to do. It would be impossible for him to keep up with nets and lines that required daily attention. He did manage to bait a couple of lines near the dock, where he caught enough fish for supper several times a week. Firm, lively catfish like this one.

A blow on the head from the butcher knife's wooden handle stunned the fish. Then Adam slit the bluish-white skin just below the bony protrusions on each side of the skull. He went through the movements swiftly, without thinking. Placing the knife on the cleaning board, he picked up the blunt-nosed skinning pliers. Had to be careful making that switch; one or both could slip out of his hand into the water. He sold plenty of replacements for the knives and skinners that got buried in bayou mud.

Four passes with the skinners, and the blue cat was peeled like a banana. Nothing to it. Back to the knife again, he opened the belly from the throat down with one quick thrust. Holding the head in his left hand and the body in his right, Adam gave a twist. The insides pulled away with the head, leaving a firm white column of meat with the back and tail fins intact.

Just the right size for frying whole, he thought. Everyone nibbled off the crisp fins first thing, and Adam knew that a fish longer than ten or twelve inches would turn out greasy if cooked whole. It cooled down the boiling fat too much.

He squatted to swish the small carcass in the bayou before flipping it into the granite dishpan, where it plopped softly on top of a pile of identical white bodies. After lowering the wooden cage back into the water, he hoisted the dishpan and carried their supper toward the house.

Shadows were long across the yard. The fire left over from the washday laundry was now burning under a smaller black iron kettle, the one reserved for fish. Adam had placed it there to heat while he cleaned the fish. Now he stepped into the smokehouse and scooped a pound of lard from the pork barrel into the hot kettle. While it melted, he took the pan of fish through the kitchen door.

Fate, Val, and Loyce were playing an Irish waltz on the porch—"The Star of the County Down." Their music flowed right into the kitchen where he was working, bringing Josie to mind. How gracefully she had waltzed to that very tune! Hearing it brought home how much he still missed her.

He couldn't remember the first time he saw her, but she was probably right there toddling around the dock, likely peering around Mame's skirt, when he stepped out of the boat. He had been taking in his own fill of the strange new sights. Yessir, Bayou Chene was a boy's best dream. About as far away from the confines of city life as you could get. Not that there was anything wrong with Nashville—it's where his father's family had lived for generations.

But this swamp—this was where Robinson Crusoe could have had an easy time making do. Natty Bumppo would have been at home tracking game through these very woods. Who could say for sure that some freshwater Moby Dick wasn't hiding in the depths of the Atchafalaya? Or 'Chafalaya, as Adam grew up pronouncing it. He didn't realize the word started with an A until he missed it in a fifth-grade spelling bee.

Back in Nashville, when Papa came home weak from that boring but most effective wartime killer—dysentery—father and son spent their days downstairs in the library. At first Adam listened to his father read, but as the man grew weak and the boy learned the words, they exchanged places. In this way he read aloud his father's favorite stories from childhood, plus all the new books they could purchase in the hard times after the war.

Adam figured that in two years he spent more hours with his father than some sons get in a lifetime. By the time Papa died, all those adventure books had convinced Adam that life was best lived on the outskirts of civilization.

Later he shared those same books with Josie. The old volumes transported the two youngsters from Bayou Chene to the most exotic locations on the planet. They sailed to India and England through *The Moonstone*. *King Solomon's Mines* took them to Africa. As newlyweds, they braved the frozen wilderness of *Frankenstein* while tucked snugly under the covers of their bed.

Adam's mother—Eugenia Snellgrove—didn't have family in Nashville; her people had come across the Appalachians when she was small. So, after her husband died and a missionary came to church telling about the Bayou Chene Primary School needing a teacher, it seemed like the perfect adventure for mother and son. The first thing Adam packed was boxes and boxes of his beloved books.

When they arrived in Bayou Chene, Mame and Elder Landry put them up over the post office until the teacher's cottage next door to the one-room primary school was ready. A new schoolteacher was a big event for the isolated community. Neighbors whitewashed the walls, built a new set of steps, and made fresh moss mattresses for the teacher and her son.

While the grownups were busy, Josie and Adam clambered around the post office, inside and out. Several times a day they trotted along the path to check on the work at the school. They were left alone to entertain themselves. Alligators, snakes, and washday fires were the only taboos. Other than the water, of course.

Water—it's the boon and the bane of swamp communities. Giving life but also taking it—one or two a year around the Chene, sometimes more. Mostly children. Josie and Adam learned quickly not to play in the water or even hang off the dock to stir in it with a stick. They didn't climb into any of the boats tied along the bank for fear of a switching. Like the rest of the mamas, Eugenia and Mame kept sharp eyes on their children when it came to the water.

Come September, the teacher's cottage and the schoolroom were fresh and ready. For three years after that, Josie walked through the woods to school. Then she quit, just like Lauf would quit when he finished third grade.

Mame refused to let them ride the school boat across Lake Mongoulois to the upper grades. The trip took better than an hour each morning and afternoon, depending on the weather and the steamboat traffic. During that time a storm could blow in, or the school boat could overturn in strong current. All of Eugenia's arguing about the benefits of education was no more than the bawling of a calf to Mame. She refused to loosen her grip on Josie's safety.

Adam suffered right along with Josie when her education stopped. He made up for it as best he could, bringing her books from his father's collection, which also served as the school library. She read them faster than he could find new ones for her. Postal customers grew accustomed to their magazines and catalogs being creased open before they were delivered. Josie stopped short of actually opening letters, but Adam suspected she would have if she could have gotten away with it.

The most difficult time for Adam had been when he left for college in Nashville. Education was a tradition in his family, so there was no question about whether he would go. While he had been glad for the experience, Adam missed Josie and life in the swamp so much that he could hardly wait for vacation. His valise was always packed with as many books for Josie as everything else. When he graduated and returned to the Chene, Adam brought all the books he had collected during his school years. He joked that his library was the reason Josie married him instead of one of the attentive swampers who lingered at the post office counter. She never corrected him about that.

Adam listened to a lot of people on the trips back and forth from Nashville. Slightly hard of hearing, he had to pay close attention to lips or risk losing the gist of a conversation. It made others think he was a good listener, and he supposed in one way they were right. The better you listen, the more people want to tell you, or at least that had been his experience.

Passengers traveling with the slender young man often mistook him for a lawyer or a judge. There was something in the calm, loose-jointed way he stood or sat. Comfortable in anyone's company, never fidgeting, he was relaxed but attentive. Fact was, he did come from a cadre of scholars in his father's family, but they mingled with the fur trappers, mountain men, and trading post proprietors on his mother's side. Adam could have lived in either world, but he had made his choice years ago. Having grown up surrounded by the majestic swamp, life in Nashville seemed crowded and squalid in comparison. The fast pace wore him down, and he never felt so peaceful as when he stepped off the steamboat onto the bayou bank once more.

Besides, the Chene was a good place to raise a family. Sure, it was out of the way, but it had suffered little from the war and had a better future than many landlocked communities. If Josie hadn't drowned, their lives would have been all they hoped for, maybe more.

But that April in 1907 all the good times seemed lodged in Adam's past. With his handlebar mustache and iron gray hair the same color as his eyes, people who didn't know Adam might guess him to be a decade or more beyond his forty-five years.

Finding a crockery bowl, he cleared a place on the table for it and began the search for the ingredients, eventually locating cornmeal ground nearly as fine as flour, to which he added a handful of salt and a half-hand of red pepper. He stirred the dry ingredients around in the bowl with his hand, rubbing the mixture together with long slender fingers to distribute the seasoning.

Humming along with dance music from the porch, he placed a fish on the table and cut three diagonal slits in the thickest part of the flesh. He turned it over and made three more slits in the other side before rolling the entire fish in the seasoned corn meal. Thinking about how the hot grease would bubble up in the gashes to quickly cook the fish tender on the inside and crunchy on the outside made Adam's mouth water. It also pushed back his loneliness. Cooking could do that for Adam, especially if there were other people around to enjoy a good meal with him.

By the time he had restacked the fish in the pan, Adam's gloom had lifted some. With a lighter step, he carried the pan back outside to the fire, where the lard was just beginning to smoke. Sssst. He dropped a fish into the boiling kettle. He squatted back on his heels and admired the hot fat roiling around two, three, then four of the fish. Twirling a long-handled fork, he waited. The remainder of his melancholy began to dissipate, crowded out by anticipation. At just the right moment he flipped each fish with the fork so that all four were the same perfect shade of golden brown.

Adam had just flipped the last fish and was studying their progress when the woman appeared. She stepped out of the woods on the path from the boat dock. He might've thought she was a ghost except she was carrying a valise in each hand. Something in the off-kilter way she toted them made him think she wasn't used to carrying her own baggage. She worked to keep the valises from dragging on the ground despite her good size. "Full-figured," the catalog called it.

Wrapped tighter than a bale of cotton, he thought. No wonder she was breathing hard, or trying to. She was girded some tight into that traveling suit! Adam noticed her bosom heaving against the maroon worsted jacket held in place by two rows of covered buttons, military style. The thick fabric, the extra row of buttons— any dry goods dealer would spot that outfit as coming from the high-priced section. In fact, he had never carried goods so fine, only seen them in the catalog. There was no call for such in Bayou Chene.

They stared at each other—the tall, loose-jointed man and the tightly bound woman. When he saw she wasn't going to speak, he gave it a shot in his best storekeeper's voice.

"Ma'am, can I help you with those?"

Her chest continued to heave but not deep enough. From her waist, which looked no bigger than a coffee can, to her neck, which looked to be about the same size, she was caught tight by whalebone and fabric. Adam, who had helped enough women order clothes to know that necks and waists should not be the same size, also knew she was getting ready to topple. He reached her in two long strides just as she was going down. As he caught her in the crook of his left arm, he began unbuttoning her high collar with the fingers of his right hand. There was nothing he could do quickly about the rest of the bodice below the neck, since the fabric was simply a cover for the laced corset. If lying down with her collar unbuttoned didn't give her enough breathing room, Adam was prepared to slice open the corset with his knife. But for every reason he could think of, he didn't want it to come to that.

"Did anyone see that?" were her first words. Not a thank-you or pardon me.

"Not that I can tell, but I'm a little too busy keeping your head out of the dirt to check right now," Adam said, making a cushion of her straw traveling hat before setting back on his heels to look at her. "Don't talk, just breathe."

She relaxed a little at that and worked on drawing whiffs of air past her corset.

He noticed that her black hair was pinned so tight in place by a whole set of jet combs, it had not come loose during her long walk or the fall. Her eyes, just a tad lighter than her hair, focused on the trees overhead. Soon color returned to her cheeks, but the rest of her skin remained pale. After a few more shallow breaths, she lowered her eyes from the trees to look at him. Her gaze was as reserved as her speech.

"Thank you. I'm Roseanne Barclay. If you are Adam Snellgrove, I've heard you may have a room I can rent. I won't need it for long, as I'm waiting for my husband."

The mention of a husband dampened Adam's pleasure of watching her and brought him back to the reason he had been in the backyard.

"Ooooh, the fish." He sprang from his squatting position and went back to the kettle over the fire. "Just a little bit brown, but that'll make 'em crisper, don't you know," he said as he began dipping them out with the long-handled fork.

An old copy of the *New Orleans Times Picayune* waited in a platter to receive them. Adam knew to plan ahead because fish are perfect only for the time it takes to dip them out. Waste time looking for something to drain them on, and you might as well throw them to the dogs to start with because they won't be fit to eat. When he was satisfied that the first batch was perfectly placed, he began dropping another round of fish into the kettle.

She watched every move, but Adam didn't let her rattle his concentration. Only after both sets of fish were situated did he reply.

"I'm not in the boarding business, and it's probably not what you're used to, but I have a room that might do for a time if you got nowhere else to go. How'd you come to be here?"

Her eyes were set deep, which made them even harder to read. Maybe it was her angled face or the high-bridged nose. But when she shifted that dark gaze back to the treetops, Adam thought of red-shouldered hawks. He'd seen them with that same look when they were scouting places to build their nests high in the cypress trees, where their eggs would be safe from predators. Finally she appeared to light on a story she judged would be safe with him.

"I left New Orleans to meet up with my husband, who's on a business trip in New Iberia. Our boat had to detour around a logjam, and Bayou Chene was as close to New Iberia as they could drop me off. I'll just be here until I can get word to him to pay my passage from here to New Iberia, since I don't have money."

Squatting down to turn the second batch of fish gave Adam

time to decide how much of that might be true. Didn't she know anybody with the brains of a fox squirrel would wonder why a woman dressed so fine would be traveling without money in the tapestry reticule hanging from her wrist? The little bag cost at least two dollars if it was a penny. That surprised him almost as much as a husband who would let his wife travel alone on a steamboat across the swamp. By the time he finished turning the fish, Adam had made up his mind it was safest to just change the subject.

He extended one hand and then the other to help the woman to her feet. Then he picked up the little traveling hat (another dollar, even without the dark red feather trimming the ribbon band). She dusted the hat and cocked it just so on her head, as well as if she was looking in a mirror. By the time he had finished forking up the second batch of fish, her collar was buttoned to the top, and she looked like she was ready to seat callers in her parlor.

"Well, first let's go in and do these fish justice," Adam said. "Then we'll see what we can do. Fate will come get your bags; you just bring yourself."

Breathing restored, she walked ahead of him to where he indicated the screen door leading into the kitchen. Whether it was the whalebone or her backbone, Adam couldn't tell, but from the set of her spine, he figured this was a woman who'd break before she would bend.

"So you don't *have* to cook outdoors," Roseanne said. "But I can see why you do." The beak-like nose jerked in a small sniff.

Adam looked around at his cooking gear stashed here and there along with the rags, water buckets, and other necessaries that make up a kitchen. Trying to take it all in at once like she was doing, instead of gradually like it had accumulated, he understood how the sight might prejudice a newcomer.

Once again her nose jerked in a sniff, maybe over the basket of sprouted onions on the floor next to the stove. He probably should have used them by now. And the strings of red peppers hanging from the ceiling. He'd never noticed before that after a few years past drying out, they start to look like talons of dead birds. A spoon stuck straight up out of a container of honey that had gone to sugar. How long had it been there? He didn't even remember seeing it before. Well, she was either hungry or she wasn't, and the way she had been watching those fish fry made him think she could put all this mess behind her in a flash.

"Ah, Mrs. Barclay," he said, with all the confidence his fish deserved, "you won't care where these little darlings were cooked when you taste them."

With that he breezed on through the kitchen door to the porch. He could hear the tippy-tap of her shoes trying to keep up with his long strides.

The music stopped when they entered, the squeeze-box and Fate's fiddle first, then a few more fiddle strokes before Loyce noticed she was playing alone.

"Young'uns, this is Mrs. Barclay, who has been stranded by a logjam and will be passing time with us while she waits for her husband to send her passage," Adam said, with a proprietor's flourish. "Mrs. Barclay, meet my daughter, Loyce; my nephew, Fate Landry; and Valzine Broussard, first mate of the *Golden Era*."

Val looked up from where he was putting away his squeeze-box. Always interested in what's happening on the water anywhere, he and Fate took every opportunity to talk about boats.

"That'd be the logjam over around Plaquemine or Simmesport?" he asked.

"Uhhh," Roseanne hesitated. Adam couldn't tell if she was stalling for time or was overcome with the good smells rising up from the table. It did appear her corset strained with her trying to breathe them in.

Finally, she said, "Simmesport," but her voice lacked confidence, in Adam's opinion. No wonder, since Simmesport was north of Bayou Chene, opposite from New Orleans, where she had told him she was from.

"Yeh, that makes it a trial to get from Natchez this time of year," Val said.

Natchez was the city *above* the Simmesport logjam. Adam saw that Val was too occupied with serving Loyce's plate to notice the woman's discomfort over her mistake.

"How about some of those English peas you spent the morning shelling?" Val went on, holding a spoon over Loyce's plate. With the other hand he moved fringe from his vest out of the way. Val's clothes were a little on the colorful side for Adam's taste, but he appreciated the young man's good-hearted attentiveness to Loyce.

"Since I did all the work of picking and shelling, give me a double helping, but wait till I put this biscuit down," Loyce replied.

Val waited while she split a biscuit and placed it on one side of her plate. Then he covered the biscuit with tiny green peas and the sauce made with butter and pure cream.

Other dishes passed around the table in the same fashion, with either Val or Fate serving Loyce as needed. Along with the creamed peas and biscuits, their plates were soon heaped with the fried catfish, rutabaga chunks smothered in a brown roux, and leaves of wild spinach wilted with hot bacon grease and splashed with vinegar. The conversation flowed to the rhythm of their congenial dining. Adam noticed that the newcomer ate as heartily as the boys.

"Your Bayou Chene surprises me," she said to the table in general. "I wasn't expecting to see so many houses, picket fences, and even a store way out here."

"Oh, *cher*, there's nowhere else like it, for true," Val answered. "I go up and down these rivers, and I know them all. The Chene, she got most everything except roads in and out."

"How do you get around?" she asked.

"There's paths on each island," Val said. "Usually along the banks, sometimes across, depending on how close kin the families are on the other side. And everybody, they got boats for going to another island."

Then Fate jumped in on his favorite subject. "We got boats for anything we want to do. Mostly we use push skiffs like you see tied up along the banks. You can stand up and see where you going for one thing, and a man can row a pretty good load by himself pushing on them long oars. Now, for tight places you can't beat a pirogue—so light it can float on a dew. It's narrow built and pointed at both ends so you can back up as easy as you can go frontwards. And believe me, sometimes backing up is the best thing you can do."

"Like that time you talked me into toting that beehive over to Cow Island," Val said, picking on him now. "I knew better than to put a hive of bees in a pirogue or any other boat, as far as that goes!"

"That should have worked!" Fate shot back. "The water was level with the bank, and it could've saved a lot of time and work to move it that way if we'd done it just right."

"Well, slamming the pirogue up on the bank so sudden it knocked the hive over missed being just right by a long shot," Val replied. "You backed up, all right, but you plum forgot about the pirogue, yes. Just jumped out and left me, *enh!*"

Adam noticed that Fate didn't let Val sidetrack his education of Mrs. Barclay, whether she was interested in boats or not.

"The thing you got to remember about pirogues is they turn over faster than a frog can snatch a fly," he went on. "You don't want to try to carry a lot of stuff you care about, like fish or game or family. The push skiffs are wider than a pirogue, and the stern—back end—is flat, not pointed. A kid or two can hop around in that without turning you over. And you can get some traveling done in a hurry standing up pushing on both oars. Yessir, for plain old hunting or fishing or going down to the dock for a card game, give me a push skiff any day."

Adam could see Mrs. Barclay's interest was waning. When Fate started yammering about boats, it was hard to fetch the conversation back in line. The conscientious host was still trying to break into the stream of talk when Loyce took control.

"Is this your first trip south of Natchez?" she inquired.

Adam settled back in his chair. If anyone could head Fate off, it was Loyce, and boats didn't rank high with her for conversation.

Then Adam noticed the question made Mrs. Barclay choke on a bite of biscuit and reach for her handkerchief, fine lawn with a little tatting around the edges. A dollar a dozen if he remembered correctly. He couldn't let her stumble like that and ruin her meal, so he spoke up for her.

"I do believe Mrs. Barclay told me she *lives* in New Orleans but just happened to be visiting relatives in Natchez, is that right?"

"That is so, Mr. Snellgrove," she nodded from behind her handkerchief. "And I must say I have not had a better meal in the finest establishments of either city. How did you learn to cook?"

That was as smooth a subject change as anyone could pull off, Adam thought. He acknowledged her skill with a nod. Cooking always made good conversation in his opinion.

"Well, ma'am, after my wife, Josie, died, I didn't care whether I ate or not, but I had those two young'uns and Mame out there depending on me, so I just kept tasting and trying until things came together. Learning to cook was a necessity, but I didn't realize it would also be a comfort. Turns out I even enjoy reading cookbooks. Did you ever read that *Fannie Farmer* book from up north? They eat some different things from us, and I can't say I've cooked much out of it, but it makes good reading all the same. Sort of like taking a trip without having to leave home."

He took another helping of fish and passed the platter to her. She looked interested but shook her head.

"Thank you, but I can barely breathe as it is."

He noticed her seams did pull ever so slightly more than they did earlier, so Adam didn't press the offer.

"Keep that coming 'round this way," said Fate. "This is just the size I like best, the ones too small to sell."

"Talking about people eating different," Val spoke up. "On the Monongahela last trip a buyer come aboard looking for scale fish. Says whole communities up there won't eat catfish. Got to have fish with scales. They're Jews, just like in the Bible."

"Jews!" Fate said. "I thought they were all gone like the Philistines and such. You mean they still around and living here in the United States?"

"Mr. Landry, Jews live all over the United States, including right down the river in New Orleans," said Mrs. Barclay. "All the big cities along the East Coast have sizable Jewish populations, and their faith prohibits them from eating fish that are bottom-feeders such as catfish."

"Now, if a fella could just come up with a way to get loads of worthless buffalo fish to them, he could make some money!" Fate said.

Adam knew what was coming next.

"There you go again, just as predictable as a squawking hen who's just laid an egg," Loyce jumped in.

Talk about predictable, Adam thought. Did Fate say things like that just to rile her? He could tell by the pitch of her voice she was winding up for a long spell of it.

"All you can think of is how many pounds mean how much money. You don't give a thought to how much work that fella would have to put in hauling those buffalo out of the river and then how he's going to get them to those big cities."

"Loyce got a point," Val chimed in. "A load of buffalo would be a powerful weight to row any distance, for true, and they don't live in a fish cart like catfish will."

By then even Adam had to break in with his opinion.

"Depends on the time of year, for sure. A powerful lot of water pours down the 'Chafalaya in the spring. Back in '82, when those surveyors came to measure the rivers around here, they said Bayou Chene was thirty feet deep in places. Alcide claims he's fished places in the 'Chafalaya that's a hundred and fifty feet deep. You won't row upstream long in high water, that's for sure. But what I don't understand is how can someone not eat catfish? I just can't seem to get past that notion. Why would God make a creature as tasty as catfish and then tell people not to eat them?"

Then he noticed the newcomer. She appeared exhausted amid the heated opinions about boats and fish. Adam nodded to her.

"I see you're finished eating, and you must be thinking about stretching out. Let's go see what we can do with that room before dark. The young'uns'll take care of the cleanup."

He led her to the breezeway and held open the screen door. He noticed she stopped on the threshold, just like she'd done in the kitchen. That woman had a problem with doorways.

"What happened?" she finally said, her voice breathless and tinged with wonder. Adam chuckled when she pulled her skirt closer as if to protect it or maybe herself.

"Well, it's a little untidy, now that you mention it," he said. "Things just sort of got out of hand after my wife, Josie, died."

He led the way, kicking boxes, boots, and unpacked inventory aside until they reached the stairs.

"Hadn't been much call to go up here for a while since Mame and Fate moved onto the houseboat, but I think once we get a path opened up, we'll find it has weathered the years."

"Who's Mame?" she asked, breathing close behind his back as if afraid of going astray in the jumble.

"My mother-in-law. Loyce and Fate's grandma. She went daft after her children, Josie and Lauf, drowned."

He told her more about it while picking their way around the packages on the stairs. She followed, holding up her skirt to keep from tripping. The room looked just the same as it had for years. A little bed with a moss mattress set headfirst against the outside wall. A cedar robe and a sewing rocker from the Landry side of the family were on the near side of the bed. On the far side a crockery basin and pitcher waited on a small table. The emptiness of the room made it look larger than its counterpart downstairs.

Adam watched her eyes toting up the lack of carpet, curtains, upholstered chairs, gas lamps, or other nice things she was used to back home in New Orleans or Natchez or wherever she was really from.

"I believe at one time Elder Landry stored extra goods up here, but since the plantations never came back after the war, there's no cause to keep that much stuff on hand," Adam offered, by way of explaining the bareness. "But we should be able to keep you comfortable until your husband sends for you."

Suddenly he stopped trying to raise the window and looked

hard at her face from the side. She was peering into the armoire, sniffing as if a score of rats had died inside.

"He won't be coming, will he, Mrs. Barclay?"

Without looking up from the empty armoire, she said, "I don't know, Mr. Snellgrove, I just don't know."

— 6 —

Roseanne woke the next morning to the screech of nails being pried from a shipping crate in the store below. The sun was high. Several conversations floated up through the plank floor. She could make out the voice of that gray-haired gentleman, Mr. Snellgrove. Despite his backwoods appearance, there was something courtly about him. The way he tilted his head and looked directly at her brought to mind a good priest holding an audience.

Of course, he looked just as attentive when the young ones were playing and singing. The young man with the curls had as pure an Irish tenor as she had ever heard. The dark one—Fate— had stage presence, if nothing else. Whether he was playing, singing, or just standing there, he drew all the eyes in the room. And Loyce, where did she learn to play violin like that when she couldn't even see to read music? How many more surprises did this Bayou Chene hide from the world?

She stretched one more time. The sheets were rough—muslin maybe? And the mattress made crunching sounds whenever she moved or even blinked. It smelled good, though. How had she slept so soundly, when sleep was usually elusive? It must have been the long walk, she concluded. Roseanne Barclay wasn't accustomed to physical exertion and certainly not while carrying her own valises! Someone had always been around to take care of her needs.

Just before collapsing in front of Mr. Snellgrove, she felt perspiration beading on her face, pooling in the crook of her elbows, which were locked against the weight of the valises. How humiliating, even if he was old enough to be her father! It was unseemly for a lady to perspire, and she knew from a lifetime of living in New Orleans that any exertion between April and October would have sweat running down her corset seams and between her thighs, which were encased in long drawers tied over the corset and beneath the corset cover. Stockings, two petticoats, the ankle-length skirt, and long-sleeved blouse completed her informal everyday costume. If she went out, a jacket covered the blouse, no matter the temperature. Even in bed she wore a sleeping corset beneath a high-necked nightgown.

She wondered what Loyce's nightclothes were like. Probably another version of the ugly sack thing she was wearing yesterday— a shapeless cotton housedress vaguely held in place by an apron, which probably would have clashed with the color of the dress if they hadn't both been faded to a muddled gray. Who knows, maybe her day and night dress were the same garment? It was wrinkled enough to have been slept in. Maybe blind women could dress however they liked, or maybe it was the swamp. After all, who would ever see her to care what she wore? Just thinking about it made Roseanne's nose convulse.

Then she sniffed again, on purpose this time. Cream, butter, and vanilla—three of her favorite fragrances—wafted through the cracks in the floor and enticed her out of bed. Even though her stomach growled and she rushed through her morning toilette, it was nearly an hour before she felt presentable enough to go down the stairs. A night of hanging in the armoire had not taken the wrinkles out of her most casual outfit—a blue and black plaid linen skirt with a dark-gray blouse closely buttoned at cuffs and collar. She smoothed the fabric as best she could with her hands, but her nose still jerked when she looked in the armoire mirror. To make up for the dishevelment, she took extra care coiling her hair and securing it with additional pins. Roseanne's spine was also straighter than usual as she descended the stairs, trying to pull the wrinkles out of the clothes with her body.

Mr. Snellgrove had finished with his customer and returned to the kitchen. "Mrs. Barclay, you're just in time for a fresh batch." He greeted her with a wave of the spatula he was wielding over an iron skillet, where four pieces of French bread sizzled in butter.

She knew the bread had been soaked in sweetened cream and beaten eggs, giving the breakfast dish the name "lost bread," or *pain perdu* among the French Creoles of her hometown. Some people said the name came from the fact that the recipe reclaimed stale bread that would otherwise be lost, or thrown away. Roseanne preferred to imagine the dry crusts losing themselves in the rich custard, transformed until they were unrecognizable—truly lost bread. Her stomach growled once more as she watched the bread puff until it doubled in thickness.

Roseanne was always hungry. Her heavy, form-fitting clothes discouraged eating more than a few spoonfuls at a sitting, and she rarely left a table feeling satisfied. Even so, she was constantly having to cut back on what she ate. Once she turned thirty, it seemed that every meal added another inch to her waist and hips. Now that she was thirty-five, every meal left her looking more like her mother's side of the family. So said her trim stepmother, Clothilde.

"Thank you, Mr. Snellgrove, I will have a piece," Roseanne said as casually as she could muster with those fragrances swirling around, confusing her thoughts.

Clothilde's sharp features and nagging voice faded from her mind as she settled into the chair pulled out for her. Once seated, she surveyed the kitchen table made of cypress planks worn smooth by years of dishes sliding across it. Her chair was in front of a small clearing just large enough for the plate and a cup of coffee. The rest of the table was littered with a milk bucket, spools of twine, several wooden shuttles, a few unopened tins of fruit, two boxes of fishhooks, five dirty coffee cups. She sniffed and flicked her handkerchief ineffectually at dried spills.

Without asking how she took her coffee, Adam set a sugar bowl and small pot of scalded milk next to her cup. "You just help yourself, Mrs. Barclay. I hear someone across the way," he said, and was gone through the screen door.

Even though she always took coffee black, the scalded milk and the bowl of sugar had been put out just for her. She didn't want to offend her generous host. It was the first meal she had ever eaten alone. There was no one to supervise her choices. Darting a furtive glance right and left without moving her head, she quickly stirred in a generous spoon of sugar. Then she watched the rich milk swirl the black coffee into a caramel color. She lifted the cup to her lips. It was a different drink from the bitter brew she had known all her life.

Purposefully, deliberately, Roseanne Barclay turned to the lost bread. Instead of the one piece she had asked for, Adam had set the entire platter in front of her. She slid one slice onto her plate. Her fork broke through the brown crust into the golden center of custard-soaked bread. The next thing she knew the platter was empty.

This would not do. Clothilde said the Garnier women always kept their figures, no matter what. In fact, it was rumored that Roseanne's cousin Celestine Garnier nearly died from surgery that removed her bottom ribs so her corset could tighten another fraction of an inch.

Clothilde said Roseanne needn't resort to such drastic measures, even if her mother's side of the family did tend toward roundness. She could just set her mind to follow the Garnier example of self-control. It was only a matter of training herself to eat very little and to always wear close-fitting waists. Even though other matters of discipline came easy—she had the most perfect cursive handwriting in her class and the most precise satin stitch in her embroidery circle—Roseanne's self-control fell short when it came to food.

To get her mind off the empty platter, or maybe to hide the evidence, she picked up the dishes and carried them to the porcelain dishpan, only to find that it was already full of dirty cups and plates. Before she realized what she was doing, she had filled a kettle from the water bucket on the counter. While it heated on the stove, she started clearing the table of non-kitchen items. Fishing gear went into a wooden crate by the back door. The shuttles were stacked neatly in a basket that had held only a dirt dauber's nest and husks of dried garlic.

When the water was hot, she poured it over a bar of Octagon soap in the dishpan and breathed in the fragrance she remembered from washdays, when the kitchen girl would haul baskets of laundry from the clothesline. Later the clothes would be stored away in armoires and linen closets throughout the house, carrying their fragrance with them. When no one was looking, Roseanne would refold every piece in her own armoire so that each set of stockings, individual handkerchiefs, and every pair of drawers were precisely creased and stacked. Then she would make her way through the house from room to room, linen closet to armoire, bringing the folds up to her standards. She didn't know why she kept this self-imposed duty a secret or why it made her uncomfortable to hear her stepmother brag on the kitchen girl's attention to detail.

Order, order, Roseanne had to make order. When she was still in braids, she would check the ribbons throughout the day to make sure they were evenly placed and tied exactly the same way. Roseanne had looked forward to wearing her hair up and not having to keep an eye on the braids throughout the day. But the grown-up style brought no relief. She stabbed more pins into her hair throughout the day, chasing down any curl that sprang out of control. By nightfall her head ached. She went to bed earlier to get relief from the pins.

Order. That was the reason she couldn't walk out of the post office kitchen without washing the dishes, even though she told herself it was just a good way to express appreciation to Mr. Snellgrove for the breakfast. It took three kettles of hot water to wash all the dirty crockery and utensils, and when she finished, the chaos in the rest of the room looked even worse.

Roseanne kept moving, making order despite the tight waist, which was even more constricting after the heavy breakfast. She bent to pick up a pair of muddy boots from the floor and became light-headed. She put a hand on the table to steady herself until it passed. She swooned again when she stretched to lift a broom under the cobwebs drifting from the ceiling. There was no way to take a deep breath. She would stop in mid-stride, lean on something, and breathe shallowly until the dizziness passed.

When Adam came to cook the noon meal, he stopped in the doorway. "Oooh, Mrs. Barclay! What have you done in here?"

"Just a little spit and polish, Mr. Snellgrove," Roseanne said, smoothing down her straining waistband and surveying her work with satisfaction. She had made order out of chaos and cleaned up the evidence of her extravagant breakfast. If only a life was as simple as a kitchen, she thought, and all secrets so easy to keep.

— 7 —

"Drifter, cow pen!"

Fate's voice carried to the porch, where the dog was stretched out by Loyce's foot. She rolled her eyes in his direction and slapped her tail once, but that was all. She'd been that way ever since the snake fracas—claimed her spot next to Loyce and wouldn't budge. When even Loyce gave up trying to shoo her off, Fate knew the little dog possessed extraordinary determination and concentration. All he had to do was figure out how to make that work for him.

"Drifter, cow pen!"

This time he waved toward the pen to give her a hint, to at least start her looking in the right direction. So far the Jersey, who stretched her neck over the picket fence and mooed in Fate's direction, was showing more interest than Drifter. This brought hoots from the porch.

For four days in a row every trifler and rattlehead on the Chene had been educating each other on the fine points of dog training by pointing out what all he and Drifter were doing wrong. All he wanted her to do was learn the names of places in sight of the post office and then go there on command. It just didn't seem like so much to ask, when he was the one who saved her life.

Oh, he knew Loyce and Val both claimed to have had a hand in it, but they got all closed-mouthed when Fate asked them plain and simple who pulled her out of the water and pumped on her till she coughed up that belly full of bayou. Without that, none of the other would have amounted to a hill of beans. But the way she stuck by Loyce now, anyone would think Fate had been just a bystander that day, like all those gawkers and jaybirds on the porch right then that didn't have nothing better to do than interfere with his dog training.

The sun climbed higher and hotter, but that wasn't the only reason sweat was running down Fate's shoulder blades. The few times that ungrateful pup did snuffle in the direction he told her—whether it was the dock, the outhouse, the clothesline, the picket fence, or the cow lot—those knuckleheads all whooped it up and swore that her change in direction was more accidental than intentional.

He was just about ready to give it up when he had one more idea.

"Maybe if you'd come down here and act like you *wanted* to go somewhere, she'd catch on," he yelled up at Loyce.

"I got better things to do than fool with a dog, and so do you," Loyce yelled right back. Fate heard the slap on her thigh and how it made the speckled butter beans dance in the pan on her lap. Of course she couldn't stop there.

"Shouldn't you be running nets today?" she went on. She could be real bossy for such a little thing.

"Awww, they're full of buffalo, and it'd be a lot of work for nothing," he explained, even though he shouldn't have to. They were *his* nets. "Alcide ran his yesterday, and even after selling to the cook of the *Teche Trader,* he had some left over. No one wants to eat buffalo when there's catfish."

As you'd find out if you talked to an expert like Wambly Cracker, he wanted to add and would have if there had been time enough to enjoy his cousin's reaction to the peddler's name. Wambly had figured it out, wrote it down on paper and everything— buffalo weigh in at ten, even twenty pounds each, and sometimes when the water's high, they'll pack into a hoop net so tight you can't run a knife blade between 'em. But fish buyers pay just two cents a pound for them and only buy a few each week. Mostly what you can sell goes to feed the riverboat crews, who don't have much say about what gets put in front of them.

Catfish, now, that's a different story. They taste better, buyers pay four cents a pound, and they can live in the fish cars riverboats tow alongside. Buffalo die right off in a tow car, so they'll never make it to a market in New Orleans or Morgan City.

It just didn't make sense to waste time with buffalo unless a fella was to get up extra early and beat someone like Alcide to the next riverboat cook that docked at the Chene. Fate was not aiming to be that fella. Of course, if a fella could think of a way to get buffalo to those Jews that Mrs. Barclay knows about, it would be a different story. He needed to ask Wambly. You could bet if there was anything to it, Wambly would know.

Fate would have said all that and more just for the fun of riling his cousin, but right then he needed to concentrate on dog training.

"C'mon, Loyce, let's just try one more thing," he pleaded. "Help me out here—I know she'll do it for you."

"Just once, I mean it!" She set aside the pan of beans and started feeling her way to the banister.

Fate watched Loyce toe her way down the steps. Like always, her shapeless dress was pulled in around her middle by apron strings—probably in knots already. He had been unknotting them for her since they were kids. She got impatient and jerked the strings, then before you knew it, there was a knot so tight you had to fetch an ice pick to pry it open.

As usual, there was more of her hair outside her braid than in it, making sort of a fringy frame around her face. He figured her eyes would have been the same blue-gray even if she wasn't blind. The color fit with her light-brown hair, kind of like a great blue heron wading along a sun-streaked bayou bank. That comparison was one of the few things she didn't mind him saying about her looks. She never could catch on to the notion of color, no matter how many times Fate tried to explain it, but she did understand that everyone likes to watch blue herons fishing along the bank.

Her skin brought to mind the Jersey cream he watched her skim by touch. Beat anything he ever saw the way she could slide a big spoon right between the cream and milk, feeling the space between them. He didn't know what she'd make of that comparison, so he played it safe and kept that likeness to himself. Not that he ever paid much attention to what she looked like. Loyce was just Loyce, whether it was the sight, smell, or sound of her.

What really got to him was watching her come down steps. She didn't look at her feet like sighted people do. No sir! She came chin up, head high and tilted to one side—listening like—tapping for the next step with her toe a little bit ahead of the rest of her body. To him that listening stance made her seem more tuned in to the workings of the universe, like she knew something other people, especially Fate, didn't know yet. Add that bossy voice, and you got the notion she was a force.

Yet at the same time she was so little, bones like a chicken. It was all Fate could do to leave her alone when he thought she needed help. After all, she was his cousin, more like a sister really. He'd watched out for her since back when she was taller than him, not that she ever heeded any of his warnings about anything.

"When are you going to start acting like a blind girl!" he had admonished when he found her dangling from a pothook in the kitchen.

That was the day she had climbed up to the cupboard to put away jars of figs Adam had left to cool on the counter. When she slipped, only the knot in her apron strings kept her aloft until Fate reached her. Was she grateful that he saved her from landing in a pile of broken jars and sticky figs? Not unless you'd call bloodying his nose with a kick grateful, which Fate certainly did not. Even though his eyes stung and his breath caught at the unexpected blow, he managed to keep a grip until she was safe on the floor again.

Another time he found her swatting from tree to tree behind the cow lot, where she had wandered off the plank walk trying to find a setting hen's nest. She could have ended up in the woods or stumbled into one of Val's beehives. She thanked him that day with a thrown egg, which he dodged because he knew to be on guard for it. Plus, not being able to see played the devil with her aim.

There were countless other times he stepped between her fool-heartedness and danger. Her response was always the same: "Who are you to tell me how a blind girl is supposed to act? How many do you know? I think when you get right down to it, I'm the authority on this!"

She learned words like *authority* up there at the Blind School, going all the way through the grades like it was nothing. Book learning came easy for her.

Fate put aside his thoughts and met her at the bottom of the steps.

"Here, let's get set up in the right direction," he said, taking her by the hand and facing her toward the cow lot. Drifter turned with Loyce and looked from side to side.

"I think she's catching on!" Fate said excitedly. "Now just hold this rope while I put the other end around her neck."

Fate carefully arranged both ends of the rope, took one more look at his subjects, then pointed while shouting, "Drifter, cow lot!"

The black tail waved, but nothing else moved.

"Maybe if there was something to get her attention," Val said from the porch.

Fate narrowed his eyes at Val, trying to determine whether his pal was making fun or being helpful. Well, nothing else had worked. In one smooth motion Fate picked up a stick and tossed it toward the Jersey cow. Just as quickly, Drifter shot after it, hit the end of the rope, and flipped backward, jerking Loyce down on top of her.

Drifter's squeals were nearly drowned out by "Fate Landry, what'd you do!" Loyce pushed against his hands as he lifted her from the ground and dusted the back of her dress before leading her back to the porch.

"Whoahoa! I'm guessing someone taught her to retrieve. This here is some kind of retriever dog. Loyce, we could make some money just renting her out to hunters. I've seen pictures in the papers of rich men who pay to—"

"No one in Bayou Chene is going to pay to rent a dog!" she said, plopping hard into the seat of the rocking chair for emphasis. "For the last time I'm telling you to find that dog a home."

Loyce's fuming was cut short by the scraping of Val's chair on the porch floor.

"Would you look at that?" He stood up and took off his cap as if it helped him see clearer. He always did that. Fate thought maybe it was something they taught him on the river.

Val squinted again and continued, "Some real sights have drifted around that bend, but this might be the strangest of all."

"What? What is it?" Loyce tilted her ear, her version of Val taking off his cap.

"Is that a silk parasol? What color would you call that outfit?" Fate said, adding an extra dose of wonder to his voice. He knew he was aggravating her but couldn't help himself.

"Fate Landry, you tell me what it is this second, or I'll sic Drifter on the seat of your baggy britches," she said. Drifter thumped her tail at the sound of her name.

"It's a flatboat, Loyce," he explained. "Just a regular old flatboat poled by a regular-looking fella. Looks like they got everything they own with them."

"He's toting a parasol?" her voice slid up, suspicious, alert, feeling her way one step ahead of Fate.

"Nope, that's the girl with him. Or woman. Can't tell which. Skinny, skinny little ol' thing. Sitting on a chair in the middle of the flat dressed in something shiny about the color of a lemon. Holding a purple parasol like she's scared to death of the sunlight hitting her face, which from here looks white as a catfish belly. Her mouth is moving, but it don't appear he's paying any attention to what she's saying. Just keeps poling that flat like his life depended on getting to our dock."

"Chartreuse, Fate. That color is chartreuse." Mrs. Barclay had heard the commotion and walked out to the porch. "I've seen fabric samples like that but never imagined someone buying anything that color. And that violet parasol!" She sniffed and went back inside the store.

Fate and the others watched as the man squeezed past the woman in the chair to reach the bowline at the front of the flat. He hopped onto the dock and snubbed the line to a post. The woman continued to talk, but instead of replying, the man walked silently to where she sat and took her proffered hand. Then he led her carefully through their stacked possessions. After helping her onto the dock, the man stood back to let her pass. He followed her up the plank walk, blocked from view by her parasol.

"Josie Landry?" was the first two words out of the man's mouth.

Before anyone could say anything like "Josie's been dead for more than ten years," Drifter shot off the porch, just like Fate had been trying to get her to do for days. She scooted around the woman, right into the man's arms. From that vantage point she licked his face while squealing in a high-pitched way. Her tail drummed against his thigh. Fate noticed the stranger didn't back away from her tongue; in fact, he looked like he might start licking her back.

"Maggie! Maggie! Girl, I thought you drowned, but I guess you thought I did too! How'd you get here before me?"

The man talked as if he expected an answer from the wriggling black mass in his arms. The dog squealed louder, sliding into a yodeling howl. If it was too loud in the stranger's ear, Fate couldn't tell it by watching. Before the man buried his face in the fur under Drifter's neck, Fate saw he was covered with fresh pink scars as if the skin had been peeled away from his forehead, cheeks, and nose. The dog didn't notice the man's face had moved; her tongue flicked the air above his head, unable to stop the frenzied greeting.

"I guess you own a blue and black skiff? I'm Lafayette Landry, but everyone calls me Fate. Where you coming from, and how'd you lose your rig? What kind of boat is that anyway?"

The stranger blinked slowly, looking for all the world like one of Mary Ann's calves, thought Fate. The whiteface kind with the wide-spaced eyes. The bovine resemblance grew when he blinked a few more times before answering.

"Sam Stockett of St. Louis, and my wife here is C.B. McKernan Stockett of Natchez. Is Josie here?"

Fate noticed that besides being taller, the flamboyant woman was also somewhat older than the man, who appeared to be in his early twenties. Putting on his best manners, Fate nodded to her in greeting and then opened the screened door into the store.

"Please to meet you, ma'am. Mrs. Barclay's in there to take care of you. Tell her to send Adam out, if you don't mind."

"Thank you kindly," she said as she swept through the door, flourishing the parasol closed only after she was safely out of the sun.

Fate leaned against the screen door frame in order to follow the conversations in both places. Mrs. Barclay looked up from the far side of the room, where she was unpacking canned goods and putting them on a shelf. This was gonna be worth paying attention to.

First of all, Mrs. Barclay didn't bother saying "Howdy" or "Kiss my foot" or anything else but just sniffed and stood looking at the woman from the flatboat. Even if that had not been Mrs. Barclay's reaction to most anything new, it was easy to get struck dumb at the sight of the stranger.

Her skin was pale to begin with, even lighter than Loyce's, who never went outside. But on top of that, Fate noticed her face was coated with something like whitewash. It caked into the creases around her lips and eyes and then ran kind of ragged around her ears and jaw. There were bright orange spots on each side of her face and dark smeary circles around her eyes. He thought her yellow hair was right jaunty but so thin in some places that her pink scalp showed through. Pieces of hair that had squirmed loose from their pins were uneven and cottony like singed feathers from a yellow parrot.

She twittered around the store, her chest jerking from side to side without ever touching the stiff top of the low-cut frock, which anyone could tell had been made for a full bosom like Mrs. Barclay's. The bodice had a mind of its own, too, pointing straight ahead no matter which way the bony little chest turned inside of it. She flitted around until her eyes lit on Mrs. Barclay standing in the gloom. She never noticed the sniff nor the glare coming from that direction but just launched right into talking as if she had been invited to speak her mind.

"Howdy! You must be Roseanne. I'm proud to meet you. My name's Cairo Beauty, but everyone just calls me C.B. Named after a jar of pickles, I was. By the time Mama had eight boys she was wore-out and about half-crazy. I guess the surprise of having a girl baby was just too much for her, and she saw that pretty little label on a jar in a store and just stuck that label on me as well. Never could afford to buy a jar of pickles in her life, but being poor didn't keep her from looking." She stopped for breath and then added, "Oh, that young man out there said to send Adam out."

"I'll have to go get him," Mrs. Barclay said. Then she nodded as much to tell Fate to keep an eye on things as to excuse herself across to the kitchen.

While waiting for Roseanne to return, Fate cocked an ear toward Val and the others on the porch, asking questions of the stranger. The man, Sam, talked so low Fate couldn't make much of the answers.

When Adam stepped out, trailed by Roseanne, Fate noted the stranger offered his hand right away. Even if he didn't talk much, Sam Stockett had his manners; Fate would give him that. Adam finished wiping his own hands on the flour sack tucked in his pants before accepting Sam's greeting.

Fate also noticed that Mrs. Barclay didn't waste any time getting back inside the store to keep her eye on the woman.

"I'm looking for Josie Landry—ain't this the post office?" The stranger just couldn't get past that subject, Fate thought. Well, Adam would put him straight.

"Landry was my wife's maiden name." Adam's voice was soft, even for him. "She died more than ten years ago. How did you know her?"

"She and my granny wrote back and forth for years. Granny being housebound, her biggest pastime was reading letters people sent her from all over. Pen pals, she called them. Said you found out stuff newspapers didn't think worth printing. Josie's letters made this sound like a place where a fella with not much but gumption could make a go of it. After Granny died, I kept her box of letters."

"What do you know about that!" Adam shook his head and smiled at the memories the man's story jostled up for him. "Josie couldn't get enough of reading and writing. She found pen pals like your grandma listed in magazines that came through the post office, and she sent her own name and address to every magazine that kept pen pal lists. I teased her that she was the reason the post office saw fit to keep a branch open way out here."

Lost in memories, Adam stood silently for several moments. Never one to let a conversation lag, Fate jumped in to keep the talk moving. It was a job that fell to him uncommonly often, but he could handle it; in fact he was good at it.

"How'd you know to find Bayou Chene? Did Aunt Josie draw your grandma a map?" he prompted.

"I worked at a shoe factory in St. Louis since I was a kid. Got a map from the Corps of Engineers office right there near the wharf. I could tell it was all downstream from St. Louis to Bayou Chene and with any luck at all I should be able to find my way. When I saved enough money, I bought a used skiff and started saving again for food. The other stuff I scrounged from alleys and along the docks. When I figured I had enough to make the trip, I just went to my skiff one morning instead of to the factory."

Sam seemed worn-down by the long spell of talking, so Fate pitched in to give him a rest.

"That's the one I found, Uncle Adam. The blue and black one. I told you it come from up north with them high sides and wide bottom."

By now Sam was squatting on the porch. Fate noticed that his heels were flat on the porch floor. Most men around the Chene squatted in just the same way. They could sit on their heels for hours, giving them a solid base for running lines or working with nets. Fate never could get the hang of it, blaming his long legs for taking up too much room under his chin.

Right then he noticed that the dog—Drifter or Maggie, whoever she was now—sat as close to Sam as she could get. Her head was tucked under his arm for good measure.

"What's Drifter—uh, Maggie—got to do with it?" Fate asked.

"She was hanging around the factory. I used to throw her a bite of my vittles now and then. On the day I left, she seemed to figure there wasn't much of a future there without me, so she just hopped in the boat. We did pretty good coming down, made it off the Mississippi and into the Atchafalaya with no trouble."

He stopped to rest again. Fate opened his mouth to stir things up with another question, but Sam had gathered up enough words for another run at his story.

"We was so close to here when trouble hit. Right up there above Bayou Tensas. It was mainly for Maggie I tried to rope that deer for supper one evening. Swum across right in front of us. Venison seemed pretty good to me, too, after days of beans and bread. Almost worked, too, if that buck hadn't wrapped the line around my arm and liked to pulled it out of socket. Next thing I knew I was on a showboat heading back upriver, every mile undoing the work I had already put in. The crew said they found me on a sandbar being dragged around by one mad buck. I don't know if they'd a stopped just for me, but they had in mind getting some of that deer for supper. Natchez was their next stop. They put me off there."

"Whew, boy! And a sight he was too!" His wife had joined them on the porch. Now she jabbed the folded umbrella in Sam's direction. "We'd just closed down a show, and there wasn't nothing to do till we got to Natchez, so I took him upstairs to my cabin for the rest of the trip. Skin was rubbed plumb off his hide everywhere except his privates, which I guess even unconscious it's a man's instinct to protect. There's this Royal Princess Face Cream that's really good for bruises and cuts—I used it plenty of times, myself. He didn't seem to be in a position to put up no fuss about what I smeared on him. Kept saying the name Maggie over and over. Well I figgered that was his woman, but as days went by and he got better, I found out Maggie was his dog! My own situation had recently turned sour as a green persimmon, and it was time for me to get off that boat, if you know what I mean."

When she stopped to take a breath, so did the listeners. Then she was off again.

"Working the boats is a good way to save money 'cause there's nowhere to spend it. It didn't take long for us to figger out that throwing in together made more good sense than bad. Since he'd lost everything trying to prove hisself to a black dog and a wild-ass buck, we used my stash to buy this flatboat and some supplies. Got married on the way out of Natchez."

Heads bobbed back and forth following the violet umbrella as it punctuated the rest of the story about their trip down the rivers to the post office dock. The only contribution Sam made was an occasional affirmation in response to "Ain't that right, Sam, you correct me if I'm wrong," before she was off again. Sam blinked slowly but never corrected her on a single point.

When the newcomers asked about a place to tie up and settle in, Adam gave them directions to an old homestead up Graveyard Bayou.

"Been vacant as long as I can remember—you'll see it just past the cemetery," he told them. "Won't take much work to make that old dock sound, and there's even a slab shack on the bank until you build something better. A houseboat's your best bet until you decide where you want to stay for good. Find out where you going to be fishing and such."

Val and Fate helped them load supplies the woman had purchased. The dog scurried back and forth in excitement. Sam settled C.B. into her chair and then, without looking up, made a little clicking sound with his tongue.

"Load up, Maggie."

Drifter bounded down the plank walk, but when she reached the dock, instead of jumping in the boat, she stood and barked. Then she ran back up the bank to the porch, looking behind at Sam. She flew back and forth twice more without stopping.

"Maggie, git on in here now. We need to go," Sam called.

Obediently, she jumped off the porch and headed back down the walk but not with abandon this time. She walked purposefully but then stopped halfway. Her eyes locked onto Sam's. She strained with stillness. Only the tip of her tail moved back and forth, ever so slightly. He blinked. She didn't.

"Maggie, I mean it. I'm untying this line." He bent over the knot. She watched. He held her eyes briefly, once more, before turning his back.

"Well, stay if you want, it matters none to me," he said, but his voice sagged.

He turned his back to her and pushed the pole against the dock; the flat eased into the current. Sam continued poling them away without looking up to wave good-bye. C.B. made up for his dismissal by shouting, "Ya'll come see us when we get settled," and waving madly until they disappeared around the bend. The dog whined and watched until they were out of sight but didn't move to follow along the bank.

"Whew, what a trial to be trapped with that woman on a flatboat day and night!" Adam said, shaking his head as he turned toward the kitchen. "No wonder that man doesn't have much to say."

Roseanne stood with her arms folded across her bosom, sniffing in the way Adam had come to know. He stopped in the doorway and turned.

"I wonder what he'd have to say if he knew she was in here wanting to buy French female pills to get rid of her baby," she said.

— 8 —

"Mr. Snellgrove, this just won't do!" Roseanne bustled into the kitchen, where Adam was standing over a black iron skillet. "I'm not a person to just sit and wait for disaster to strike!"

"And I'd be amiss to take you for one, Mrs. Barclay." Adam couldn't look up at that crucial moment of stirring a handful of flour into a pool of melting lard. He knew it had to be quick and smooth. Let the tiniest bit of flour scorch, and the roux would turn bitter as quinine. Nothing to do with it then but throw it out. He knew enough about that from the times he had tried to sneak in some reading while cooking.

"And what impending disaster might this be?" he asked, when the roux had smoothed to silk. Nothing to do now until it turned the color of chocolate on bottom and needed stirring again. He glanced up at Roseanne's flushed face.

"Humiliation, Mr. Snellgrove," she sniffed. "I'm in danger of being severely humiliated."

He had come to recognize her sniff and knew that sometimes she also used it to breathe in the fragrance of something he was cooking. He could tell that skillet of browning roux was on her mind in a powerful way. Adam's gaze stayed on her face when he dropped in the chopped onions, then the bell pepper and garlic. She didn't even know what he was making, but those smells were getting the best of whatever she was upset about. He lowered his eyes so she couldn't see the merriment in them. Mrs. Barclay didn't take kindly to not being taken seriously.

She drew in another breath as deep as her waist would allow, which wasn't much. In fact, it was tighter than when she had worn it the week before. He remembered it because the russet color made her eyes less black, warmer somehow. Adam knew all about russet, just another one of those things you have to know if you are going to help women shop from a catalog. Don't let them order russet if they really want plain brown or bright red. You'll be sending it right back.

Right then Mrs. Barclay's eyes were as black as the jet combs holding up her hair, and her cheeks looked rosy like she'd been running. Then he remembered the sound of crates and barrels dragging around the store all morning. She must have been putting away stock whenever there was a lull between customers. He'd never had a chance to get ahead like that since the drownings. Was that a decade ago? As far as he knew, some of the things she shelved might have been sitting there since that fateful night.

Roseanne blew out a breath, and a curl that had sneaked out of her combs puffed out with it. She must have kept on talking while he was thinking about russet.

"I know we agreed that I would assist in the store in exchange for room and board until my husband sends passage for me," she said. "But I find my clothes are not suited to the work. Why just now I had to open a bottle of smelling salts to keep from fainting. Not only does that deplete the inventory, Mr. Snellgrove, but what if I had fainted and someone saw me fall out right onto the floor, with my skirts all askew and my hair falling down, unconscious, not even knowing who was looking at me?"

She sniffed at the image. "I might well die from the humiliation."

He pondered the scene for himself, and it wasn't until she "ahemmed" with another puff of air that he ventured into the stream of that particular conversation.

"Your husband will probably send for you before it comes to

that, Mrs. Barclay—didn't you write him a letter about your mishap? Surely he'll be sending passage for you soon."

"Well, most certainly," she snapped, with more force than seemed necessary. Her eyes glided up and to the side in that way she had, bringing to mind how a fish in a trap swims right past your hands until sometimes you have to drain all the water out before you can catch it.

"But there's no telling how long it will take for that letter to find him," she continued in that slippery way. "Perhaps he's not even staying at the same establishment this trip. The reality is, Mr. Snellgrove, I may be here longer than I first expected, and my traveling clothes simply won't do. I propose that you consider adding a small wage to my food and lodging in exchange for me taking on more responsibility for your business. Even you must have noticed more goods are actually being sold now that it's easier for your customers to find what they are looking for and that I am on hand to actually collect payment, rather than allowing people to just pay when they feel like it. Mr. Snellgrove, as I've heard my own father and husband say many times: 'When it comes to profit, management wins over product any day of the week!'"

"Well, Mrs. Barclay, I won't argue with you there," he admitted. "I never did have a head for this stuff, and it just came to be too blamed much for one man to stay on top of. I tell you what, how's $1.75 a week sound? We can keep it up as long as what you are doing around here brings that much extra. I can advance you two weeks' wages to order them frocks."

"You have yourself a manager, Mr. Snellgrove," she said right back. Then she stuck out her hand to seal the bargain. He passed the cooking spoon to his other hand and held hers but a moment. Then she swept away across the dogtrot, leaving him to ponder what he had just done.

— 9 —

Loyce was still mulling over the business transaction she'd heard from the kitchen when Mrs. Barclay tap-tap-tapped across the dogtrot to the store. In two more seconds she was tapping back again and settling into the chair across the porch. Loyce knew that when people had something to read, they sat with their back to the outside, so she wasn't surprised when pages started rustling across the way. She could tell it was the catalog used to order everything from the canned goods on the shelves to mule harnesses.

She hadn't learned much about Mrs. Barclay in the few weeks the mysterious woman had lived upstairs, but one thing was sure—if something needed doing, she hopped right on it. No jawing and worrying or trying to talk herself out of it, like some people do. Loyce had lost count of the times Fate had hit on a scheme to make quick money and then talked it over, around, and upside down until the notion passed. His mouth ran away from his brain every time.

Mrs. Barclay, now, she was just the opposite. Some idea for an improvement would come to her, and she would dive in without stopping to tell Adam or Loyce. The next thing they knew, pattern books and sewing supplies were all together in one corner of the store. Mule collars, saddles, and other bulky items hung from the rafters instead of lying in heaps on the floor.

Loyce couldn't imagine going back to the way they lived before Mrs. Barclay. She knew how to keep things moving in the right direction, for sure. They never ran out of clean clothes anymore. Loyce didn't have to worry about grabbing a handful of fishhooks that weren't supposed to be on the kitchen table or next to the washbasin. Despite Mrs. Barclay's quick way to jump to conclusions about some things, Loyce dreaded the day her husband would come for her.

Now catalog pages snapped from across the porch, signaling another project launched.

"Loyce, I've never ordered a ready-made dress." Roseanne's voice was matter of fact. "I'm leery of the whole process—working from drawings, size charts, and fabric descriptions. I'm accustomed to seeing the fabrics and feeling them against my skin. Back home a seamstress measures me for every new dress, and we have several fittings before it is finished. I just don't know about this."

"How can it be that complicated?" Loyce queried. "Other people have always decided what I'm going to wear. Just so it's short enough that I don't trip over the hem, nothing else matters much."

"Of course, how could you know?" Mrs. Barclay rose from her chair and tapped across the porch. "Here, feel my bodice."

She picked up Loyce's hand and guided it to a high collar, stiff as bark, pressed into the skin beneath her jaw. More unyielding fabric pulled across her collarbone into sleeves tight as winter stockings but without the stretch. Her middle was hard as a china doll. A corset! All the grown women at Loyce's school had worn them. All except the cook whose big soft bosom used to be as comforting to a sick child as the cocoa and toast she brought to their beds.

"My word, Mrs. Barclay, how do you get anything done girded up like that?"

For the first time Loyce heard her break into a deep laugh. At least her voice had taken off some layers.

"Just call me Roseanne, Loyce," she said, still laughing as she quick-stepped back to her chair. Then she took a sniffy little breath of air and started over. "Things are so different out here. Back home dressing is not about getting things done. It's about looking appropriate for the occasion."

"What occasions do you dress for like *that*?"

"Oh, just about everything—outings of any kind, art exhibits, musical performances, plays, lectures, as well as just gatherings of acquaintances for dining and visiting. Entertaining is important for my family's businesses."

Loyce's attention jerked to a stop at the mention of music. "Oh, what I'd give to hear some of that music!" She sounded wistful. "We used to go to concerts a couple times a year when I was at school. I even heard a woman sing from an opera once, and the magic of it just opened me all up inside. Now, sometimes when a showboat comes through, I'll get to hear a fine piece of music, but I can't remember it long enough to get back home and try to play it. And Val brings me tunes he picks up on the river, but it's not the same kind of music."

"Oh yes, we attend operas regularly," Roseanne said. "I can't say many of them resonate with me. Mostly it's about the dresses, the hats, the hairstyles." She chuckled again.

Then Loyce heard her sigh and turn more catalog pages, stopping now and then to take a better look. The turning slowed, then was broken by spells of silence.

"Where are the housedresses? Here we go! Not just a straight sack style like you wear nor a tight bodice like I customarily wear. Sort of in-between. Slightly gathered top caught in at the waist. I can do whatever a day's work calls for and still look decent. Just to make sure it fits, I'll even get a size larger than usual," she said. "What do you think about a russet—that's always one of my best colors. And maybe the dark blue."

"You're asking the wrong person about that!" Loyce couldn't help but laugh. Sometimes the people who were around her the most forgot she didn't see.

"Pardon me, you are right about that," Roseanne chuckled. "But you can help me with another decision. After ordering two dresses, I'll have enough left out of my $3.50 to buy either a larger corset or a pair of comfortable walking shoes. My feet hurt all the time, but the looser dresses won't bring much relief if I'm still wearing a tight corset. You just don't know what it's like to never be able to take a deep breath. You are so slender you can get away with just a chemise under your dresses. If you had a curvaceous figure like mine or if you ever start wearing fitted tops, you'll know what I'm talking about."

Loyce was only half-listening now. She was still thinking that it might be worth girding up her bosom or any other body parts if it meant she could sit in a big crowd of people listening to beautiful music. Not that she was ever likely to get that chance. She was jerked back to the reality of the porch when Roseanne turned a page and gasped.

"Oh my goodness, look—I mean, listen to this, Loyce! The drawing shows what appears to be a corset with the bottom cut off, leaving the midsection completely unbound—a secret that would be all too plain to anyone who accidentally brushed against a woman who dared to wear such a thing. Really, all it amounts to is a sling contraption that simply pillows the bosom! The caption under the drawing says it's a *brassière*. French—no surprise there. It's described as a 'healthful' alternative for vigorous exercise. Of all things! It's a scandal, that's what it is!"

She sniffed and quickly turned the page. It was Loyce's turn to chuckle again as she picked up her shuttle and cotton line.

After more scratching and erasing on the order form, Roseanne finally sighed and settled on the shoes.

"I'll just eat less and try to let out my old corset strings until I can afford a larger one," she said. "Well, Loyce, this catalog order marks the first time in my life that I have spent money I earned myself. It's a good feeling; I just wish there was more of it."

Loyce paused in her work and tilted her head to one side as if hitting on a brand-new thought herself.

"Tell you what, Roseanne. I have some money saved and nothing to spend it on, so how about I give you enough for that new corset. In return you take my measurements and order me a new dress as well. Do they have one my size colored like a great blue heron?"

It was a morning well into June when the dresses were delivered in a crate of dry goods from Morgan City. By that time Roseanne had caught up with stocking the store's backlog of inventory. She opened the crates the same day they arrived, a novelty for the customers, who were accustomed to scavenging for items they wished to purchase. Roseanne would have the goods displayed on shelves or tables by the next afternoon, but first she had to run upstairs to try on the dresses.

Her bedroom door had barely closed when she removed the fitted bodice and unlaced the old corset with a sigh of relief. There was a zigzag of cord across her skin where she had let it out way past modesty's sake. She laced up the new, larger size, guessing at how tightly to draw it in so that it would just fill out the new bodice. Then she pulled the lightweight, cotton print dress over her head. While buttoning the bodice front, she shifted her bosom from side to side and found there was still room to loosen her corset even more. Oh, could life get any better! She didn't take the time to loosen it at the moment since she could already breathe more deeply. Besides, there was a crate still waiting for her to unpack. She flew back down the stairs, feeling unfettered for the first time in years.

A few hours later the flow of customers thinned out as people began heading home to start afternoon chores. The new frocks had launched Roseanne into a celebratory state. Loyce was out front to keep company with any customers who dropped in, making this the ideal time for Roseanne to wash her hair. She stopped by the porch to tell Loyce and then whisked out to the cistern with two buckets.

On the porch Loyce's rocking chair creaked to fit the rhythm of her shuttle. Knitting could be satisfying like that. Put the twine in your left hand, then the right hand moves on its own, in and out. She didn't even think about it. Val had told her that the shuttle she used and the knot it made were the same all around the world.

The very same! He read to her about it one afternoon from that magazine of the National Geographic Society. Now wouldn't it be fine to just pick up something like that and read about shuttles on her own? But she wouldn't stop there.

"Hmmph!" She had butted in to his reading. "If I could read, I'd be learning more than shuttles and knots. I'd read about explorers and thinkers. What people eat in other countries. I'd find out how cotton goes from being a plant to a piece of cloth. And what about thunder? No one on the Chene can explain to me what makes that booming noise during summer storms and why we don't hear it in winter when it rains every day. There's smart people out there who know so many things, but they're not likely to come here and tell me about it."

Val hadn't said anything, just turned another page. For some reason that vexed her even more. People liked to watch her demonstrate how braille worked, but truth be told, most of what she could get in braille was for youngsters learning to read—there wasn't much for grown-ups. Oh, Adam was happy to read to her from his books, but even she understood that was easiest done by daylight when he was already so busy. And Adam's books were mostly novels from a much earlier time. What did she care about old stories and make-believe characters? She wanted to know real things!

After stewing awhile, she had felt ashamed for cutting in on Val, who could have been doing something other than sitting on the porch reading to her. Whether or not he really was sweet on her, as Fate kept saying, he clearly thought about her even when he was away from the Chene. Her room was decorated with little gifts brought back from his travels. Things no one else would guess she was interested in. A smooth rock from the Ohio River because there were no rocks in the swamp. The face of a tiny monkey carved into a peach seed. He even guided her fingers around the features to give her an idea of what a monkey looked like. Val understood her restless curiosity the way no one else did, and he got such a kick out of bringing the world to her. At least as much of it as he could carry in his own hands.

"I do appreciate you reading to me and telling me what you see up and down the rivers," she had said by way of apology, "but that only makes me want to know more. Like that World's Fair in St. Louis that even Wambly Cracker went to and learned all kinds of things that he won't do nothing with but botch up. Imagine the things I could have learned there just by listening, touching, and smelling. It wouldn't matter that I can't *see*—I just need to get to where it's going on!"

How high-handed she had been with Val! They were used to listening to each other sound off, but maybe that day she did make him feel a little guilty about being able to just take off and go places while she was stuck there every day of the year. Other than a few dances at the schoolhouse or a showboat passing through now and then, there wasn't much at Bayou Chene for a blind girl to do.

Oh well, for every time Val had listened to her complain about being a prisoner, she had listened to him wish he could get off the river and settle down. He had even hinted that he'd like to settle down right here on the Chene. Fate said if Val did that, the next thing they'd know he would be asking Loyce to marry him! That's Fate for you, thinking up stuff that might bring more complications than it would solve. Loyce figured it all came down to everyone wanting what someone else has, even for a little while to see how it fits.

Suddenly through that quiet afternoon—so quiet she could hear fish rippling just under the water, not even breaking the surface—she felt someone watching. Not close, not like the kids who sneaked up behind her chair and had her guess their names. It was like a furtive breeze on the back of her neck. She felt it the way she could feel a hand passing close but holding back from touching her face.

Why watch someone rocking and knitting a net? She stopped rocking, tilted one ear up, and held her breath to get a better listen. Was she imagining it? No, a low growl was purring up from Drifter's throat. Loyce felt the little dog ease up from her napping position to her feet, softly, just like when she was creeping up on a

82

lizard. Both of them tensed, waiting for the person to step out and yell a greeting. Seconds ticked by. She couldn't stand it any longer.

"Who's there?"

No answer.

"You! That's watching me. Who are you?"

Drifter growled again. Across the bayou on Indigo Island—a stagnant hole of no use to anyone—unseen by Loyce, two buttonwood bushes eased back into place.

After that afternoon Loyce strained to hear any new sound through the usual clamor around the post office. An unfamiliar voice or a new step that could explain her uneasiness. Days passed, and nothing out of the ordinary happened. Eventually, she shook it off and even blamed her own imagination for Drifter's continued anxiety. The little dog went beyond keeping her company, staying so close underfoot that Loyce stepped on or tripped over her several times a day.

— 10 —

The pan slapping against the picket fence was enough to break into Mame's thoughts. Some days it didn't take much. Other times she kept her mind shuttered from daylight to dark. That day she stopped stabbing the earth and watched the hens tackle the pile of corn shucks. They finished scratching for stray kernels and then went on to block Loyce's way on the plank walk, hoping for better pickings. The little black dog rushed back and forth, back and forth, barking, trying to make a path for the blind girl.

"Shoo, shoo, you're just making it worse," Mame heard her fuss in that voice so much like Josie's.

The sound of that voice almost sent her back, but then she was caught up watching how expertly Loyce kicked one foot at a time out in front, fighting her way through the chickens and dog. *Determined*, Mame thought. Like Fate says, a force. That boy might as well try to smooth the hackles of a coon caught in a leg trap as to watch out for Loyce.

The shuffling, barking, pecking crowd, absent a few feathers, was almost to the house when Mame heard the pony cart coming faster than usual down the woods path. She squatted back on her heels and pushed her bonnet up to see.

"That's it—he's done it now!" The voice was even louder than the rattle of the cart shaking to a stop at the edge of the garden.

The old woman squinted up. Mary Ann. Married to York Bertram, son of Mame's brother, Martin Bertram. Wasn't she usually

smiling? Mame couldn't remember for sure. Maybe she had someone else in mind.

Heat or no heat, Mary Ann wore a long-sleeved shirt tucked
into men's pants that flared out and then dipped into the top of her
rubber boots. She mopped her face with a bandana that was hanging around her neck. Blue eyes burned from under her hat. Pirates
came to mind, and Mame glanced around to get her bearings. It
didn't take much for her to drift off track. She wanted to keep up
in case there was something she could do to help.

Mary Ann's goat Fredette bleated from the back of the wagon,
hooves clattering to keep balance through the stop. Shiny brown
like a mink, a black stripe bristled straight up from her backbone.
She tossed her bony little head bearing a swoop of horns sharp as
daggers.

Looking every bit the demon York swears she is, Mame
thought. Or did she say it out loud? So hard to tell anymore after
years of talking to the dead.

"Has anyone around here seen or heard my litter of red hogs?"
Mary Ann shouted to anyone in hearing distance. "The gate was
open, and nary a one was around this morning. I know he did it a
purpose—that's the spitefullest man I know."

Fredette cut her short by crashing into the back of her knees.
Mary Ann scrabbled for balance in the rubber boots but plopped
down anyway. Anger whooshed out of her. That seemed real
enough to Mame.

"Mame, does meanness just run in the men of your family?"
The wagon seat groaned under her shifting weight. Fredette clattered back and forth.

"Oh, I'd say it's mellowed some in the passing down." She removed her bonnet for an unobstructed view of Mary Ann's face.
The younger woman's eyes softened and focused back at her.
Mame took that to mean she really was talking out loud, so she
worked more on that thought before it got lost again.

"York's got a ways to go if he's gonna catch up to his daddy
in meanness, better yet his grandpa—Father Bertram. Since you
didn't grow up here, you had the pleasure of not knowing York's

grandparents. Martin and me had to call them Mother and Father Bertram, if that tells you anything. I still got the scars on my knees from the hours we spent kneeling on shell corn as young'uns. I tried to shield Martin from the worst of the whippings, but when the notion would take over, there was no stopping Father Bertram."

Mary Ann's eyes shifted from Mame's face to the path ahead. Did that mean her words had already curved in on themselves and were thoughts again? Whether she was thinking or talking, the stream had to run its course.

"And Mother Bertram was no bosom of kindness for her part," she kept going. "Many's the time she not only whipped me but made me do the entire day's wash over again because of one bird dropping on a piece of clothes. Like I could help that! And while she was too frail to do a lick of housework herself, she could get around good enough to crawl under the beds with a candle to make sure I got all the dust. She'd even whip me for whistling! Said a whistling girl and a crowing hen were headed for a bad end, or some such. No wonder Martin and me both left home as soon as we were able. I went to work for Elder and took over raising Josie like she was my own. Never regretted it a minute."

"I didn't know you wasn't Josie's mama," Mary Ann said, a little calmer. Mame pushed ahead through the fog that was closing in.

"Of course. I suppose you wouldn't." Even she could hear her voice beginning to drift.

"All that happened so long ago, most people who were born here don't even remember it. Elder's first wife, Maudie, died of the typhoid right before the war. She was as jolly as my own Mother Bertram was mean. Fact was, I called her Ma. It was short for Maudie and made up a bit for having to call my own mama Mother Bertram. I found reasons to hang around the store even before Maudie came down sick. Josie was born around that time."

Mame's voice dropped to a mumble, but her mind kept running.

Still happens a lot out here—what with no doctors, even young women die, leaving a husband with kids. And what with drown-

ing, hot tar, snakebites, card games, and such *afflicting the men, some wives outlive two or three husbands. People marry up again, and after a few years no one keeps track of who the different kids came with.*

Especially that year Maudie died . . . '60? '61? I can't remember for sure, but it was so pitiful. The typhoid was like an epidemic that spring—so many people got sick and died. Right about that time Father Bertram just seemed to sprout meanness like the horns on that goat. My brother, Martin, took off for the war, along with Josie's brothers and most of the other young men around here. I started out taking care of Maudie till she died and then raising Josie.

It worked out for everyone when Elder asked me to stay on permanent by marrying. Not one of Elder's boys made it back from the war, so Josie and I were all he had. He was some proud when Lauf come along so quick the next year.

Lauf was a good baby and a happy boy. Maybe because he got so much attention. Anyway, whatever the reason, when he got older, he liked helping around the store like Josie did in the post office. He just never did get the hang of fishing and swamping like most of 'em do around here. Storekeeping seemed to suit him better than that hard dirty work.

He would have made good with the store, and Adam could have kept on fishing and swamping if things had stayed the same. Beatrice and Josie shared the care of their young'uns, making it easier on both of them. Those were happy years.

I remember the night they found the last of the bodies. Beatrice. I finally went to bed. I was tossing around trying to rest somehow, but my mind was just too tortured. Then all of a sudden I heard crackling, just like willow sounds when it burns. My scalp felt like it had ants crawling all over it. I didn't think no more about it until a few weeks later—Adam noticed my hair was growing out white as cotton at the roots.

Everything was different after that. Adam couldn't be gone off fishing if we was to keep the store and post office open. I wasn't any help; my spirit just left me. I couldn't rouse up even to help with the young'uns.

Mame noticed Mary Ann was looking at her like she was expecting something. Was she talking? Was Mary Ann? The old woman brought all her mind to bear and finally caught it—Mary Ann's question about York's temper.

"I swore I'd never treat my kids like Father and Mother Bertram treated Martin and me," she said, snatching up the thread of conversation before it unraveled even more. "But I guess Martin might of forgot because I heard he was mighty hard on York growing up. I was so glad to have family again when you and York moved here, but sometimes it does seem like he is Father Bertram come back in the flesh."

"So, what's that got to do with me?" Mary Ann fumed. "I married York; I didn't take him to raise."

"I guess what it means is, it's probably for the best that you and York don't have no young'uns. Just stop that mean streak of Bertrams right here and now."

Mame's voice dipped again as her train of thought wobbled back on itself. She couldn't tell whether Mary Ann heard her over Fredette's hooves on the floorboards, but then the young woman slapped the reins and yelled, "Well, I can tell you right now, I ain't got no babies on my mind. I'm just thinking on some way to get him back. I can give as well as I get!"

Fredette spread her legs and braced. Devil eyes flashing, bleats trailing behind, they were gone around the bend.

Mame was left standing, bonnet in hand, still thinking about Martin living up there in Plaquemine all those years. Could've seen his son, York, every day but didn't. She never treated Josie and Lauf like that, but she lost them just the same. Just the same. There was naught to do but get back to digging.

— 11 —

On a July afternoon two weeks after Mary Ann's angry visit, Roseanne was carrying buckets of water from the cistern to the kitchen. Early afternoons were generally quiet, so she had asked Loyce to mind the store. Now that the business and household were set up to run smoothly, Loyce could be there for customers while Roseanne enjoyed a few hours off.

Roseanne's help, in turn, gave Adam a chance to return to fishing after more than a decade of being land bound. How he had missed prowling those quiet bayous! In their shadowy depths he found more than catfish, blue crabs, and river shrimp. He rediscovered a vitality he had thought was gone forever. These days his step was quick and light on the boardwalk to the dock. His arms muscled up from rowing boats and pulling nets. Shirt buttons strained across his chest, until he had to leave the top ones unbuttoned. The sun bronzed his face, making his gray hair and eyes shimmer in contrast.

He rowed home smelling of green cypress, bringing a merriment Loyce barely remembered and Roseanne had never seen. Just last evening he had been whistling softly while cleaning fish on the dock. Roseanne walked out to bring him the dishpan.

"Ah, Mrs. Barclay, you always anticipate my needs," he said, with a mock flourish of the fish skinners. "Have I told you how much you relieve me of burdens I didn't even know I carried? I'm a century younger than before you stepped out of the woods. Was that just two months ago?" His gray eyes twinkled to match the playfulness in his voice.

"You probably didn't think events were headed in that direction when you saw me dragging those valises!" she said, catching his humor. "If you had laughed at me that day, I would have died of humiliation! How did you refrain?"

"You clearly were a damsel in distress, Mrs. Barclay," he continued in a theatrical voice, opening the screen door to the kitchen with another gallant flourish. "Seeing as how I learned to read on the great chivalric novels, I couldn't shame my heroes by making light of your situation. And now you have repaid me many times over."

Together they looked around the neat kitchen, so different from the chaos she had stumbled upon back in the spring. Gone was the jumble of goods, clothes, and papers strewn across both floors of the old house. No more iron pots of scorched food soaking at the water cistern until the insides turned to rust. They both took in the serenity of the well-ordered household. Likewise, they both avoided the question of how and when it might end.

Now as she easily carried two full buckets of water across the yard and up the steps, Roseanne realized she had changed as much as the household, maybe more. Before coming to the Chene, Roseanne had never lifted more than a croquet mallet and then only when she couldn't get out of a Sunday afternoon match. She was grateful that her family and friends couldn't see how she spent her time now. They'd probably try to rescue her!

Truth be told, she didn't mind the work. It was satisfying to help customers shop for the things that made their lives more comfortable. She particularly enjoyed researching various catalogs for specialty items. And there was real satisfaction in balancing the sales against the cash on hand at the end of the day.

With the increased mental stimulation and physical exercise, Roseanne felt more alive than any other time in her life. At times she found herself in spirited arguments with Adam over books that she had yawned through in school. She also felt free to express her own opinions with Adam, Loyce, and the customers in a way she never could back home. But she had to be careful about that, she reminded herself. Talking too much about her past could lead to trouble. The most important thing was to make sure no one from her old life found out where she was and what she had gotten herself into. Toting her own bathwater was nothing compared to that!

Roseanne filled two kettles from one of the buckets and set them on the stove, before adding a stick of dry ash wood to the firebox. She poured the remainder of the water into the dishpan. Watching the pan fill brought to mind the first time she had done that—the morning she cleaned the kitchen and nearly fainted from the exertion because of her corset. Surely that was a lifetime ago! In her looser corset and soft shoes, she could breathe and move with near-scandalous alacrity.

Now, as the water heated, she removed the pins and shook down her hair. Bending from the waist, she vigorously brushed it out, reveling in the freedom of its movement. She removed her dress and corset, folding them neatly over the back of a chair. Then standing in only her chemise, she poured the hot water into the dishpan and swirled it with her hand before bending again. Her hair floated like a dark cloud on top of the water. She relaxed with her scalp below the surface for a minute, enjoying the sensation of warmth. Then she lifted her head and poured liquid castile soap into her palm. Starting from the scalp, she massaged the suds through her wet hair, working toward the dripping ends.

She dipped her entire head beneath the surface again, swirling the hair around and then squeezing the soapy water back into the pan. As she lifted her torso to pour the used water into the pail, warm streams coursed down the side of her face and neck under the thin cotton chemise. By the time she bent again into a fresh pan of water, the wet cotton plastered the curve of her bosom.

Had her head not been under water, she may have heard Adam's step at the screen door. His breath caught at the sight of her breasts swinging in the sodden cloth, the ridge of her spine, still straight, even as she bent from the waist. Her hands scooped water that ran across her white neck.

Adam caught the door for support. When his strength returned, it seemed the most natural thing in the world to walk in and rinse the spot of suds she kept missing. Instead, he forced his arm to close the door, and he walked around the back of the house to the store entrance. Where was that damn fool husband of hers?

Out front Drifter lay panting under the roof overhang, where the sun had moved from the east side of the porch to the west.

"C'mon, Drifter," Loyce said. "The clothesline is in the shade by now."

The little black dog stretched and yawned as Loyce felt her way down the steps to the plank walk connecting the porch to the back lot. Before Loyce had made it to the walk, Drifter was already sniffing ahead of her on the path. When the walk forked—right to the cistern, left to the outhouse—Loyce bore to the right and counted six steps before leaving the security of the planks. Angling her body even more to the right, she felt ahead with each foot before committing her weight behind the move. Coals from the washday fire gave her plenty of warning with their heat, but experience had taught her that tubs, buckets, logs, or a sleeping cat could be anywhere in the lot. Steps were not precise on the open ground, so she didn't bother to count but relied instead on waving her outstretched arms slowly up and down, until her fingers brushed the first stiff, sun-dried garment. She continued following the clothesline and feeling the ground with her foot until she located the wicker basket.

Laundry was a communal task. Soon after daylight Adam built the fire under the cast iron washpot he had filled with rainwater from the cistern. As it heated, he carried more water for the two galvanized rinse tubs. Roseanne did the actual washing, while Adam waited on customers. She grated Octagon soap into the tub of hot water and agitated the suds with a paddle. Stains were rubbed on the washboard with an extra dab of soap. Each piece was dropped into a tub of cold water and rinsed once, then again in a second tub. During lulls between customers, Adam helped with the wringing, wrapping long pieces around a young sapling to squeeze them nearly dry. Sometimes Mame would wander up to help with the washing or pinning the individual pieces to the cotton lines stretched between cottonwood trees. This time of year the sun dried their combined labor in a few hours.

Now feeling her way along the lines, Loyce removed clothespins from the garments, placing the pins back on the line before dropping each piece into the wicker basket on the ground. She pushed the basket along with her foot, often bumping into Drifter, who snuffled around the yard under the lines. When she felt no more weight on the lines, she lifted the basket to her hip and turned left, feeling her way back to the plank walk, finally making her way to the porch. Well, that was her big excursion for the day, maybe even for the entire week!

Placing the basket on the bed Fate had slept in as a little boy, she removed each piece of laundry, making stacks for each person. She folded her own stack as well as the items for the linen closet. She had noticed that linens were refolded and stacked precisely on the shelves since Roseanne's arrival, but she didn't take it as a rebuke on her own casual folding. Before Roseanne came, Adam and Mame didn't think to do laundry until everyone was wearing dirty clothes. When they did get around to it, one tub full of washing could take all day to complete, what with Mame wandering off and Adam tending to customers. Yessir, Roseanne's past was a mystery, but Loyce hoped she'd come to stay.

Loyce settled into the porch rocker and tested the rolled-up newspaper in the palm of her left hand. She was waiting for the lone bee droning around the porch rafters. Otherwise, the afternoon was so quiet she could hear the *chk, chk, chk* of Mame's butcher knife coming from behind the house, where she was weeding a patch of lilies.

Suddenly she felt that prickle behind her neck, the one she had come to think of as The Watcher. While she couldn't comprehend visual observation, she understood that someone was deliberately withholding all cues from her. She felt vulnerable and exposed for the third time in as many weeks. It always happened when there was no one around except Drifter. She held her breath and concentrated on listening.

Then she heard the swish of a paddle. It was followed, seconds later, by Fate's voice coming from the dock.

"Hey Loyce, is the coffee water on?"

Relief flooded the tension out of her muscles, and she let out the breath she had been holding. It must have been her imagination after all. Maybe that's all it ever was.

"Well, it's three o'clock, so where'd you expect it to be?" she replied, slapping the rocking chair arm with the newspaper for emphasis. "Roseanne should be down to drip it in a bit. I think she's pinning up her hair now that it's dry. The *Golden Era*'s docked, so Val should be along too."

The boat clunked against the dock, and she heard Fate's step, hollow sounding as he walked from stern to bow and then more solid as he strode the plank walk toward the porch. She couldn't stop herself from counting the twenty steps. When Fate bounded onto the porch, she stood up from the chair but kept her grip on the rolled newspaper. He swept an arm around her waist and untied her apron, hugging her to him when she tried to retie it.

"Get on now," she said. "I've been laying wait for that whining old bee since morning, so don't go scaring him off."

"What makes you think it's a he and not a she?" Fate queried. He held her close until she returned the hug. His familiar body was a comfort after her scare, and she stayed in his embrace longer than usual.

"'Cause he just makes noise and never produces anything useful," she laughed.

"Hey, there's no cause to say that. I'm on to something useful right now! Been up to Atchafalaya Station, where Wambly showed off about smoking fish—not the way the Indians do it but the way scientists do it."

"You mean like bacon?"

"That's right, Loyce. It's another one of those things he learned up at that World's Fair in St. Louis. Take most any of your big fish and cut it into strips. Soak it in a brine, then lay it on these racks over a smoky fire. No different really from making bacon. Be able to keep it for the longest time, so you don't have to sell it right away. Get more for it than for fresh too! I'm gonna make me some money—I can feel it."

"Ugh, fish bacon sounds like the nastiest taste I can imagine. Who's gonna buy it?"

"Wambly says the government will buy it to feed prisoners. Plus, other people might develop a taste for it if we can talk them into trying it somehow."

"Not around here, they won't. Why would they eat something that nasty when there's fresh fish any day you want it? Might be a caution against going to prison, though."

"Well, another thing we could do is ship it to places where they don't have fresh fish. Once they get that railroad finished up at Atchafalaya Station, won't take no time at all to send it north. Plus, it'll keep."

Loyce jabbed the front of Fate's shirt with her index finger, a gesture he knew well.

"If you keep listening to Wambly Cracker, you'll never—"

Ka wooom! A blast shook the trees in the woodlot between the store and York's property. Loyce's finger stopped in midair, and she cocked an ear toward the sound. Drifter leaped protectively in front of her.

"That can't be nothing but York's still!" Fate shouted as he jumped off the porch onto the ground.

— 12 —

Loyce plopped down but didn't rock. She needed to concentrate on listening. It was easy enough to follow Fate's footsteps down the woods path a piece, but then they jumbled up with other boots pounding from every which way. Seemed that everyone in hearing distance was running toward York's, but Loyce would have to wait until someone thought to tell her what had happened, even if somebody was hurt or dead. She slapped her thigh until it stung and started up the rocking chair again. Rocking always helped unknot her frazzles.

Shouts rang out from every direction until she was dizzy with sound. Then the noise settled down in one place. After that the voices mixed up with scraping and thudding. Wood? Metal? She was trying to puzzle it out when the shouts got louder. Headed toward the post office!

"Loyce, clear off the downstairs bed and get some water!" Adam's voice rose above the other noises.

She didn't waste time asking why but flew down the breezeway to the room Fate had used before he moved into the houseboat with Mame. As she felt across the top of the mattress, she heard Roseanne's shoes running down the stairs. Only a bundle of newspapers and a few of Adam's books cluttered the top of the neatly made bed. She kicked them under the bed and felt across the top of the quilt again. As a final step, she fluffed the pillow and caught

Fate's scent, even though he had moved to the houseboat years back.

Boots clomped up the back steps as she finished dipping water from a bucket into a basin. Adam, Fate, Val, and Alcide were all talking at once. Loyce grabbed a towel and caught up with the commotion just as they were stepping through the bedroom door. She squeezed inside, on the edge of the noise, waiting for someone to notice the basin and rag. Adam grabbed them.

"It's York!" Roseanne explained to Loyce before switching to questions of her own. "How bad? What happened? What do you need?" Roseanne continued, throwing the questions at anyone who might know.

"A doctor would come in handy," Adam answered. "But since we don't have one, Mrs. Barclay, bring me a tin of that yellow ointment from the store."

Roseanne didn't take time to answer but ran across the breezeway.

"I'll fetch Mary Ann!" That was Alcide's voice already coming back through the door. "But some honey and Mame's comfrey leaves would be better. That store-bought medicine ain't as good when it comes to a bad burn."

"Whoooeee, he looks mighty bad, Adam." Val's voice came from the other side of the bed. "Do you think we should take his clothes off, or will the skin come with it?"

"Don't matter if it does, they have to come off. Let's be quick before he comes to," Adam said.

Boots shuffled, the mattress rustled, and the bed frame creaked. Loyce backed into a corner, out of the way. She smelled something like burnt cotton and scalded chicken mixed with whiskey. Roseanne's skirt brushed past, trailing a carbolic fragrance Loyce recognized as the ointment Adam used when he picked up a hot skillet by mistake.

"York's still blew up? How does that happen?" Roseanne asked, when she came back to stand out of the way with Loyce.

"No one seems to know," Loyce said. "How bad is it?"

Roseanne took stock of the injuries a moment longer before replying.

"Well, there's blisters already full of water and looking to be swelling even more inside of his thighs. I can't imagine how he got burned like that. His palms look pretty raw, and the tops of his hands are sprinkled with smaller blisters. His face looks like it was splashed with hot water. I don't know what would cause that pattern of injuries unless he was sitting astride his still when it exploded. Is that part of the distilling process?"

"I don't know," Loyce replied. "I can smell the difference when he's using corn or sugarcane to make it, but that's all I know about it."

"Well, it doesn't look life-threatening, but he's going to be in pain a considerable amount of time. If he hadn't been wearing thick underwear and pants, his privates would be badly burned."

Just then steps pounded up the back path and burst through the open door.

"Oh Lordy mercy! How bad is it?" Mary Ann threw her brown felt hat on the floor in exasperation. "I didn't mean for to hurt him. I just wanted to get him back for turning loose my hogs."

"Whaaat?" Adam asked.

"I put an old dirt dauber nest in that pressure relief valve to cause him some aggravation. It must of started the still to jumping, and that fool straddled it to hold it down."

Her footsteps crisscrossed themselves. Then she stood, fists on hips, at the foot of the bed and leaned over to get a better look at York, as if he were the runt in a new litter of pigs.

"He's had a case of the mean-as-a-snake-itis for the longest time, and I just got tired of it. Turning my hogs loose was too much, and I was bound not to let him get away with it. I never done a thing to deserve the way he's been treating me."

"Mmmph." As York's senses returned, his voice was muffled and weak but angry.

"Mmmph," he said again.

Mary Ann picked up his pants. "What? Is there something in

here you want? You want to see if anyone stole something while they were hauling your burnt-raw carcass over here? Here's your billfold, see?"

She held up the worn black leather rectangle. York reached toward it. Wincing with the effort, he yanked the pocketbook from her hands and clumsily opened it with his burned fingers. Slowly he withdrew a small envelope. It wavered in his shaking fingers as he lifted it toward her.

Mary Ann opened the envelope and took out the page of unlined paper. She read aloud.

"Michaud, by next year this time there will be three of us. Please send me passage as soon as you get this letter. I'm looking forward to being in France when my time comes so we can start our family in your country—ours is falling apart. All my love, Mary Ann."

"Who's Michaud?" Mary Ann puzzled.

"You tell me." York blinked his eyes, which were lopsided because of a growing water blister on the right side of his face.

"You think I wrote this?" She waved the little blue sheet of paper, which looked incongruous in her broad calloused hand. "You don't even know what my handwriting looks like! York Bertram, you're an even bigger ass than I took you for. How'd I get to know anybody in France?"

"Don't know. Maybe someone you met at your daddy's shop, same as I done?" Yelling was easier now that he was coming to his senses. "Why would anyone sign your name on a letter you didn't write?"

"I ain't got an idea about that, but I know this ain't my letter, ain't never been my letter, I never saw this piece of paper before." Concern had left her voice. Now she just sounded mad. Loyce winced back from the noise.

"Can I see it?" Adam took a step between the warring couple. Mary Ann handed him the letter and envelope.

He walked to the window and examined the two paper items. "It was mailed from Bayou Chene all right. 'INSUFFICIENT

99

POSTAGE, SOUTHERN LETTER UNPAID,'" he read aloud. "I've never seen a blue postal mark like this. What's this? June 21? Today's only June 13. Wait a minute—the year stamped on this is 1861!"

No one had noticed Mame's slight frame in the open doorway, clutching a bundle of comfrey in one hand. She dropped the comfrey, shuffled forward, and wordlessly took the letter in her left hand. She gently passed her right index finger across the address.

"Michaud," Mame finally said in a kind of whisper. "So that's what happened."

All eyes in the room turned to her. Loyce tilted her head in that direction. As Alcide would describe the scene later, "Right then, the Angel Gabriel himself trumpeting into that room couldn't of broke our concentration. There was nowhere else to look or listen for any of us, let me tell you!"

Mame's thin shoulders began to shake, but instead of crying, she was chuckling. The bonnet slid off the pink and green–streaked bun onto her shoulders as she threw her head back and cranked up a laugh like no one had heard since before the drownings. After a while the bed creaked, and York yelped as the old woman dropped onto the foot of the mattress, still cackling with mirth. Then she told them.

"Michaud came the spring before the war started. Wanting to learn all he could about growing indigo, of all things. Where he was from in France, they made their living selling some kind of seashell that blue dye was made from. He said when the indigo plantations over here started taking away that market, it just made sense to try to get into the indigo business themselves—not just his family but the whole region there. Oh, he was quite the figure—tall, with that black hair and green eyes. Swept me right off my feet." She chuckled again at the memory.

"He was staying right here with Elder, that room up over the store where Roseanne stays now. Bought up a whole sugar plantation and planted it in indigo all at the same time. Everyone told him sugar was the thing to plant out here then, but he was bound and determined for indigo. I was taking care of Josie—it wasn't long since Maudie passed. Elder knew Michaud and me had taken up together. Two youngsters like us, wasn't no surprise. And Michaud was a ruckus all by himself, could cheer up a funeral if you gave him a chance. We was all glad for the merriment he brought after what we'd been through.

"He left around Easter and was supposed to come back at harvest time to see how the indigo was processed. But the war started in early summer, and everything changed—I mean everything! For one thing they broke loose that big logjam up where the Red River comes in. When the extra water started coming down the 'Chafalaya, it covered Michaud's plantation plum up, which was on low ground to start with. He never did come back, so I guess he never knew. I reckon he give up on his blue dye when the war started. That's when they started calling it Indigo Island, though. I had about forgot that's where the name came from."

Mame's attention swerved away from Michaud back to the envelope.

"I remember when they started using that blue stamp, stopping letters that had postage paid with Confederate money. A few of those letters made it back to the post office during that time, mostly letters meant for our boys gone to the war. It would've meant a lot for them to get news from home."

"Ol' Michaud!" Alcide said. "Tall fella, Frenchy speech, but not like the Cajuns around here. Sure, I remember him."

Mame took up her telling again. Her voice was stronger and not so far away as it usually sounded.

"Once the war started, I could understand him not trying to come back, but I wondered about him not answering my letter. Now I see it never got to him. As time went by without us hearing anything from Michaud and my condition got more noticeable, Elder was the one who came up with the idea that we could solve both our problems if him and me would just go ahead and get married. It made sense because I was already taking care of Josie. It was Josie who started calling me Mame, 'cause she couldn't say "Mary Ann." I was growing up so fast in the midst of all that and the war to boot, so it wasn't long before Michaud was as much a part of my childhood as my corn shuck dolls. I haven't thought about him for years."

"When Lauf turned out to be one of them *early* babies, everyone kidded old Elder to no end," Alcide broke in with a laugh.

"That's right, he didn't back up from taking the credit," Mame chuckled. "He made a good daddy—better'n I was raised with, that's for sure. Treated Lauf like he was his own."

"So that's where Lauf and Fate got them long legs from!" Alcide chortled. "Might be where they got their dislike of hard work, too, seeing as how they came from a line of high-falutin' business stock."

"I don't care where anybody got anything," York spoke up. "I'm an injured man; do I have to drag myself down to the dock and get a deckhand to help me out?"

This brought a round of argument about the merits of the comfrey and honey compared to the tin of ointment. Loyce didn't have an opinion because her mind was still on Mame's story.

"Maybe we should mix them all together so as not to miss anything," Adam suggested.

"*Mais non!*" Val offered. "Put the store medicine on one side, with honey and comfrey on the other. See which one works best, once and for all. Me, I'll go get the honey."

"Whatever you put on it, what's he gonna wear until it heals?" Mame asked. "He's not stepping into pants for a long time, I can tell you that much."

"Well, I can tell you something else; I ain't laying abed till it heals!" York's voice was taking on its normal belligerent tone. Loyce could hear the change even through her distraction.

"The best thing I can think of is a dress," Mary Ann spoke up. "I don't have any dresses, but I have an old nightgown that will do. In fact, what difference does it make whether it's a nightgown or a dress?"

"A dress!" York exploded. "I ain't putting on no dress or a gown, I'll tell you that right now."

"Well, what other ideas you got for covering your blistered privates for the next few weeks?" Mary Ann shot back.

In the noisy debate over how to treat and dress the injured man, only the blind girl noticed that Fate had slipped from the room without saying a word to anyone.

— 13 —

It had been three weeks since the explosion. No one needed to spread the news that York was recovering under Mary Ann's reluctant care. Their arguments could be heard by anyone who paddled past the front of their big house or walked the path behind it. Eventually, the patient was seen stomping around his compound, spraddle-legged under a voluminous nightgown.

The letter that led to the blast shook up more than the Bertram marriage. It shook loose something in Mame, like a clock that gets jarred back into motion after being stopped for too long. That first night she and Mary Ann took turns sitting up with York. The next morning, when her nephew went home in the pony cart, Mame rode alongside Mary Ann, carrying a fresh bundle of comfrey and the jar of honey.

She tirelessly nursed her ailing nephew through the first critical week without coming home. When she moved back to her houseboat, she brought meals to York and Mary Ann from Adam's kitchen. She tended to York during the days, while Mary Ann kept up with orders at the sawmill and charcoal pit. People began to notice that Mame's eyes focused on the present, and she carried her end of conversations as if she had not withdrawn for more than a decade.

When asked about the change, she shrugged and said, "I've grieved long enough. We lost so many during the war. After, when the sugar didn't come back, whole families left. Losing Josie, Lauf, and Beatrice on top of the others, it was too much, I reckon." She stopped and thought a moment before continuing. "All those years I paid notice only to the ones leaving and dying. But there was life coming back too. Some young people like York coming home and bringing a wife from outside. New people like the Stocketts moving in from other places. I can't do anything to help the dead and gone, but these young ones are my family too. It's time for me to come back. Past time."

If the letter dragged Mame back into the life of the community, it seemed to drive Fate away. Because of Mame staying with York, several days passed before anyone noticed that Fate wasn't living at their little houseboat tied up at the post office dock. Debris tangled in his nets as the water fell. No one saw his boat maneuvering the bayous around the Chene. Even though he had often visited around to the other swamp communities, Fate had never been away from the Chene for long. Just when Adam started to worry that they may need to drag the bayous for him, word came that Fate had been spotted upriver around Atchafalaya Station.

The sighting brought as much speculation as his disappearance. Was it a coincidence that he just up and left the very day that letter arrived? Did he think anyone cared that his grandfather wasn't really Elder Landry? Mame, herself, said she had not kept it a secret from him; she just never thought to mention it. Maybe it would have come up if Lauf had lived, but what with the drownings and all the grief that followed, she just never thought about it. Ever. Even if the news of his father's paternity startled Fate, why would he just up and leave?

No one felt Fate's absence like Loyce. She rocked and wondered. Other than when she was away at school, she had never been separated from her cousin for so long. Cousin? Not exactly. What was he now, anyway?

Her little family just kept on shrinking. Somewhere along the way—she didn't even remember when—she had found out that Josie's parents were Maudie and Elder, making *them* Loyce's real grandparents, not Mame and Elder. The news didn't affect her one way or the other. How could she miss someone she never knew?

It wasn't like losing her mother. Loyce still tried to summon her voice, her touch, the smell of her skin, but the sensations faded more each year. Even so, being lonesome for her didn't fade. It simply changed from the practical needs of a child to the deeper yearning of a young woman needing guidance into the world of adults.

For most of her life Adam, Fate, and Mame had to supply all Loyce had in the way of family. With Adam so busy and distracted, Mame so absent, she depended on Fate for help learning to tie her shoes or navigating the plank walks. He was there for whatever she needed, without ever reminding her that he had lost *both* parents.

Now the letter had changed all that by taking away Fate—one-third of her remaining family. If Mame and Michaud were Fate's grandparents, then Fate wasn't even her cousin. The more she thought on it, the more her anger grew. How was she supposed to act around him now if they weren't even kin? Is that how he was feeling about her? Was that the reason he was making himself so scarce?

As Loyce mulled over these questions on the porch, inside the post office conversations settled back into routine happenings. Customers were catching up with each other in a steady hum. Children chased around the front yard, bare feet thumping whenever they touched down on the springy plank walks. Chickens fluttered out of the way, sometimes even launching into short flights to the porch banister or a low branch in an oak tree. Boat whistles and bells sounded through the trees. Three steamboats had docked at daylight, their cooks, crews, and passengers adding to the bustle in the store.

A breeze stirred through the open window. Leaf-shaped light filtered through the sycamore tree onto the neat shelves lined with goods. Bolts of bright cloth contrasted with the sun-bleached bonnets and dresses of the customers. The smell of tarred nets and fresh fish wafted through the window to blend with fragrant cheese, coffee beans, leather, and soap inside. Layered scents of trees, soft earth, and the cow lot drifted in from the back.

"Adam, a body can look forward to coming here now that we don't have to dig through boxes and barrels for every little thing," said a customer with one child on her hip and another holding onto her skirt.

"Well, I'd be amiss to take the credit," Adam replied good-naturedly from the post office corner, where he was bent over a piece of lined paper, helping Madame Gilchrist write a letter. "That's Mrs. Barclay's doings; be sure and tell her before you go. I saw her pick up a comb and head out to tackle Loyce's braid," he chuckled.

Out on the porch Roseanne was untying the twine and separating Loyce's lopsided braid into three soft tangles.

"For someone who knits nets, you surely can't make a braid," she was saying. "Most of it comes loose and falls around your face."

"Well, it's not like it gets in the way of my seeing," Loyce said, but with none of her usual spirit. "Mame, on her good days, used to braid it up high like you do, but she never showed me how. So I just wind it up, tie it off, and let it be. It's good enough."

"For one thing it's too soft," said C.B. "What your hair needs is some body."

She'd arrived unannounced through the back of the dogtrot. Roseanne sniffed. Loyce tilted her head in greeting but didn't offer a comeback.

"If you'd get you some of that olive wax pomade, you could make it stay in place a week or more," C.B. continued, patting her own frizz, which Roseanne thought leaned even more toward the greenish side of yellow this morning. "When I couldn't afford olive wax pomade, I'd use egg white mixed with water, but that can get to smelling after a few days. Even so, when I barely had enough to eat, I'd save an egg in case I needed it for my hair."

Roseanne sniffed again.

"You ain't getting sick, are you, Mrs. Barclay, what with all that sniffing?" C.B. prattled on, without stopping for a breath herself. "You being such a robust sort of woman and all, I wouldn't think you get sick much. In fact, if I was put to it, I'd have to say you are even more robust than you were last time I came over. I always been delicate, myself. Got bones like a chicken. Look at this wrist. Wouldn't you say that brings to mind a little ol' chicken neck? Just ain't never been able to get no flesh on me. I even tried Dr. Earling's Weight Gain Tonic that was guaranteed or my money back. I didn't gain even one little bit. Well, what did I do? Got my friend Minnie to write that doctor asking for my money back. She wrote a good letter too. But we had to leave that place, St. Louis maybe, before my money ever came. Sometimes you gotta leave a place before you're good and ready, if you know what I mean. Hey, you could write to him again for me, Mrs. Barclay; it was guaranteed. I'll even pay you for your time out of what I get."

"C.B., you fall for anything anyone wants to sell you," Roseanne said, stopping short of another sniff. "Like those French female pills to get rid of your baby. You could have died if you'd actually found some for sale."

"Well, you ain't telling no tales there, Mrs. Barclay," C.B. said, perching on the edge of a porch chair, her small belly barely showing under her skirt. "My friend Pearl's teeth plumb flaked off to nothing one time when she took 'em, but she said that was small enough price to pay for not having a young'un to raise. Barely able to keep her own body to soul as it was. Don't know how I got so careless, myself, but I'd just started suspecting it was on the way when Sam came on the scene. I knew I couldn't work much longer, and nothing had gone right for me in Natchez anyway. This here was the first store we came on since I knowed for sure. Even if I could have got 'em, by that time it'd probably be too late.

"Sam, now, he's looking forward to it. He said a fambly's a fambly and most men never know if the kids they raising is theirs or not. He said at least he'll know this one ain't, which he figures puts him a step ahead of most men. I reckon I'll make my mind up to do right by it, but I ain't looking forward to it."

"Roseanne, I've picked out the fabric for my dress." A voice rose above the din in the store. Giving Loyce's hair a final pat, Roseanne whisked back inside the store with a proprietary air, taking her place behind the counter.

"I'll be glad to order that gabardine for you, Viola, but you know, for just seventy-five cents more, you can get that dress ready made." Roseanne paged to the clothing section and slid the catalog back to the customer side. "When you think about how long a gabardine dress lasts and the time you'd put in making it, you might do better that way. You'd be saving the cost of buttons and thread too."

"Hmmmmmm," Viola mused and pulled the catalog closer. Roseanne turned away to take care of other customers while the shopper made up her mind.

The bell, another one of Roseanne's ideas, tinkled as a new customer entered.

"Well lookee here! If it ain't the bamboozler from New Orleens!" A sooty deckhand removed his hat with an exaggerated bow in Roseanne's direction and grinned with checkerboard teeth.

"I thought you'd be long gone to meet your thieving, slippery-assed card shark of a husband by now. How long's it been since we dumped you off—two, three months? Reckon maybe he found someone else to help him spend all that money he stole?"

The murmuring sounds of commerce stopped as heads turned first to the man in the doorway and then to Roseanne. They saw the blood drain from her cheeks, making her eyes even darker.

"You should be ashamed to even look me in the face after abandoning me in the middle of the swamp!" she spit back.

The stranger didn't flinch.

"I'd guess you'd be the expert on shame seeing as how your man left you behind to face the crew and passengers when he took off in the night with our money and our lifeboat to boot. You mean he ain't even got in touch with you about where to meet? Or are you just waiting until you steal enough from Adam's cash box to join him?"

"Well, Mrs. Barclay, we got more in common than I thought." C.B. peered around the stranger in the doorway. "I used to run a scheme like that, too, started it early with the peddler. See, we'd come on a boat all dressed in poorly clothes toting nothing but a little croaker sack of belongings. We'd carry on something fierce about being so scared 'cause we couldn't swim and we's so poor cause we'd lost the farm and was on our way to stay with relatives. Well, about two miles upstream from some little town, I'd start hollering that my daddy had done fell overboard. I'd jump up and down and point toward a spot in the current by the wheel. Oh, people'd gather 'round and hug me and point with me, looking for him. Before you know it, some guy would whip off his hat and start passing it around, taking up a collection for the poor little orphaned girl. I'd get off at that next town, and there the peddler would be waiting for me."

"How'd he not drown for real?" someone asked.

"Well, all he did was just wear a rubber life vest under his clothes," C.B. continued. "He could swim ashore in about two miles. Only once did he miss his bank and ended up at the next town and like to never caught up with me. It was during that two weeks I figured out I could do even better on my own!"

"My husband and I did no such thing!" Roseanne slammed the pattern book on the counter. "I just woke up, and he was gone. I don't know what happened to him. I don't know about any money. All I know is that he was not on the boat when morning came."

With that she swept around the end of the counter and up the stairs.

— 14 —

The last customer had paddled on down the bayou and Adam was sweeping up when he heard Roseanne's door open and softly close. Her step was hesitant coming down the stairs, so different from her clattering and slamming ascent that morning. Adam kept his eyes on the pile of dirt he was corralling toward the breezeway. He followed the little mound, stepping and sweeping, until it was whisked into the evening. He had never bothered to sweep before she came to live with them. There wasn't time or energy back then, or so it seemed.

"I guess you'll be wanting me to leave," she said.

"Don't know why that would be the case," he said mildly. "There's two sides to every coin."

The unexpected kindness in his answer deflated her, and she collapsed into the nearest chair.

"It's not at all like he said," she began. "It's true that boat forced me off under a cloud of suspicion, but I don't know what my husband is up to; he's never done anything like this before. He had been excited, agitated even, about winning a lot at *bourre* that last afternoon. Apparently, some of the men sitting in hadn't played before."

Adam chuckled. "Oooh, Mrs. Barclay, now that's a card game where you can lose a pile of money quicker than a frog can snatch a fly."

She relaxed even more and continued.

"Charles said they were a bunch of rubes and sore losers. He said he wasn't going to play anymore, but after dinner he went out for a walk and a cigar."

Roseanne smoothed her waist down and sniffed. She took an additional breath before confessing.

"Mr. Snellgrove, this was not the first time Charles had been accused of improprieties during card games. The heat of argument seems to be what he enjoys most about playing any kind of game, be it croquet or cards, even dominoes. He is ruthless about winning."

Roseanne was silent a moment. Was she examining her husband in a new light or just pausing while she made up the rest of the story? Adam couldn't tell. She continued.

"He didn't come back, so I assumed he had decided to play cards after all. The next morning I discovered he had never come to bed. By making some inquiries, I also found out that he had once again won a great sum from a group of men who were set on getting their winnings back. When my questions led to the realization that he was not on board, a search of the boat revealed the lifeboat was also missing. That's when everyone jumped to the conclusion that he had escaped with his ill-gotten goods, leaving me in the wake of his troubles. Bayou Chene was the next stop, so they put me off here. It was so humiliating to be dumped off with only what I could carry—I still don't know how I summoned the nerve to walk over here. Don't you see why I couldn't tell you what happened? It was just too embarrassing. And now everyone knows! Or worse yet, they think I'm a thief!"

Adam combed the left side of his gray mustache with one finger, a sign he was giving serious thought to the situation. He regarded her with the same open gaze and inclined head that made customers tell him things they didn't tell other people, even those closest to them. His voice was kind but frank.

"My advice is to write your family and let them know your predicament. They'll send you money; you can go home."

Roseanne breathed as deeply as her corset would allow and decisively placed both plump hands down flat on the table.

"There's no way I can go back there, Mr. Snellgrove. There's something else I haven't told you. While Charles was truthfully on a business trip to New Iberia, we were also on our wedding trip."

Adam gazed thoughtfully at her face, smoothing his mustache twice, deciding whether to inquire further.

"Pardon my saying so, Mrs. Barclay, but that doesn't sound very romantic."

Roseanne shuddered and narrowed her eyes. "It was far from romantic, Mr. Snellgrove. I never wanted to marry Charles. I would have been content to stay on at the convent and take orders. In the short time we were man and wife, I'm sure he wished I had done so."

"You don't strike me as particularly interested in religion, Mrs. Barclay."

"That's discerning of you, Mr. Snellgrove," she said with a wry smile. "In fact, I'm not in the least religious, but it seems a safe and orderly life."

"And I have noticed your fondness for order, Mrs. Barclay," he added with a nod and a small smile of his own.

She went on as if he hadn't spoken.

"To tell you the truth, my first feeling was relief when he could not be found. Later, of course, I began wondering what was to become of me."

"Become of you? Surely your family will not hold you accountable for his actions!"

"I don't even have to wonder about that, Mr. Snellgrove. My marriage was a business deal between the Garniers and the Barclays, not a matter to be taken lightly, especially when the bride is thirty-five years old. For me to try to return now—a shamed woman—would be humiliation beyond what I could bear, even if they would take me in."

She paused as if considering whether to say more. Then with a shake of her head, she plunged on.

"Charles was the second son of a wealthy English family. Since he didn't inherit anything when the patriarch passed, he sold everything he owned to buy passage on a steam ship to this country. Upon arrival in New Orleans he began making the rounds to likely individuals and lending agencies. It wasn't long before he met my brother, and they became friends.

"Charles borrowed enough money from my family to purchase a share in a shipping company. Through his own connections in England, the venture was such a success that he was able to pay back the loan in less than a year. He was so much more serious about business than my own brother, that Father began thinking of him like another son. He was always at our house. As time went by and I remained single, Father put more pressure on me to respond to Charles's suit. To tell you the truth, I never felt that he had a personal interest in me but that our marriage was no more to him than another business deal with permanent opportunities for both families."

"Was there another young man you preferred?" Adam asked. "Surely your family would have allowed you to marry any worthy suitor?"

"No, there wasn't." Her eyes slid off to the side in that evasive way that made him think of catfish looking for escape through slatted wood.

There was more, he was sure of it. He waited for the revelation, but it didn't come. Instead, she shook herself as if coming awake, and her voice took on the professional tone she used in the store.

"So, you see, I can't go back and have everyone look at me as a soiled and discarded woman! I will make my own way before I could do that!"

"And how do you plan to do that, Mrs. Barclay? You're not going to live like you're used to on what I can pay, for sure." Adam's voice was kind but certain.

"I could help you expand your business, Mr. Snellgrove," she said, some of the spunk coming back into her voice.

"Expand?" Adam looked from the left side of the breezeway to the right. "Make the store bigger? I don't think we'd have enough customers to warrant that, Mrs. Barclay."

"Not the store, Mr. Snellgrove, your *cooking*! There is nowhere for a traveler to get a meal around here. Just think about it; for example, you could multiply the profit on a can of syrup by selling it over hot biscuits. I must say you make the lightest biscuits I've ever tasted, Mr. Snellgrove."

Roseanne had missed lunch. Her stomach rumbled at the thought of Adam's biscuits.

"Catfish, squirrels, venison, eggs, milk, vegetables from Mame's garden. These are all free for you, Mr. Snellgrove." Roseanne's stomach rumbled louder at the thought of what he could do with those ingredients. "You could turn these into meals, while I run the store and help you in the post office. It wouldn't be that difficult to convert Fate's old room into a dining area; it's right next to the kitchen. I do believe you could double the profit you are making now."

"You may have something there," he said thoughtfully. "Maybe it's time for me to think about putting something by for Loyce's future."

Then, as if to dispel the dark cloud of her past, he added, "Let's go whip you up a batch of lost bread for supper, Mrs. Barclay."

— 15 —

Loyce closed the outhouse door and felt around for the wooden latch. Out of habit she turned it so that a stiff breeze couldn't swing it open and make it a danger to small children, who could fall headfirst through the hole. A useless caution in this case, she thought. She had been the last child born on the place, and there weren't likely to be any more in the future. As for breezes, they were as scarce as tits on a boar hog, and it would be that way until the September storms blew in. No relief for a month! The heat pulled on her shoulders like a net anchor.

That's why everything's askew, she told herself. If it would just cool off a bit. She didn't have the energy to even brush out her hair but just bundled it up and retied it every morning. If Roseanne didn't notice and find time to brush and braid it, the knots stayed another day. Now and then she even slept in her clothes, something Roseanne had accused her of in the past.

Her nets were tangling up even more than her hair. Some days she had to rip out yards of the knotted string. Nothing had been going right for weeks, not since the day York's still blew the lid off her family.

She couldn't remember when her family tree had been set in her mind; that went back way too early. She had always known more about Josie's side. She could recite it like the alphabet, without even thinking. There was Great-Grandpa Wash Landry and Great-Grandma Viney, who had given birth to Grandpa Elder.

On the other side Great-Grandpa Bertram and Great-Grandma Bertram produced Grandma Mame. Then Grandma Mame and Grandpa Elder married and had birthed Josie and Fate's daddy, Uncle Lauf.

Well, that's what she had thought until somewhere along the way she found out that Josie had belonged to Grandpa Elder's first wife, Maudie. That didn't matter back then, but now it just added to the quicksand feeling that came over her whenever she tried to untangle her family ties. The same quicksand that had taken away her cousin and best friend.

Fate and Loyce had clung to each other when all the grown-ups in their lives disappeared—three of them lost forever under a steamboat and the other two just temporarily, although Mame stretched the meaning of the word *temporary* to new limits. Adam came back first, but he was like a hen too small for an oversized clutch of eggs. He tried to take care of all of them, but there wasn't enough of him to go around. Meanwhile, Mame seemed as lost as her drowned children.

So, it came down to just Fate and Loyce. By then their school went all the way to the sixth grade. Every morning they walked across the island together. Ambling home, most days she could remember more of the lessons than Fate did, especially when it came to spelling. She couldn't see the writing and reading but made up for it by listening, something Fate couldn't do if his life depended on it.

By the end of the third grade the teacher suggested that Loyce would benefit by living at a special school for the blind in Baton Rouge. By then writing and reading took up so much of the school day, it did seem like a waste of her time to just sit while the rest of the class scratched away on their slates. Still, it was only because Fate wouldn't shut up about it that she decided to try one year— fourth grade—away at the Louisiana School for the Deaf and Blind in Baton Rouge.

Oh, was she homesick! The sounds and smells were so different. And the food—it wasn't really bad; it just lacked Adam's special touch. She made it through those first days by practicing in her head how she would describe everything to Fate. The years flew by, and before she noticed what was happening, she had finished not just the fourth but the fifth, sixth, seventh—all the way to the eleventh grade. And all because of Fate.

She had always thought of Papa's side of the family as the strangers. Grandma Eugenia Snellgrove was the outsider who had moved to the Chene, bringing little Adam. There were no other local connections for that side of Loyce's family, and to make it worse, Grandma Eugenia moved away before Loyce was even born. Like so many people who had moved outside the swamp, she never made the trip back to visit. Adam wrote her a letter now and then, but mostly they just all went on with their lives.

Now it seemed that Loyce knew as little about one side of her family as the other. She couldn't count the times that she had gone over it all in her mind since the day that letter came. If Elder and Mame were not Uncle Lauf's parents, then she wasn't even kin to her dead Uncle Lauf, whom she had mourned along with her mama.

And Fate! His granddaddy was not really the long-dead Grandpa Elder but some old man in France that could be alive or dead. And did all this new information mean Grandpa Elder was not her grandpa either? No, wait a minute—Elder was still Josie's father, Josie was really her mama, so at least Grandpa Elder was safely still in her family. But not Mame, whom she had loved all her life. It hadn't mattered that Mame was a bit touched. She was there every day if Loyce needed to climb in her lap.

So, Fate got Mame, while Loyce was left with only a grandfather who had died before she was born. Fate also got a grandpa in France who might even still be alive. It seemed she was getting shortchanged no matter which way you added it up.

She shook her head to clear the confusion and then tilted an ear toward the bayou. "What's that, Drifter? Sounds like a cross between a woodpecker banging on a tin roof and dried corn running through the sheller."

She felt the dog's attention rivet in the same direction. They stood listening together, until Loyce moved to ease the pull of a knot of hair caught in her collar. The noise closed in on the landing, bringing an unfamiliar smell with it. Sort of like coal oil but not quite. They sniffed the air and tried to figure it out. Then there was a thump and a familiar shout.

"Hey Loyce, you ain't gonna believe this!"

Somehow she had known it was Fate even before she heard his voice over the racket, which was now sinking down to a sputter and finally a cough before giving back the blessing of silence. Then the stomp of his boots coming up the walk. Her shoulders lifted, and an unconscious smile played over her face.

"I ain't paddling, and this ain't goat power!" Fate bounded toward her. "This is a gasoline boat, and it's gonna take the work out of working for a living."

The vibration of the plank walk thrummed his steps right through the porch into her feet. A split second more, and his hands would encircle her waist, lifting her up to his level. His embrace would tighten. She would fuss before giving up into laughter.

But the letter slid between them like a knife. She backed up. He stopped short. She felt the breeze as his hands dropped back.

"Hmmph" was the only greeting she could muster. "So, you've been off looking for an easy way to make a fortune! Suppose to be the reason you hadn't been around since York like to blew himself up? And what's that smell? Rank enough to make me go for the paregoric or peppermint water to settle my stomach."

"That's the gasoline you smelling," Fate said. "It explodes inside a jacket just like a gun shooting off inside a drum would make it raise up. Explode it fast enough, and it can move a boat as good as two men paddling together but keep it up day and night without getting tired."

"Fate Landry, you just keep setting eggs with nary a rooster in sight. Where are you needing to go in such a hurry, and where are you expecting to get gasoline?"

She couldn't help it if she sounded more out of sorts than usual. She was.

He recovered some of his swagger but stepped to the edge of the porch, away from her.

"Been thinking about what Val said about all those Jews in the cities that eat scale fish and how we got all them frazzling buffalo crowding our nets, but they won't live in a fish cart like catfish do. If I could figure out how to keep them fresh, I could make plenty of money selling something we got a lot of. So, I went to Baton Rouge and dropped in on Wambly to see if he had any more new ideas—something that tastes better than the fish bacon—he might of picked up from that World's Fair or some other place."

"Yeh, fish bacon, I remember that one," Loyce broke in, trying to recapture their old rapport. Her effort fell flat, and Fate continued like he was reciting a piece for school.

"Well, he told me scientists have found out that packing fish in ice is almost as good as keeping them alive if you don't hold them too long. And he told me the railroad's just about finished on that line that'll cross the swamp right up the river at Atchafalaya Station. Cross right on over the swamp to Baton Rouge. Supposed to be finished by fall. I figured if I could pack them in ice as soon as they come out of the water and then get them to the railroad stop at Atchafalaya Station inside a day, I could sell a whole lotta buffalo. I mean more than anyone out here ever thought of selling before. I could probably sell all the buffalo anyone catches out here. Not just me but every fisherman out here could get rich!"

Loyce felt that old toss of his head. The one that let on he was telling more than he knew.

"And so this noisy, stinking gasoline boat is how you're gonna do it? Where'd you get money for a contraption like that?" she shot back to tone him down a notch. "I'm sure no one's handing them out to just any daydreaming fool who thinks he's going to make money shipping ice and fish from the swamp way up north!"

"Wambly knows some researchers working on using automobile engines and what all to turn a propeller to move a boat through water. He even saw some up at that St. Louis shindig. I figured if the experts could put together a gasoline boat good enough to show off like that, I should be able to think my way around one good enough to haul fish from here to Atchafalaya Station. This here is what I come up with. Now all I gotta do is get some fishermen to give me their catch to sell for them."

Someone had to set him straight, and she didn't notice anyone else around who qualified.

"If you think any fisherman is going to put in the work and then give their catch to *you* on the word of *Wambly Cracker,* you're a bigger fool than I took you for. We don't have enough people out here as dumb as you. They would rather sell a few fish to a buyer with a tow car whenever a riverboat comes along than risk so much on the word of you and Wambly Cracker."

"Well, my boat made it all the way back here, didn't it? Don't that prove it works?"

"Don't prove a thing except trouble's bound to come from it," Loyce countered.

He stepped back, widening the gap between them. For the first time Loyce could remember, Fate Landry didn't have one word to say.

The kitchen screen door opened, and Adam stepped into the breezeway.

"Well, look who found his way home!" he said, with way more welcome than Loyce thought the visitor warranted. "Did all that noise have something to do with you? And look at that—is that Sam Stockett's old skiff? I noticed it had gone missing but figured it just broke loose and drifted off."

"You got it, Uncle Adam!" Fate said. "I talked a mate on the *Annette* into hoisting it onboard and dropping me off at Atchafalaya Station."

"Is that a pump sitting in the middle?" Adam was working at sounding hopeful.

"Well, it *was* on a pump one time." Fate was stepping all over himself in his excitement. That usually meant trouble was hot on his boot heels. Even if he couldn't tell, Loyce could.

"Now it's my boat engine!"

Just as proud as if he had given us a new Jersey calf, she fumed to herself. He blathered on.

"Those high sides on Sam's boat wasn't good for fishing, but it's just what you need for running in big water with a load, especially if you gonna get some speed up, like four or five miles an hour."

"And where are you planning to go so fast?" Adam sounded somewhere between interested and worried.

"Hauling fish, Uncle Adam, hauling fish—buffalo mostly."

It was like old times again with the pacing and the waving. Drifter stretched out on the floor, and Loyce sat back down to hear where this was going. She didn't catch much of the talk because the two men followed the plank walk back to the boat dock. Only a word or two drifted back up the bank. Once they cranked up the noisy engine, she went indoors, slamming the screen door with enough force to bounce the old spring off its catch.

Supper wasn't any better. Fate talked. Adam and Roseanne asked questions. All of it centered around that hubbub up at Atchafalaya Station and the railroad. Then they got off on the price of ice and what fish might sell for in New York City, of all places.

Before the night was over, Adam said he would keep a drum of gasoline in stock for Fate's trips upriver to Atchafalaya Station. He said he knew some packet boats that could bring it, but only by special order, since a stray spark from the smokestack could make it blow up like a drum full of dynamite.

Loyce wanted to tell Adam he might as well throw that money in the bayou because Fate wouldn't be in business long enough to use up one drum. The last she heard, her ex-cousin was rattling on downstream to let Sam know that his discarded skiff had made him a partner in the latest doomed-to-fail scheme in the swamp.

— 16 —

Adam dropped the coffeepot and waved his burned hand. Scorched coffee smell hung on the morning air. He tossed the contents out the back door with his good hand and was trying to refill the kettle when he noticed customers lining up in the store, at least twice the usual number, certainly more than Mrs. Barclay could handle alone. He clanged the kettle onto the stove and crossed the dogtrot to help out. Too much, just too much going on at one time.

Adam wanted Fate's bold venture to succeed, but Loyce's warning proved true, at least for the first run. While most mornings at the post office started off slowly, building speed until midday, then slacking off again through the afternoon, Fate's big event had skiffs and pirogues jockeying for space around the dock shortly after sunup. When there was no more room to toss another bowline, they started tying to each other, leading Alcide to exclaim, "If one line had broke, we'd a lost the whole fleet!"

Looking ahead with a good manager's eye, Mrs. Barclay had figured that most of the men would come inside either before or after delivering their fish.

"Be ready from that first day. Invite them to think of this as their meal stop on fish trading days," she had pronounced with authority.

That's how Adam found himself trying to cook dinner before breakfast was finished. And that's how the coffee boiled over. Confound it! How did he let that woman talk him into trying to cook for customers in addition to running a store, post office, and fish dock! It was more than one man could tend to, even with her help.

During a lull he stopped by the kitchen to pour boiling water over the new pot of coffee. Then he hustled down the walk to weigh his own fish. First, he kneeled on the wooden dock and pulled on the cotton line. His burned fingers bumped into everything he didn't want to touch, but finally the slats of the fish cart broke the surface.

"That's a fine crop of blue cats you got there, Uncle Adam," said Fate, jiggling around with excitement.

Even though he planned to ship mostly buffalo, Fate was sending a sampling of catfish up north to test the market.

"Not bad for low water, but don't know how much longer they'll last," Adam replied.

Adam knew that only about half the fishermen milling around had actually brought fish with them. Most were holding out to see if Fate made enough to pay out. He hoped his own confidence in Fate was well placed.

A hesitant voice broke into Adam's concentration.

"Mr. Snellgrove, can you put a dime's worth of coal oil in here before I leave. I almost forgot it." Wuf Neeley held out the gray, spouted can identical to the one every Chene family had on their back porch. It held the precious fluid that kept the lamps burning and started cook fires on damp mornings.

"Sure, Wuf, hand it here." Adam started to get up, but his foot slipped on fish slime, and he crashed into the tub, sending his catch spilling onto the dock. Everyone pitched in to re-catch the fish before they splashed back into the bayou.

"Tell you what, how about taking it yourself and filling it from that barrel," Adam panted. "Be sure and turn it off tight, now, so it won't drip. Mrs. Barclay can write it down on your daddy's bill."

"Yessir, I can do that," Wuf said. "Come on, Drifter, gimme a hand."

"Now, where'd that big blue cat go," Adam muttered. "Alcide, you hiding that big one in your overalls?"

"No such thing! You already put 'em in the scale."

The wet slap of flapping fish drowned out conversation for the next minute.

"Wuf, what you got there?" Loyce's voice was louder than usual.

"It's okay. I told him to fill it up himself," Adam shouted up the bank.

"If they put that stuff in a lamp, won't it blow up the whole house?" Loyce replied. "It's that gasoline you keep for Fate; I can smell it."

"Lordy, I think she's right!" Alcide had stumped up the plank walk and was sniffing the spout of the gray can. "It smells different from usual. Is this that gasoline, Adam?"

"Let's see it, Wuf," Adam said, reaching for the can. He smeared a few drops over his burned fingers and sniffed. Coal oil was a good treatment for burns. But this wasn't oily; it was thin. Vapors shivered off it.

"By god, she's right! Which drum did you get this out of?"

"That one on the right, same as usual." Wuf pointed to the old drum raised on a dais made from a cottonwood stump.

Adam's spine shivered like the vapors off his hand.

"Mrs. Barclay, has anyone else bought coal oil since the delivery yesterday?" He shouted up the bank in what he hoped was a calm voice. No sense in adding more fractiousness to the morning.

"Mary Ann filled up a can, that's all," she replied.

Just the one! Adam breathed a sigh of relief.

"Wuf, you're quicker on your feet than the rest of us—run tell Mrs. Mary Ann not to use that can, run now! Don't go in the house, just yell from outside."

The men on the dock stood still as death watching the boy disappear into the woods. Adam held his breath for every second that ticked by without the second explosion of the year coming from the Bertrams'. He didn't exhale until the pony cart came rattling through the woods. A welcome sight! Wuf sat tall next to Mary Ann on the seat, his bony chest reared back straight and proud through his overall straps. Even that brown goat bleating and stomping looked beautiful to Adam.

The cheering from the dock brought Roseanne to the porch.

"What's going on?" she asked.

"Wuf saved the Bertrams from getting blowed up is what happened!" Alcide shouted. "That's right! That boy always did have more gumption than the rest of them Neeleys put together."

Now that the danger was over, banter on the dock picked up again.

"Remember when the church ladies pitched in and made O'Lamp Neeley a moss mattress?" a voice started off. "Someone had seen that the young'uns was sleeping on bare floorboards."

"I remember that," someone else chuckled. "Well, those church ladies was some mad when they found out O'Lamp didn't do nothing but rip it open and sell the moss to buy a watermelon!"

Laughter rang out over the water and up the bank. With all the commotion no one heard Loyce slap the arm of her chair.

"Hey, don't forget I'm the one who smelled it and saved the Neeleys as well as the Bertrams," she grumbled. "And Fate's the reason that frazzling, dangerous stuff is here anyway. Him and his fancy boat. Gonna just cause trouble for everyone."

— 17 —

August came to a close with no more mishaps at the dock during the weekly fish transports. Fate chugged in, loaded up, and disappeared in a cloud of fumes and noise. During the few minutes he was weighing fish and paying out money, Loyce could hear his voice, as usual, over everyone else's. But something was different.

Men were not just laughing at his carrying on as they once did. They were asking questions and hushing for his answers. What were fishermen pulling in at other spots in the river? What was selling best up north? And of course there were umpteen questions about that gasoline boat. How fast, how far, how much time, how much load could it carry, on and on. Seems like they all had a notion of what could be done with such a contraption. Loyce knew what she'd like to do with the noisome, foul-smelling thing if anyone asked, but no one did.

"I bet you don't know who this is." The voice broke into her thoughts. It came from the path rather than the dock.

"Cairo Beauty," said Loyce. "Even a seeing person could pick out the only Mississippi drawl on the Chenc, and I don't need Drifter's nose to follow the trail of your Blue Waltz perfume. Come on in and let me feel that baby." Her mood lightened when Cairo Beauty dropped by.

Cairo laughed and climbed the steps to the back of the breezeway. Entering the porch, she stood in front of Loyce, who felt around her stomach. It had expanded since Cairo's last visit just two weeks ago.

"Well, how you doing there?" Adam spoke up from where he sat peeling potatoes and reading a book propped against the dishpan. "What's the water doing down on Graveyard?"

"Come up just a tad the last few days," she replied, settling into another chair on the porch. "That's how come Alcide was out that way setting some lines. I caught a ride to the back side of the island and walked up. I wish it'd raise faster and make it easier to tote things from the shed to the cabin we're building on the flatboat. The bigger I get, the harder all that hauling gets to be. That's what I come for today, some bigger clothes. Done let out all mine far as they'll go."

She patted the bodice of her chartreuse frock, which was filled to capacity and a little more. Then she tugged at the buttons gapped open at the waist.

"I still have what Josie wore before Loyce was born," Adam said. "Let me go see if I can find 'em. That'll save your money for building the houseboat and putting together Sam's nets."

He sat the book on top of the potatoes, placed the pan in the seat of his chair, and left the porch. Soon the women could hear him moving boxes and barrels inside. Presently, he came back with two cotton jumpers designed with tucks over the bosom that spread out into roomy skirts. One was a slate blue, and the other was dark green. Each jumper came with a long muslin shift that could be worn as a nightgown or as a blouse-petticoat combination. The garments were well made and strong.

"I'll look like a schoolmarm—won't that be a wonder!" C.B. said as she held the blue jumper in front of her and grinned at Adam. "Me, who ain't never seen the inside of a school. I 'spect you haven't either, huh, Loyce?"

"Well, I certainly didn't *see* the inside or the outside," she said, "but I did go to school in Baton Rouge for eight years. Fate's the one who talked me into giving it a try. I missed home, but it's a good thing I went, or I'd a never learned anything. I learned to read by touching the words punched in paper. That's where I learned to knit nets—they called it occupational therapy. I learned to swim and ride a horse. I learned to play the fiddle and the mandolin. Music! Of all the things I learned, that's what I wish I could have kept up."

"Did you go to school, Mrs. Barclay?" C.B. turned companionably toward the doorway into the store, where Roseanne stood, arms folded over her bosom.

"Of course I went to school. I graduated from the Sisters of Evangeline in New Orleans," she said, fingering the top button of her high collar, making sure it was still properly fastened.

"What'd you learn there?" C.B. asked.

"Deportment, the classics, catechism, some piano and singing," she replied.

"I reckon the first thing I learned was how to open oysters without cutting my hand," C.B. went on. "Don't know about that 'portment and classics, but we did have some cats hanging around that dock, and there was plenty of singing—fighting too—when the boats come in. So, I guess we got some background in common, Mrs. Barclay."

Roseanne sniffed loudly, but C.B. rambled on.

"We was living down there at Dunbar where the oyster luggers come in. I started out standing on a bucket to reach the shucking table. The bigger kids blocking the wind off us little ones and the littlest one of all sitting in the middle of the oysters on the table. Mama was one of the fastest shuckers on the dock, so that's why they let her bring a baby too little to be any help yet. I know you're thinking about how tight a oyster closes their lips and that no shirttail kid could pry 'em open. But what you learn right off is it's not the strength in your hands but putting that oyster knife in just the right spot and twisting it just so. I wasn't more than four years old, which was a little young. Most didn't start till they was about school-age, but Mama didn't have nowhere to put me, so there I stood, starting my schooling two years early, you might say."

Roseanne had taken a step back and refolded her arms over her chest.

"We have nothing in common, nothing at all," she said, with

more wonder than anything else. Loyce was also puzzled at the connection only C.B. could see.

"Well, what did you do after schooling?" C.B.'s voice was more than inquisitive. Loyce felt something building.

"I lived with my father and stepmother until I married Mr. Barclay." Loyce heard Roseanne's voice change from proud to uncertain in the middle of the reply. She realized Roseanne never talked about that time.

"See! Me and you's a lot alike, Mrs. Barclay," C.B. said, way too innocently in Loyce's opinion. "I was passed from my daddy to a peddler man when I was twelve. See, he'd reached the point of figuring out how many kids can you feed even when they all shucking. The numbers wasn't coming out so good. So, when this oyster peddler took a shine to me, it seemed like a good chance for all of us. He taught me how to do the things that please a growed man. I got pretty good at it too. So good that he started loaning me out to pay debts to men who beat him in card games. By the time I was fourteen, I'd found out that making my own living got me a bigger dip out of the pot than just hanging around someone else's pot hoping for whatever they saw fit to pass along to me. So, I struck out on my own one night when the peddler was sleeping off a drunk. Your daddy passed you along to Mr. Barclay. I just got an earlier start at being kept."

Roseanne sniffed loudly and turned back into the store without a word.

"C.B., you oughtn't fool with Mrs. Barclay like that," Adam admonished.

"Tell me why not?" she chuckled. "Someone's got to, or she'll drown next time it rains with her nose so far up in the air. Oh, speaking of drowning, did you hear about Fate's boat? Sam told me all about it. Fate paid him and eight more fishermen for a day's catch. Then he laid all them fish on ice in his boat and covered 'em with it too. So loaded down it was just about flat in the water, or so Sam tells it. He aimed to tote all of it to that railroad at Atchafalaya Station. You know he'd made two, maybe three trips already.

Thought he could save some time and make more money by taking a bigger load."

Loyce's hands stopped on the line she was knitting, but she didn't say a word. It was Adam who asked, "What happened?"

"Well, from the way Sam tells it, Fate miscalculated the amount of that gasoline he needed to make it all the way upstream with such a load of fish and ice. Most they can figure out is that the extra weight and going against the current sucked up all his gasoline along about two-thirds of the way. But he didn't give up. He just set about tryin' to paddle that big load upstream, even though he should of knowed better. Sounds like he made it a ways before the current pushed him into the bank, where he broke his paddle trying to get back out into the water. By the time the *Mollie B* came by the next morning and gave him a tow, his ice was melted and that whole load of fish was stinking to high heaven. He dumped fish overboard all the way back. They left him up there at the big dock in Atchafalaya Station washing the slime out of his boat."

"This is the first I heard about that!" Adam chuckled. "It does seem like his mishaps always end in a powerful smell."

"Well, you know he's got Sam working with him now." C.B.'s voice was muffled by a hairpin clamped between her lips. She swept a handful of frizz from the nape of her neck and re-pinned it into the bundle of yellow, which now had dark auburn roots.

"Yessir, they both gonna be rich someday, according to Fate. See, Fate don't like being out here in the swamp so much anymore. Once ever'thing's working right, Sam's gonna run Fate's boat—a bigger one he's building—with the fish in it to Atchafalaya Station, stopping along the way upriver to pick up fish and pay out the money. Fate bought a scale and tub that Sam can take right along with him. Now that suits Sam just fine; he don't like nothing better than just easing around from net to net, dock to dock, handling them fish like they were some kind of treasure.

"See, Fate says he likes running the bizness end, as he calls it. Fate'll meet Sam at Atchafalaya Station, where he'll have the ice ready to bed 'em down for the trip. A man right there at the depot buys ice out of Lafayette and stores it until Fate needs it. Both of 'em making money, too, according to Fate."

Loyce's keen ears picked up the clatter of a horse cart before Adam or C.B. could hear it.

"Fredette, you stay right there—I won't be a minute." Mary Ann's voice floated through the breezeway, followed by the thud of her boots across the floor.

"Come on in here and tell us about York," Adam said by way of greeting.

"Doing better now that he can wear pants again," she said. "'Course, this heat don't help him any. It's so hot I'm fearing the wax is gonna melt in Val's hives and flood the island with honey. Now won't that be a mess and a half? And talking about honey, you know it made York's skin grow back just a pretty as a baby's."

"Now, don't you wish you hadn't been so hard on him?" Adam asked, returning to the cane-bottomed chair and settling, with the pan of potatoes on his knees.

"Well, I didn't expect it to be that bad—I just wanted to make him sit up and take notice." Mary Ann's voice sounded remorseful, then she snorted. "All he'd had to do was look at me to see I waddn't going to have a baby, even if he didn't want to bother asking! That man's seen enough animals born around our place to know what to expect. And to think he thought I had the time to take up with another man! Who does he think would have been raising his food and cooking his meals? Cleaning lamp globes, washing clothes, and scrubbing floors? And now I got the extra trouble of keeping up with the sawmill."

Her boots picked up speed back and forth along the front of the porch, reminding Loyce of how Fate used to pace when he talked. Thoughts of him crowded out the rest of the conversation around her. Why had he disappeared from her life? What was so all-fired important about selling fish that he didn't stay home anymore? A new scheme with Wambly Cracker to hatch disaster throughout the swamp? If so, why wasn't he here telling her about it? He'd been facing off with her for as long as she could remember. Without Fate, Loyce seemed like a stranger to herself.

She felt a pang at how they had parted the night he came to tell them his plans. Why had she been so angry? Deep down she knew the reason. It was the letter. Once he found out that they weren't kin, he didn't feel responsible for her anymore. He had been obliged to watch over her while they were kin. Now she was just another girl—a blind one at that.

— 18 —

Two pair of boots thudded along the planks from the bayou. Lost in her own reverie and the noise of conversation on the porch, Loyce hadn't heard anyone landing at the dock.

"Went down so fast, they didn't even save any of the cows," said a voice she recognized as a deckhand from the *Iona*, a small steamboat that serviced the timber camps dotting the swamp.

"What about the crew?" asked a second voice.

"Saved about half of them. Lost one that you might know, that curly-haired mate from the *Golden Era*."

"Valzine? From Morgan City?"

"Yeh, that's the one. Damn shame."

"Damn shame is right. He played a fine squeeze-box. Gonna miss him at the dances."

Loyce's face went cold. Her voice caught in her throat, forcing her to try twice, three times before her lips could shape the words.

"Val? Who says?" She rasped just above a whisper.

Conversation stopped, then Adam's voice was strident with denial.

"Can't be! The *Golden Era* was here a few days ago, and he was on it."

"Sorry, Miss Loyce, Adam. I forgot he was a friend of yours, or I would have broke it better," the young man said. "His captain loaned him out to that sister boat *Golden Crescent* needing a crew member that could talk French. They was hauling a load of cattle from them prairie cowboys west of the swamp on Bayou Courtableau. Hit a snag in Grand River. With such a load, once it started taking on water, wasn't nothing to be done but every man look out for himself. Val was one of the ones that never came back up."

The conversation faded for Loyce. First Fate, now Val. The realization that she had lost both of them swept over her. She slumped in her chair and buried her face in her hands, letting the shuttle fall to the floor.

"Loyce, Loyce." Roseanne's voice was gentle, but her hand was firm on Loyce's shoulder, shaking her awake. She had only a moment to wonder why Roseanne was in her room before the awful truth came back. Val was gone. She had rolled over to get up but now buried her face in the pillow again, so like the way she used to bury her face in Val's curly hair.

From the time they were children, Val had bowed his head for her to feel as soon as he stepped on the porch; it was his own special greeting for her. When she playfully hid her face in his curls, she could smell the places he had visited, smells not common to Bayou Chene. Pine trees from upriver, the red clay of Natchez bluffs. She could identify the cargo that shared his space and even tell him something about the passengers. Cattle, cotton, sugar, or a traveling photographer's chemicals smelled as different to her as an apple pie from a bar of soap. It tickled him that she could often tell him what dishes Tot had cooked earlier in the day.

How could it be that she would never hear him bantering with Fate, taking her side against her sparring cousin? She would never have the chance to find out if Val was sweet on her, as Fate had claimed.

"Loyce, you have to face up to this," Roseanne's voice persisted. "Everyone is meeting at his beehives before noon, and you'll regret it if you don't go."

Of course, we have to hang black crepe on the hives so the bees will know their keeper is gone, she thought. No one really believed that old superstition anymore, but it was a ritual that was just as important as the funeral itself or the all-night eating and drinking at the wake.

"No, I can't," the girl insisted. "If I go, it means he's really gone." The moss mattress crunched as she turned over and sat up against the feather pillows.

"Here's coffee with extra cream and sugar," Roseanne said, as she guided the thick mug between the space of Loyce's hands. "You didn't have supper last night."

Loyce waved her hands gently until they felt the heat of the cup and closed around it.

"Our last conversation," she said. "When was it? Was it the day C.B. and Sam arrived? No, it was later. He helped carry York to the bedroom the day the still blew up."

A new wave of sadness surged through her. That was the day the letter surfaced. That piece of paper sliced through her life like a knife neatly divides a mound of dough into two loaves. The first eighteen years, when Fate was her cousin, her liaison to the rest of the world. And now the bleak rest of her life, adrift without Val or Fate. The double loss hit her again, and she felt more alone than any time in her life. She pushed the cup out in front of her as fresh tears began to fall.

Roseanne caught the cup and waited just a moment before leaving the young woman alone to make peace with her grief.

The dry autumn days mirrored Loyce's life. She didn't knit nets. She didn't bother to comb the tangles from her hair. She wore the same shapeless shift day after day. Most days she wouldn't even go out to the porch. If she did sit out for a while, she slipped back indoors if the *Golden Era*'s whistle blew an approach to the dock. If someone stopped by while she was sitting on the porch, she was as likely to get up and leave as she was to rock silently in their midst.

Conversations swirled around without meaning for her. Why should she care whether water rose or fell? Or if fish were biting on shrimp or cut bait? The price of cotton line didn't matter. The friends who had joked and argued with her about all those details of their community—the two who enlivened her small world—were gone. She would live the rest of her life hearing about the mundane happenings of her relatives and neighbors, but none of it would matter.

Like the day Dot Verret brought the news that C.B.'s baby boy had arrived. Dot had spent two days out on Graveyard Bayou nursing C.B. through the birth and recovery. Then Sam brought the midwife as far as the post office before heading out to raise nets. While waiting for Alcide to fetch her up on his way home from picking moss, Dot visited with customers and helped Adam cook and serve meals.

"Well, I declare, it's good to be this much closer to home!" she said by way of greeting when she arrived. "Don't know what's the hardest job—picking moss for a penny a pound or delivering babies for two dollars."

"How's everybody doing down that way?" Adam said from where he was turning venison sausage at the stove.

"Well, I tell you now, C.B don't seem to be taking to it yet," Dot worried. "Some takes longer than others to get the hang of it, but poor little old C.B. seems plumb put off by the little fella even being close to her. She didn't even rouse up enough to name him, but Sam was proud as anything to call him Sam Junior. She'll come around—I never seen it fail. Some just take longer than others."

And so it went throughout the day. Dot dished up plates and washed them when they came back, passing along news from customer to customer. Loyce, who usually looked forward to Dot's company, stayed in her room. And so the weeks dragged out.

"No sense in getting your feathers ruffled, girls, I'm just here to take some of the pressure off of you." Adam's voice was familiar to the chickens, and they settled back down on the roost.

"Sorry, girls, I wouldn't be out here so early except I was just too dadblamed tired last night to wait up for you to go to roost." He felt for the wooden latch and turned it, before gently opening the henhouse door. Warm, downy chicken smell wafted out along with a few sleepy murmurings.

"If I had put these roosters in the coop for the night, I could have waited till later this morning, but I'll never catch them once daylight comes."

He ducked under the low doorway and stood for a moment to get his bearings. The proud tail feathers of the flock guardian shone white in the predawn light. Skip that one. With deft skill that comes from long practice, Adam picked up one young cockerel with his right hand and transferred it under his left arm without even waking the bird. Then he ducked his head and backed out the open doorway. Removing the top from an old fish cart, he placed the bird on the slatted floor. The sleepy rooster would probably just sit in the darkness, but Adam didn't take that chance; carefully, he replaced the lid. Good thing he did. The next bird slipped out of his grasp and flapped noisily; his squawks set off bedlam among the rest of the flock. The bird in the crate woke up and joined in the racket. Finally getting the frantic bird under control, Adam backed out the doorway and placed him in the fish cart. He propped the coop open so the rest of the birds could step over the threshold when the rising sun told them it was time.

Adam picked up the box of roosters with one hand and made his way to the dock. They would sit quietly under the tree until he returned after breakfast to dispatch them for the noon meal.

Roseanne had kept an eye on the tomato gravy and biscuits for Adam, and by the time he stepped into the kitchen, three places were set at the table. However, Loyce didn't join them until they had nearly finished eating and were planning the rest of the day. Adam and Roseanne exchanged a worried look at the way a sack-like dress hung from her thin shoulders. She toyed with half a biscuit on her plate but didn't eat any with her coffee.

"If one of you will fill the dishpan, I'll wash up," Loyce said listlessly, as she pushed back her chair and felt around the wall where several clean aprons hung from hooks beside the door.

Adam lifted the kettle from the stove and poured hot water into the dishpan. Then he dipped cold water from the bucket on the counter, testing the temperature with his own hand before leaving it for her.

"The rest of this can heat up for scalding while I put an edge on this knife. No sense in hauling water and starting a fire in the washpot for just two roosters," he said.

For a few minutes the silence was broken only by the rattle of dishes in the porcelain dishpan and the *shsk, shsk* of the blade on the whetstone. Adam had given up trying to prod Loyce out of her gloom and had learned to settle in with her mood. The pall of grief that hung over the house brought back to him the atmosphere after the drowning of his wife, except now it was relieved somewhat by Roseanne's careful attention to order.

When the blade was sharp enough to suit him, Adam slid the knife into the scabbard on his belt and picked up a kettle in each hand. Steam trailed behind him down the plank walk in the October morning.

In less than a minute he had each bird hanging by its feet from a massive oak limb that curved out over the bayou. He sliced the head off each rooster before they had a chance to squawk. As they bled into the water, he poured the contents of each kettle into a bucket. By the time the birds had bled out, the water had cooled to just the right temperature. Too hot, the skin would cook. Not hot enough, the feathers wouldn't release. He dunked each bird up and down, soaking all the feathers equally.

As he was tugging on a wing feather to test it, the first boat of the day came around the bend. He glanced up to see a seated man paddling a small dugout. The pirogue was not local, looked to be an old one made in the Indian style—"un pirogue sauvage," as the Cajuns would say. The silhouette against the sunrise showed a man who was not big but with disproportionately heavy shoulders and arms. Something familiar about him made Adam stop, then stand up and stare. It looked so much like Val. He tried to recall Val's brothers and why one of them might be paddling a pirogue through Bayou Chene.

By then the little boat had reached the dock. The man didn't move to the bow to tie it off. Instead, he remained seated and paddled the light craft parallel to the logs, which he grasped with one hand. That was when Adam saw the bowline lay at the man's feet instead of coiled in the bow. He also saw the man's right leg was stretched straight out, bound in a cast made of moss and mud.

"Hey, Adam. You gonna give a man a hand or just let him flop around on your dock like a dying catfish, *enh*?" Val's voice sounded cheerful but winded.

"It can't be! How can it be? What do you mean? How did you get here? Where have you been?" Adam couldn't decide what he needed to know first, so all the questions tumbled out at once.

He tripped over the buckets of scalding roosters in his rush to reach the edge of the dock. His left hand grabbed the pirogue, while his right gathered up the line and tied it off as quickly as he had bound the roosters' feet. Then he stretched out a hand to Val.

"*Mais oui*, I think I'm gonna need a little more help than that, or the both of us gonna get wet," Val said. "This thing, she's too quick in the water for me to try to stand up on one leg. You hold her tight against the log and see if I can get me up on the dock."

Val's biceps corded and then released. Just like that, he was sitting on the dock.

"Whew!" he grunted. "Been crouched in there since early, early yesterday, slept in it last night. Bought it off one of them Grand River Injuns. You heard my boat went down—not the *Era*, no, but the *Crescent*?"

"For sure! But we heard you drowned!" Adam squatted on his heels in front of the younger man he had expected never to see again.

"*Mais*, not quite." Val took a moment to catch his breath. "It was a damn old cow, she slam my leg against something—the cookstove maybe—but I can't say nothing 'cause it was the same cow what her tail give me a tow to the bank. Pulled me all the way up, for true, before taking off and leaving me there. Couldn't tell where we was, but I wasn't in any shape to go no place anyway. "A lot of trash float by, but I never see another soul, dead or alive. Maybe two, three hours? After a while my mind she catch up with how bad my leg hurting. And how I done lost everything 'cept the clothes on my back and the pay in my pocket. Worst of all is my squeeze-box, she at the bottom of the bayou. I tell you for truth that brought me just about as low as I ever been. I just set there and thought about the trouble I done found myself in.

"Right about then, two Injun womans came by toting ropes. I knowed 'em from the Injun camp 'cause we sometime trade for fish over there. They was trailing my cow and looking for some more along the way. They took me back to camp and wrap my leg up like this. That was what, two or three weeks back?"

"Well, I can't say when it happened," Adam offered, "but we heard about it right around the start of September."

Val nodded thoughtfully.

"I figured someone was missing me by now, so I paid 'em for the pirogue and some food, with the notion that if I couldn't make it this far, I might as well jus' flip on overboard. Looks like I cheated them gators out of a meal, *enh*?"

"I don't know about that, you *smell* like gator bait." Adam chuckled as he helped Val up on his good leg. "Let's get you on to the house."

"Must be the smoked fish you smell in my sack. It'll kill your appetite if you hungry enough, but I don't think I could ever eat it regular. Might also be the gator oil you smelling. The Injuns believe it keeps *mostiques* from biting, and you know, it seem like they left me alone. I can't smell either one of them no more, but it smell rotten when I first got there."

Inside Loyce had finished putting away the dishes and was hanging up her apron when she heard the uneven steps coming down the plank walk. She paused a moment trying to imagine how carrying two dead roosters and a dishpan could change the sound of Adam's footfalls so much. Try as she might, she couldn't identify the *ka-thump, drag, ka-thump, drag* coming through the screen door. Then the smells wafted ahead of the sounds, and she took a step backward to escape the assault on her sensitive nose. The creak of the door coincided with Adam's voice singing out.

"Loyce, look who's here!"

Before Adam's words could sink in, she sensed someone's head bending level with her chest. Instinctively, she reached out to investigate. Curls, stiff with dirt and oil, sprang under her touch. Her fingers quickly passed around to the face, reading his features.

"Val?" Her voice was querulous. "Val!" It changed to a joyful shout.

Two hours later Val had told his story, wolfed down the breakfast leavings, and bathed as much of his filthy body as his broken leg would allow. It was a quiet morning. Only Alcide, C.B., and Sam Junior joined Loyce, Roseanne, and Adam for ten o'clock coffee on the porch.

Cottonwood leaves rustled in the morning breeze, and C.B. pulled Sam Junior's blanket up higher on his head before settling into a chair.

"Whew, Val, that was some close call!" she exclaimed. "You could be dead right now instead of sitting here drinking coffee."

"Well, there's plenty who think you're still dead right this minute," said Alcide. "The *Golden Era*'s done hired another mate. Hope you don't think they was getting ahead of themselves, but you know, like as not, bodies just ain't recovered when people go missing."

"That's right, and it's hard to decide which is worse," Adam said softly. "As long as they don't find the body, you can hope. But at least, once you know for sure, you can try to go on with a new kind of life."

No one spoke for several moments as his remembered grief intruded on their celebration of Val's return.

"Reminds me of that little Voisin boy." Alcide picked up his thread again. "Name was Calvin. Ten or twelve years old. His daddy sent him down to bail the boats one afternoon after a hard rain. They never saw him again. Can only figure he fell overboard. Never did find his body."

"I do remember that," said Adam. "Didn't miss him till he was called for supper. When he didn't come, his mama knew something had happened."

"And that Neeley boy, Pank. Look how he just up and disappeared," said Alcide.

"Well, that was after he shot and killed his girlfriend for walking out on a Sunday with another man," said Adam. "Don't you reckon he run off, thinking maybe someone was gonna call the law?"

"And then there's the bodies that show up that we never find out who they were," Alcide countered. "There was even one with iron cook pots tied onto him. Old man Larson pulled him up, and what a load that was! Them pots all full of water. We was on our way to this very post office—long before your time, Adam—when Mr. Larson called Papa over to help. First dead man I ever saw. Papa waving me off, telling me to keep away but me craning my neck to see for myself. They figured he was dumped off a riverboat, probably made someone mad in a card game. They even figured the cook was the one that killed 'im, since no one else on a boat would dare mess with the pots."

"Maybe the dead man *was* the cook?" offered C.B.

"No one on a boat would kill a cook, no matter what," said Cide with conviction.

"So, what happened to the body?" asked Loyce.

"Buried him right there, back from the riverbank a piece," replied Cide. "So long ago, I think Mary Ann's chicken yard is over him now."

"You know, Val, this could be your chance to get off those boats once and for all," C.B. said to him over the top of Sam Junior's head.

Loyce's heart skipped a beat. She cocked her head to catch the fullness of his answer. Val had longed to quit boats and settle down to raise bees, but both sides of his family always worked on the rivers, and he felt he'd be letting them down.

"C.B., I been sitting here thinking the same thing, me," Val replied. "I could help Adam in the kitchen even with my broke leg. After it comes better, I could pretty much start over. Raising all the bees I want, collecting the honey, selling it right here at the store. Get myself a little houseboat."

"That's what you've always wanted to try," said Adam.

"Once I start making a living—prove I can do something besides plow them rivers," said Val, "maybe Mama would understand. She just throw a fit when I talk about trying that before. She say we was always riverboat people, and that was all we knew, and the river was good to us."

"Well, if you've a mind to stay around here, we'd be proud to have you," Adam said. "In fact, to make you feel at home and help overcome your run of bad luck, I'll make you a present of that squeeze-box I never learned to play. You made it look so easy, I thought sure I could do it, but all I ever did was make the hens squawk and the dogs howl. As for Fate, he's not been around in a coon's age. Sam takes the fish from the Chene to him on Wednesdays now, so he don't come this far down himself."

"Oh, but word drifts in now and again," Alcide chimed in. "Sometimes about him making money and other times just making a mess somewhere when he takes over the run from Sam now and again. You know he ties up and spends the night at his last pickup place, different places depending on what route he's running. Heard tell he had made a deal with Dieu Cavalier to pick up some cleaned ducks on his way back upstream to Atchafalaya Station the next day. Well, the next morning he got to daydreaming, I suppose, and went right on by Dieu's dock. Couldn't hear Dieu yelling at him over the noise of his engine. Dieu was waving a duck trying to get his attention. Well, Dieu didn't have no other way to get rid of nine cleaned ducks so he just took matters into his own hands. He grabbed his shotgun and fired in that direction a little above Fate's head. Dieu, not being used to gasoline boat speed, over-guessed how fast Fate's boat was going in the slack current.

Blew Fate's hat right off, gentlemen! Got his attention all right, and they made the trade. I suppose those ducks made it to the station in time to get packed down in ice and travel first-class up north."

Everyone except Loyce enjoyed a laugh at the absent Fate's expense.

"Val, how do you feel about bunking with Mame on the houseboat now that Fate is gone? She'd appreciate the company," Adam offered.

"That sounds good to me, if Mame don't mind," Val said.

Loyce took her first deep breath in months. The fresh October air filled her lungs to near bursting with joy.

— 19 —

Val, his cast removed, sat on a low stool repairing wooden frames that held the wax foundation in his beehives. Loyce was shelling dried peas. Their tapping and rustling provided industrious background music to the conversations going on around the porch. Benches and chairs were filling up as fragrances from the kitchen told everyone Adam would soon be serving up plates for early diners. Word had spread quickly that his kitchen was open, and true to Roseanne's predictions, a sizable gathering had started milling around the porch near mealtimes. In fact, riverboat captains had been known to flirt with the wrath of their own cooks by sneaking away to sit at Adam's table.

That day Cairo Beauty squirmed in the rocking chair next to Loyce and settled Sam Junior on her lap, pulling his blanket tight against the November breeze. She had told the story so many times that most people on the Chene had heard it firsthand, and everyone had heard second- and thirdhand versions. Since interest wasn't lagging, she enjoyed retelling it with new details each time around to keep it fresh.

"Let's see, about a week ago now, the whole thing started with the mop water," she commenced. "Hadn't rained enough to keep the cistern full, so I was saving what was left for drinking and cooking. For everything else I just drew a bucket full right out of the bayou, which that morning was so muddy you could cut bricks from it.

"I remember thinking it must be raining upriver somewhere—Memphis, St. Louis, Natchez, or one of the other places I'd lived. More than likely it had been a room over a saloon, that same kind of rain pouring down on the tin roof, making so much noise I couldn't even hear if shooting broke out below. Didn't matter, I wouldn't be there for long. Seems like I was always running crossways someone whose rules I couldn't make sense of, and it was me who had to move on.

"But not now! I had me a husband and a houseboat of my own, plenty of sunshine and all the time in the world. I hauled up a bucket full of water and knew there was nothing I could do but wait for the dirt to settle before I could mop. You can't hurry muddy water.

"Like I said, I had plenty time. My beans were on the stove, had been since early. They'd be tender by the time Sam got home. I stuck in another chunk of wood and figured I might as well use that waiting time to get off my feet and let Sam Junior get some sun. But not me. I tied my bonnet good and tight and turned my back to the sun, to boot. Don't matter if I am a married woman and a mother, ain't no sense ruining my skin and looking like a field hand.

"I always did enjoy that view on Graveyard, upstream and downstream both, nothing but trees bending over the water. Now, it's true that just as I was setting down I noticed that line from the stern to that live oak on the bank was stretched tight; the water'd been falling some the past few days. Well, I wasn't about to get right back up, take Sam Junior inside, and loosen the line right then. It wasn't enough of a slant to make my beans slosh out of the pot. It could just wait until I got up again.

"We was so comfortable. It seemed like that rocking chair was keeping time with the current, so peaceful like. That old willow snag in the bend was bobbing along with us. It was getting on toward noon and had that midday quiet 'cept for now and then a thud whenever a log bumped up against the hull. Then a few seconds later it'd jostle out from under there and head on down toward Morgan City.

"I'd gotten the hang of Sam Junior suckling, and it worked out for both of us. He needed the milk as much as I needed to be rid of it. I kept him clean, full, and comforted best I could but didn't really dote on him like you see some mamas do.

"That morning in no time at all he dropped off to sleep, and I got a kick out of watching his hair lift like a little bird wing every time the chair dipped. I guess I dozed off, too, or maybe it was because my bonnet made like mule blinders. For whatever reason, I never noticed that old chair was creeping downhill toward the edge of the deck. Fact is, I was in the middle of trying to decide between rice and cornbread for supper when the next thing I knew that same bonnet was parting the water like the rod of Moses.

"It seemed like I fell forever, following that bonnet to the bottom. My skirt and petticoat wrapped all around my head and arms so I couldn't tell up from down. I fought and kicked deciding any direction was better than none. Right about the time I figured I might's well just suck up a big old chest full of water and be done with it, I broke through. That goaded me into one more good kick, all I had left in me. I lurched ahead and even touched the hull, but it swept past with nothing for me to grip, not even a splinter. Then my foot snagged a line. It was the fish cart! Well, I didn't do nothing but wrap one leg around that line. While I was working to catch my breath, that skirt tail swept downstream and tried to pull me right on to Morgan City, which was where that old chair was headed by then.

"I could feel the fish swimming and bumping in the slats of the fish cart. Funny what goes through your mind. I found myself wondering if they always bump around like that and we don't know it, or if it was just because someone was standing on them. Well, anyway, I just kept hanging on and worked my way up to the top of the cart. That line stretched and squeaked like it would break straight away, but it didn't. Then when I just started building confidence in it, the knot slipped on the spike!

"I figured then it was all over. But somehow that rigging held just enough for me to hook elbows over the edge of the deck. You know how heavy it is to pull a dress up out of a washtub and try to wring it? Now add a current to that and try to pull it up with just your elbows and with you in it, to boot! I couldn't do more; I just hung there.

"Finally, my breath came back, and I started creeping a little bit at a time on my elbows till the rest of me was finally all the way up on the deck. I laid there facedown no telling how long. I could feel them wooden planks warming my face and pushing the water from inside my clothes. I lay there a while longer wondering why feeling alive had no gladness in it. Something was wrong still. Sam Junior!

"I jumped up then and looked all around the deck. No sign of him. I didn't want to look out there in the water, but I had to, and all I spied was those rockers bobbing up through that old willow.

"Let me tell you all the air went out of me again. I couldn't even holler. And I knew if I did, there wasn't no one to hear. I couldn't even move then. I figured I never would be able to move again. How could I ever go back inside and face his crib, the blankets and little dresses? I could never look at the water again without wondering if he might still bob up. No telling how long I set there wishing I could trade places with him. How I wished I was in that cold water with the weight of my skirt pulling me on down and he was safe in his crib Sam built out of sweet-smelling willow poles. That was when I realized how much I loved him. More than I ever loved anybody, even my own self.

"Then I heard 'C.B.! C.B.? You all right?' It was Alcide paddling from down around the bend. I knew it was too late, but still I jumped and waved and hollered for him to hurry. Then I saw it—that little bundle wrapped in his shirt. It was laying on the bottom of his pirogue. Let me tell you, a wave colder than the water passed over me then. I couldn't decide whether to jump out there and snatch up that little bundle or wave at him to pass on by so I wouldn't have to see Sam Junior's still little face and body. I was froze in place.

"Alcide tied off his boat and stood up before I could move. I was still standing there when he reached down and picked up that bundle. Next thing I knew, Sam's little fist poked out and him squawling like a nest of yellow jackets got under his blanket."

Alcide had been listening intently, as if he hadn't been there in person. Now he broke in.

"I think he was mad about having his nap broken. I was baiting my crosslines when I saw this white blob coming my way. I figured for sure it was a dead heron ready to foul my lines, so I paddled around to head it off. Instead, it was this little fella with his dress all puffed out with air, floating high as a cottonmouth. He wasn't none too happy about being in so cold a bath, but when I wrapped him up in my shirt, he calmed down and went right to sleep."

The listeners let out their collective breath and started remarking to each other about the miraculous end to the near tragedy and how the story got better every time it was told. Alcide grinned, and C.B. proudly pulled back the blanket to show off Sam Junior's sleeping face. Only Roseanne was silent. She stood apart with her arms folded across her chest. Then she sniffed and turned away into the store.

— 20 —

The November sunlight thinned, keeping pace with the shedding leaf canopy overhead. A breeze stirred around Loyce's face, and the rays across her lap didn't burn like they did just a few afternoons ago. She usually looked forward to changes in the seasons but not this year. After the excitement and relief of Val's return, she missed Fate more than ever. It had been weeks since they had heard from him. She stabbed the spindle into the cotton twine and yanked the loop shut, again, then again.

Shoes clattered down the bare wooden stairs and across the hall to the porch.

"Loyce, stand up and let's look at this," Roseanne said.

"Well, you can look. I'll get by with just feeling," Loyce muttered as she stood up from the rocking chair. Her rumpled cotton shift was pinned together at the top where a button was long gone. Frayed apron strings pulled in a semblance of a waist from the folds of fabric.

Ignoring her cross tone, Roseanne surveyed the perimeter of the porch and, seeing no one, helped Loyce step out of the rag. "Hold up your arms," she prompted, pulling the maroon worsted traveling dress over Loyce's head when the girl responded. "This doesn't fit me anymore, and you could use another dress for winter."

"I can do it," Loyce said, slapping Roseanne's hands from the double row of buttons and fastening the opening from waist to collar, smoothing the fitted front as she worked. The waistband fit her slight figure with room to spare but still hung more gracefully than the shapeless dresses she usually wore. The heavy skirt skimmed her hips and fell closer to the floor than her shifts. Roseanne noticed that Loyce stood a little straighter in the tailored dress, but all she said was, "It's likely to be cold for New Year's, and this'll keep you a lot warmer at the dance."

"Oh my goodness, what is this?" Roseanne exclaimed, as she picked up Loyce's heavy braid in order to rearrange the dress collar.

Loyce raised a hand and felt the back of her neck before shrugging. "Just a tangle I can't get out."

"Here, let me see." Roseanne fingered the solid mass of hair, fine as silk and as big as her fist. "Loyce, there's nothing to do but cut this. It'll never comb out."

"Well, why not just cut it all?" Cairo Beauty stepped through the hall carrying Sam Junior on her hip. "There's plenty of 'em in the cities now just have their hair skimming their shoulders or thereabouts. Be a lot easier for a blind girl to keep up, if you know what I mean. Now some of them get these marcel waves, but with a little body like you got, Loyce, it'll just wiggle around like moss in the wind. Look real pretty to my mind."

"Cairo Beauty, it'd be just like you to come up with something like that," Roseanne sniffed. "A woman's hair is her crowning glory; the Bible says so."

"Well, does it say how long that crown's gotta be?" C.B. retorted. "Seems to me it don't signify long over short."

"If you're gonna cut a hunk out, why not make it match all over?" Loyce entered the fray. "I'd just soon have it out of my way, and I sure can't see what it looks like."

"I can do it for you—seen it done plenty times," Cairo Beauty offered. "Mrs. Barclay, you got some scissors in there somewhere?"

"If you're sure you want to do this." Roseanne sounded doubtful as she handed the scissors to Cairo Beauty and took Sam Junior.

"Go ahead," Loyce said.

Taking up the wide-toothed comb, C.B. first smoothed the

tangled hair into a white part, gradually approaching the fist-sized knot at the nape of Loyce's neck. Hair draped around the knot, flowed down the maroon worsted shoulders, and pooled in her lap. "We'll have to start with this tangle and then even it up to match," C.B. figured out loud. She closed the blades of the scissors across the knot and started sawing. "Ummph. It can't get a purchase on this much of a bite. You got a knife handy there, Mrs. Barclay?"

Roseanne carried Sam Junior into the kitchen and returned shortly, proffering a wood-handled kitchen knife. "This is sharp. Mr. Snellgrove uses it to clean fish."

"That'll do it," C.B. said. She grasped the knot again and began sawing. The hair above the knot sprang up.

"Ooooh lookidat!" C.B. exclaimed, giving it a fluff with her free hand. "Now I think I can use the scissors again."

She combed down from the part on Loyce's left side and lined up the scissors with the bottom of the fringe on the nape of Loyce's neck. Snip, snip, the hair sprang up again, about two inches shorter than the hair on the back.

"Look what you did, you fool!" Roseanne snatched the scissors away. "You pulled down too hard. Let me fix it."

She thrust Sam Junior back at C.B. and took the scissors. Working on Loyce's right side, she pulled a two-inch width of hair just tight enough to hold it still and made a cut. The result was one inch longer than the hair on the back of Loyce's neck and three inches longer than the cut C.B. made.

"It feels a little uneven," Loyce offered, passing inquisitive fingers over each ear.

"Oh, it's not so far off. All you have to do now is tilt your head to the right, and it'll look just fine," C.B. advised.

"This won't do—it won't do at all!" Roseanne waved the scissors. Loyce leaned away from the snapping sound near her right ear, but Roseanne grabbed the top of her head and held it firmly in place. "Just look straight ahead. I mean, just keep your nose pointed straight ahead, and I'll fix it."

"How can you fix it when you're the one messed it up!" C.B. countered, jiggling her hip to distract Sam Junior, who was trying to grab the scissors from Roseanne.

Distractions held no fear for someone as focused as Roseanne. The scissors clipped around the circle of Loyce's head, creating an even bob swinging around her chin.

"This side has to come up a tiny bit more," she said at the same time C.B. was saying, "That's perfect."

"No, not quite," said Roseanne, trimming another inch.

The scissors snipped away another row so that it hung precisely even with each ear tip.

"Mrs. Barclay, you getting it too short. She gonna look like a boy," warned C.B.

"It has to be straight—how can you not see that!" Roseanne exclaimed, backing away to view her work. "Just a little bit more. Oh drat, now this is longer. Just hold still, Loyce. I'm almost finished."

"Now she looks just like one of them Polish chickens of Mary Ann's," said C.B.

Loyce shook her head from side to side and front to back. Sure enough, the cropped hair sticking straight out from the center part flopped above her ears like a splayed feather duster.

"Makes no never mind to me," she declared. "It feels good, not so heavy. I won't have to bother with braids and such from now on. I don't know anyone my looks would matter to, and I can't see what it looks like anyway."

"Well, at least Fate ain't gonna be hanging 'round making fun of you." C.B. plopped down in the neighboring chair and settled Sam Junior in her lap. "Sam says that boy's so busy he can't find time to shake a stick at a snake."

"Well, he can thank me for putting the notion in his head about selling those scale fish." Roseanne stepped back from fluffing Loyce's hair and waved the scissors for emphasis.

"Oh, it's a lot more than that now!" C.B. said with authority. "Wambly Cracker told him there was a market for paddlefish eggs! It's something called 'caviar' that posh folks usually have to get from way overseas. Sam says Fate's making deals with big fish buyers from up north and lining up fish from down here, bedding it all down with ice from his own new icehouse in Atchafalaya Station. Makes it right out of river water. Sam says he don't even see Fate, except on payday. Thinks he might be living in Baton Rouge—it's just a few minutes' train ride from Atchafalaya Station, you know. Seems he's been seeing a woman Wambly knows. Sam said her name's Rona Castille and she's come to the station a couple of times with Fate."

"Well, I miss him," Roseanne said. "He could always jolly up the place; it was good for business. Customers liked to linger in the store when he was around. Not the same without him."

Loyce didn't say a word, but her feet came down harder in the rocking chair, and her cropped hair lifted on the breeze of the motion.

"You know, he ain't ever seen Sam Junior. So, I guess that's about three months since he's been around here," C.B. continued, as if Roseanne had not spoken. "He don't even know about me and Sam Junior falling in the bayou and nearly drowning."

Roseanne sniffed. "There's no doubt if Alcide hadn't come along when he did, that baby wouldn't be here today. But you seemed safe enough up there on the deck."

For the next few seconds only the rockers of Loyce's chair broke the silence. C.B.'s own rocking chair was still.

"What you getting at, Mrs. Barclay?" C.B.'s voice dipped low.

"Well, everyone knows you tried to get rid of that baby before it was born, and that was a mighty convenient accident with nobody to tell the tale but you," Roseanne countered. "If Alcide hadn't come along when he did, you'd be free and clear to go on back to your showboating life or whatever it was you did. Let me tell you right now, I'm not the only one who thinks this whole matter needs looking into by the law!"

"The law!" Loyce's chair stopped in mid-rock. "Roseanne, the law don't even come out here except during election years to talk up votes."

"Well, maybe it's time they did. That's right, now just may be the time."

C.B. jumped to her feet, slamming the rocking chair against the porch wall.

"Mrs. Barclay, you going too far this time. I put up with you looking down your nose at me and mine, acting like we ain't good enough to be in the same room with you. But you go and start messing with my baby or calling the law in here, and you gonna have more trouble than you ever expected. I was gonna wait here to catch me a ride to the turnoff, but I'd rather wait out on the dock. Loyce, I'll see you next time."

Her feet stomped down the steps and along the plank walk to the dock.

"Roseanne, that's some serious accusations," Loyce ventured.

"Well, it's a serious matter," Roseanne replied, and walked back across the dogtrot to the store.

The next day Loyce recognized Val's whistle and soft step onto the plank walk as he came out of the woods.

"Why do I smell honey this time of year?" She breathed deeply again to make sure.

"Been so warm this fall, they made more honey than they'll need to see 'em through the winter, so I relieved them of a few jars. Here's one for you, and Adam can sell the rest for me in the store, *enh*? What happen to your hair?"

"I got caught between Roseanne and C.B. Even I can tell it looks like a yellerhammer nest," she said.

"Not that bad. I never noticed how much your hair looks like mine. If you got some scissors, I straighten it up for you. I gotta cut mine all the time to keep it out of my face."

"Look in the post office over by the string."

Val returned and stood in front of Loyce's chair.

"Now sit up straight, *cher*. *Bon!* First I just rake my hands through like this," he said, so as not to startle her with his touch.

His fingers pressed her scalp from front to back and tugged her hair experimentally.

"Then I measure by the thickness of my fingers to shorten the front like this."

He started snipping ends of curls, one at a time. The bits fell to the floor around them. The effect was a fringe of light brown framing her face, with full waves lifting the back and sides. When he finished, Loyce explored the new coif with her fingers.

"It does feel like yours, just not as curly," she said.

It was the first time he had seen her smile since he returned from the dead. Impulsively, he pressed her head against his middle before stepping back. Her cheek rested briefly where his shirttail tucked into his worn canvas pants.

Loyce felt a rush of both comfort and exhilaration in the embrace.

"From what I hear, more than just your hair done got caught between those two women," Val chuckled, stepping back to look at her face. "Seem like everybody taking sides on whether the law needs to come out."

"Oh Val, I know C.B. didn't try to hurt her baby, but Roseanne is sure as anything that she did. Worse than that, she's bound and determined to make the law a part of all this. We've always taken care of our own differences on the Chene."

Val sat down in the chair next to Loyce and held her hands in his.

"Seeing as how Roseanne and C.B. both come in here from somewhere else makes it another whole mess," she continued. "If an outsider came in accusing someone who lives here, we could deal with that. But one outsider accusing another outsider of a serious crime is different. No family here has a stake in the outcome, and no one knows the facts except C.B. The word of one outsider against the suspicions of another outsider. Makes some people think Bayou Chene is getting big enough to need the law stepping in."

Loyce felt Val nod in commiseration. He always knew when to

just sit and listen. Unlike Fate, who had to talk instead of thinking or listening.

"What makes it worse is they are both good, good friends for me," she continued. "Roseanne can be testy sometimes, sure, but she has made a different place out of the store and our house. And C.B. brings so much fun when she comes. Anyone would look forward to seeing her. Anyone except Roseanne."

Val chuckled.

"For true, C.B. rubbed Roseanne the wrong way since the first time they laid eyes on each other," he said. "I see that happen on boat crews. No telling why, but now and then one person will just find another person makes them mad for no reason anybody else can see. Most often it ends with one of them leaving, but not before they mess up the whole crew with their fighting."

Loyce's hands rested on the arms of her rocker. Suddenly she felt Val gently slide his own hands beneath hers. Palm to palm, he guided her up and out of the chair.

"Ah, *cher*," he said and pulled her close. "You got youself a new dress and a new haircut to go with it. Let's leave the fighting for them two to sort out amongst them, *enh?*"

Loyce straightened her shoulders, shook back the fluff of hair framing her face, and then stepped out to the sprightly waltz Val was already humming. Alone in the twilight, they glided and dipped around the porch.

— 21 —

Some years autumn drizzled in, starting the dark, wet winter early, but in 1907 it was all a swamp autumn should be. Bayous ran blue with reflected sky. Hardwoods growing along the natural levees turned red and orange against the green background of live oaks. Flat, crinkly cottonwood and sycamore leaves drifted down and skittered on top of the current. Out in the lakes, cypress trees turned rusty red and maroon before dropping their needles in the still water.

Oaks of all kind rained acorns—small and round, large and oblong, from almost black through brown, sienna, and tan. Squirrels, hogs, goats, deer, and small furbearers grew fat and shiny on the oily nuts.

Children were sent out with buckets to vie for the muscadines and coon grapes that would be made into jelly, pies, and wine. Around the homesteads oranges, satsumas, and lemons showed their colors among the leathery green leaves. Pomegranates and Japanese persimmons filled buckets and baskets, proving that at least some of Wambly Cracker's suggestions had worked for the Cheners. Sweet potatoes, onions, hard-shell squashes, and pumpkins were set out to dry on rooftops of houses and houseboats alike, before being stored for winter eating. Even as the summer crops were still bearing, fall gardens were already bright with young winter greens that would produce leaves and roots for months to come.

The Cheners didn't put much food by, Val noted. When he had been up the river in winters past, he lived on dried beans or wilted vegetables from grocery stores, getting by just like the local residents. At the same time he knew his friends on the Chene would be feasting on fresh lettuce, spinach, or other greens tossed with green onions, a dab of bacon grease, and vinegar. Beetroots stewed in sweet vinegar spiced up plates of wild duck and turnips. Suppers on a cold night might be rutabagas cooked in a brown roux with squirrel, venison, or pork from the smokehouse. Deer, possums, coons, and rabbits were baked, roasted, or smothered in onions until they fell apart, making their own gravy. Even in winter the bayous gave up some fish, and the woods were always full of game.

The swampers prepared for winter in the simplest fashion. Children gathered wax myrtle berries for candles. Even though the candles weren't as bright as lamps for close work like reading or sewing, they reduced the amount of coal oil needed for extra hours of darkness. Men repaired traps and snares to set out in late winter, when pelts were at their finest. Women carried quilts outside and slung them over picket fences or porch banisters to air. Careful housewives ripped open moss mattresses to fluff and add more stuffing.

Some women preferred the fresh smell of corn shuck mattresses that crackled enough to wake a restless sleeper. Families that didn't grow corn bartered or bought from their neighbors. They ground most of it into meal, keeping only a portion of it whole for livestock. Great stores of livestock feed weren't needed because vines, evergreen shrubs, and some grasses grew throughout the warm winters. Chickens, hogs, and dogs also ate trimmings from the garden and the fish cart as well as a bounty of offal when game was killed.

Val had rarely stayed in one place long enough to watch seasons change. In past years he might leave St. Louis during a fresh snowfall only to arrive at Bayou Chene in a heatwave two weeks later. That autumn on the Chene he walked the paths between homesteads as much to feel the rhythm of the changing year as to deliver honey and beeswax to customers. It was the longest time he'd been around to manage the hives he had set up in different locations around the island.

As he watched his bees store the last pollen and nectar before bedding down for winter, Val pondered the fact that he could finally settle down too. No more roaming the rivers, living out of a duffel bag, spending holidays with strangers. He chuckled over the irony that his near death had provided him the chance to live out his dream. Bayou Chene would be his home from now on. *Mais oui!*

After the initial relief of not having to plan his life around the next boat whistle, Val felt a restless energy in his limbs. That was another reason he roamed the footpaths and rowed Adam's skiff along the bayous. Maybe he wouldn't feel settled until he married and built a house or houseboat of his own. Maybe he'd talk to Loyce about it.

Val had never broached the subject of a closer relationship; he assumed Loyce felt the same exhilaration he experienced when they played music or playfully argued with Fate over some unimportant difference of opinions. What if she didn't share his feeling? He thought of the other young women living around the Chene. He had danced and laughed with them. He spent time visiting when he delivered honey. But he never felt the buzz of excitement, the jubilation, he felt around Loyce. Maybe he'd bring it up tonight. If not tonight, soon.

During his rounds through the community Val crossed paths with dozens of people every day. As autumn stretched out toward winter, he couldn't avoid the growing controversy over Roseanne and C.B. More of the neighbors began taking sides. It seemed everyone was talking about the possibility of C.B. being arrested. Had Roseanne carried through with her threat to mail a letter of her suspicions to the sheriff in St. Martin Parish? Could officers be on their way right now to take C.B. in for questioning? What if they came while Sam was away on a fish-buying trip? What would become of Sam Junior? Did they let babies go to jail with their mamas? It seemed everyone had a different opinion on that as well. Some were of the opinion they needed to close ranks around C.B. and hide her from the law. Others said let her take her chances like anyone else accused of a crime in the United States. After all, she wasn't even a Chener. Val felt relief when December closed in on the community and no law officers showed up in the Chene.

The discord faded in anticipation of Christmas. He couldn't remember being so excited about the coming holiday, even as a child. He had started work on boats as a teenager, so most Christmases found him on a boat with crew members and passengers who would have preferred to be home with their own family and friends.

True to his Irish and Cajun natures, Val had always made the best of the holidays by playing music to cheer up the crowds. Soon strangers in a public hall or on a boat would be singing and dancing in time to his music. This year was going to be memorable because he had a warm circle of his own.

The post office and store started bustling early in November, with customers making special orders for gifts and seasonal food. When the first steamboats of December arrived, bananas from South America and apples from upriver filled the building with holiday fragrance. Nuts from other states, and even other countries, were measured out by the pound. Children and grandparents all along the bayous were set to work with nutcrackers and warned not to eat more than they put in the dish for fruitcake. In the final two weeks before Christmas, mysterious packages were tucked under coats or slipped into lard cans for the anonymous journey home in a pirogue or skiff.

Val knew that Mame, Adam, Loyce, and Fate usually joined York and Mary Ann for Christmas dinner at the old Bertram home. This year they welcomed both Val and Roseanne into the family gathering. Val wondered if Fate would make it home for the holidays. Most people who left the Chene to try life outside the swamp never made it back for visits. To them the Chene receded until it seemed a world from another time—quaint, backward in its ways, a place to be from. Oh, they spoke of it fondly whenever he ran into them in the towns along the river. They asked about friends and relatives. They just never made it back. It appeared that Fate, with all his notions, had turned out to be one of those.

Surely he would come back for the wedding, wouldn't he? Val couldn't imagine getting married without Fate standing next to him. He must talk to Loyce soon. They would need to plan plenty of time for Fate to get back.

On Christmas Eve, Mary Ann delivered a pork roast and a fat hen for Adam to cook the next day.

"I knew you'd be wanting to start on them before daylight, so I just brought them on over," she said with a grin. "That way I don't have to listen to York grumble in the morning when you show up pounding on my door."

"Whoooeee! This is some fine hen," Adam exclaimed. "Come see this, Mrs. Barclay."

Roseanne tapped in from across the dogtrot, where she had been closing up the store.

"So, it passes muster with you, Mr. Snellgrove?" she asked, almost playfully.

Val glanced up from where he was putting last-minute touches on Loyce's gift—a lightweight chair made of cypress that she could easily move around the porch to follow the sun or the shade.

"I'd say it could be the prettiest and plumpest baking hen I've seen in all my Christmases, Mrs. Barclay." Adam's smiling eyes lingered on hers until she glanced away, back down at the hen.

Val looked harder at the two of them standing closer together than the inspection of a dead chicken warranted. Was Roseanne blushing at that last remark? He noticed her hair was not so tightly bound as it once was. She looked softer than when she had arrived last spring, Val thought, and definitely rounder. Maybe she was feeling the same Christmas gaiety that he felt. Maybe it would extend past the season and she would get over her vendetta against C.B.

"And how many Christmases might that be, Mr. Snellgrove?" Roseanne continued to look down.

"Take a guess," he chuckled.

On the other side of the room Loyce was listening too. She smiled while Roseanne studied her father. She could feel Roseanne measuring him with her eyes. His height. The loose limbs at ease inside his long-sleeved shirt and sturdy work pants. The soft drooping mustache that tickled when he kissed her cheek. The longish hair that swooped back from a wide brow and then tried to part in the middle.

"Fifty-two," said Roseanne's voice, as if in a hurry.

Loyce chortled and slapped the arm of her chair in delight.

Mary Ann said, "You let that gray hair fool you. I've seen him out there pulling up nets full of fish."

Adam laughed. "I'll be forty-six next month."

Mary Ann, striding around the table for a piece of fruitcake, didn't notice Roseanne's eyes open wide as she quickly took in Adam's entire frame again from the top of his head down the length of his body, but Val did. He smiled to himself and went back to work.

Val also had been watching Loyce follow Roseanne's assessment of Adam. He admired the graceful, attentive postures that gleaned information overlooked by sighted people. He settled another spoke into the back of the little chair—compact and elegant like Loyce herself because he was building it with her in mind. He even designed it without arms so it wouldn't impede her playing music or knitting nets.

Maybe Christmas Day would be the time to talk to her. Maybe by next Christmas they would have a home of their own. The chair was a start, *enh?* It was going to be the best Christmas ever.

Christmas Day dawned blue and gold. The sun promised warmth, but the wind was brisk. Winter birds flitted in bare branches, and squirrels raced up tree trunks as the little group walked the path from the post office to the old Bertram house. Everyone carried something for the dinner. Adam had the pork haunch, stuffed with garlic and red pepper, then roasted in the cast iron Dutch oven until it was dark crusty brown on the outside and dripping with juice inside. Roseanne carried the baked hen nestled in a pan of cornbread dressing. Val had the raisin bread pudding and the jar of eggnog sauce to pour over each serving. Mame held the bundle of baked sweet potatoes against her bony chest, enjoying their warmth. Loyce carried a basket of rolls over one arm, while she linked Val's elbow with her other. Drifter, tail wagging in anticipation, followed her nose in and out among the savory smells.

Mary Ann threw open the door as soon as they started up the back steps.

"Well, it's about time you got here!" she exclaimed, as if she hadn't just seen them the night before. "Much longer, and I would have had to try to make York talk to me!"

"Wouldn't want him to strain himself," Adam said, his easy grin splitting the drooping mustache. "A good Christmas to you." He kissed her proffered cheek and extended a hand to York.

York shook the hand and held out a glass of wine with the other. "That's elderberry from three years ago," he said, by way of greeting.

Adam inhaled deeply before taking the first sip. In his opinion what York produced in spirits made up for what he lacked in good-will. How was it possible to capture April in a bottle, hold it there, and then release it three years later? A slight nod from York told Adam his taciturn neighbor recognized his appreciation.

The family wasted no time settling in around the long table. Dishes were passed; silver clinked on old china. Another bottle of wine added to the flow of conversation.

"I see you framed that old letter," Adam said at one point. "Does that mean it brings back more good memories than bad?"

"I guess that's close to the truth!" Mary Ann grinned. "Gotta admit, we're both more likely to bring something up for talking before we fly off the handle like we used to."

"You know, I found out where it's been for the past forty years," Adam added. "Sitting in a dead letter bin in the regional post office in Kentucky. Seems all the United States postmasters along the Confederate border states had to confiscate any mail trying to get out of the South. See, that postage was paid for with Confederate money. Most postmasters just threw those southern letters away, but the one in Lexington felt obliged to keep them. Not only that, but he made a special stamp to show why they got stopped. It was that little blue circle you saw on Mame's letter and the words SOUTHERN LETTER UNPAID. The letters and packages stayed in that bin until he died. When he died, the assistant postmaster who took over his job left the whole caboodle right where they were. But last year a new postmaster came on the job and decided the right thing to do would be to return them, just in case the senders were still alive."

"What do you know about that!" Mary Ann chortled and slapped her hand on the table. "I wonder if any of the other letters exploded a still?"

Everyone laughed, except York, who concentrated on dishing out another helping of buttered turnips.

Mary Ann went on. "Fate's been scarce ever since that day. Christmas don't seem right without him. Anyone know where he's at? We ain't seen him since he picked up that boat he had York work on. What'd you do on that boat for him, anyways?"

"Boxed off some bulkheads for ice and packed them with moss to hold in the cold," York replied.

"Oh, *mais cher!* Don't it feel off-kilter without him?" Val chimed in. "I finally make it here for Christmas, but Fate, he's missing. The last time I saw him wasn't even on the Chene. It was up around Baton Rouge right before my last trip—must have been late August. All dressed up, don't you know, having coffee at a café on the dock with three men in suits. Give me a big wave, yeh. Later, when I got off my boat and pass by there, the men—all gone, don't you know? Fate said they were investors in his new business.

They loan him money to outfit his boat and buy his first round of fish and ice. He paid them back already and was trying to borrow again to buy that icehouse. I ain't heard nothing since."

"I wonder if he's making any money with those schemes," York mused.

"Of course that's what you care about," Mary Ann replied. "I'm more worried about what kind of company he's keeping. There's some rough customers up there."

"Speaking of rough customers, doesn't he have Sam Stockett from over on Graveyard working with him?" Roseanne's tone suggested she knew Sam was working for Fate, but she just needed to express her disapproval. "I've never felt right about that pair, and now that she's tried to drown that baby I don't have any use for them at all."

"Now, Mrs. Barclay, we don't have any way of knowing what happened that day." Adam's voice was light, a feature that rankled Roseanne. He didn't give enough weight to her suspicions.

"You might not know for sure, Mr. Snellgrove," she said with a sniff, "but I'll bet you I'm right. I'm still of a mind to write the sheriff of St. Martin Parish and have him just come on out here and investigate what happened. He could get the truth out of her. And I'd tell him that she was looking to buy those French female pills the very first day she got here."

"Mrs. Barclay, there's no need to do that," Mary Ann joined in the argument, which had grown old with Adam and Roseanne. "Look at how good she is to that baby now, like a mother hen with just the one chick. She wouldn't do anything to hurt that boy."

"Me, I think Mary Ann is right about that," Val said. Then, taking a new tack, "Let me grab that squeeze-box and Loyce's fiddle for some music to help this good dinner settle, *enh*?"

In less time than it takes to tell it, the mood lifted with the music, working its magic the way Val knew it would. They moved to the sitting room, where Roseanne and Adam waltzed and chatted, carefully avoiding any mention of C.B. Mary Ann and York danced through the afternoon and evening. The warring couple did seem to be fighting less in general, Val noticed. Maybe they had learned something from the incident of the letter and the battle of wills that could have killed York.

When they played a waltz as closure, Mame took a turn with York around her old parlor. Just like she may have done with Michaud so many years ago, Val thought. He nodded a greeting to the blue paper with the girlish handwriting, now displayed in a neat frame beside the window. Mame's old letter to Fate's grandpa, its mission interrupted by the Great War that nearly brought down the country.

Loyce played her fiddle alongside Val and also thought about the letter. If the return of that piece of paper had drawn the Bertrams closer, it seemed to have driven Fate away. This was the first time she had been in the old Bertram house since she found out she wasn't blood kin to the family that built it. Everything was the same as she remembered. The horsehair sofa that prickled if her bare skin touched it. The smooth dining table that smelled like lemon oil. The lamps whose crystal teardrops Mame had taught her to tap for the tinkling sound they made. All of the textures and fragrances that belonged to the Bertram family—Fate's family—people to whom she was no longer linked except through her grandfather Elder Landry's marriage of convenience to Mame.

Walking home in the cool shadows, the little group was drowsy with food and fun. Even Loyce, who was still feeling adrift with the changes the year had wrought, was comforted by Val's arm around her waist and the warm weight of Drifter bumping against her leg now and then. If she had lost her oldest friend, at least she had found another in Drifter and, perhaps, had gained a sweetheart as well.

— 22 —

"Watch your step, Loyce, it's slippery."

Val guided her by a simple touch on her back until they reached the end of the plank walk. The wind whipped the heavy skirt of Roseanne's traveling dress around her ankles. She pulled the cloak farther down over her face before giving her free hand to Val. The other hand held her fiddle case. The boat rocked gently with their weight. Tapping her foot around for purchase, she settled on the plank seat and let go of Val's hand.

Adam and Roseanne had left earlier to help move furniture in the schoolhouse, but Val and Loyce had stayed behind to practice new ways of playing the tunes they'd performed as a trio with Fate for so many years. She could feel the pull of Val's shoulders in the stroke of the paddle as they rowed toward the schoolhouse. It was good to be out, even on a stormy night. Even without Fate.

The trip around the island took less than a half-hour, but her cloak was heavy with rain by the time they bumped against the schoolhouse dock. Once again, Val helped her navigate stepping out of the boat and safely onto the plank walk. They leaned into the wind-driven rain all the way to the steps.

Loyce shook her cloak at the door, and Val took it from her. After hanging it on one of the wall hooks, he escorted her toward the front of the room, where the teacher would stand next Monday. Loyce had played dances here since her fingers were barely long enough to reach around the neck of the same fiddle she carried tonight.

"Hey, Loyce, you and Val look like twins!" Alcide Verret ruffled her curls.

She laughed and swatted in his direction. Val grabbed her hand in the air and twirled her around for the merry crowd to admire. "*Mais non, cher!*" he exclaimed. "I'd never look so good in this fine dress, me!"

Others joined in the greetings, complimenting Loyce on her new look and boosting her spirits. As the two musicians settled themselves and their instruments on the wooden dais, Loyce reveled in being part of a couple on this momentous evening. Together she and Val would ring in a brand new year for the community. A year brimming with unforeseen joys and heartaches.

No doubt she and Val would face their share of hardships after they married. She had confidence in his steady strength to guide her through them, just as he led her through the stormy evening to the dance. She knew they were headed for a lifetime together, even though he hadn't mentioned anything yet. Maybe she should bring it up herself after the New Year.

As they tuned up the fiddle and squeeze-box, more people came through the door, letting in fresh bursts of cold air. Eventually, the latecomers were all in, and the door stopped banging. Loyce felt the heat from the coal oil lamps taking the chill off the room.

"Looks like everybody's here," Val said in her ear over the din of conversation. "What say we start with 'Gay Gordons' tonight?"

She struck the first notes of the old Scottish tune, and Val's squeeze-box followed. Before the introductory bars were over, a wheel of dancers took shape around the room. No caller was needed because everyone knew the steps, whether or not their ancestors had ever set foot in Scotland. They twirled to the marching tune, forward and back, passing the ladies over to the inside of the circle and then under the arch to a new partner. Loyce could feel the building sway with their movements.

She didn't have time to catch her breath from that vigorous

tune before Val launched into a favorite of his Irish family, "The Red Haired Boy." As he sounded the notes of the introduction, the dancers moved out of the circle and into opposing lines for a contra. Loyce's fiddle picked up the melody, and they were lost in simple steps and flowing music.

The hours flew by, and so did the dances with historic names like "Indian Queen," "Black Nag," "The Irish Washerwoman," "Jefferson's Reel," and "Washington's Quickstep." Along with the Cajun and Irish music he played with his family, Val had learned the music of every culture he encountered in his travels up and down the rivers. He also had picked up endless tales behind the dances and tunes.

He had told Loyce that when the colonies broke from British rule, they weren't about to give up their favorite dances, so they just renamed them and substituted tunes that sprang up around campfires and hearths in the New World. Descendants of those colonists brought the dances and tunes westward, which is why on New Year's Eve 1907 the tunes from village greens in England were bouncing off the walls of the Bayou Chene schoolhouse in merry company with Irish, Scottish, German, and French Canadian melodies.

"Take a break, *cher*, and go dance before we shut down," Val told her during a pause late in the evening. Families with children were already leaving so that mostly couples—courting and newly married—were left on the floor.

Loyce felt along the fiddle case and turned her instrument to fit inside its molded shape. Before her hands had finished snapping the clasps, Alcide was at her side, leading her to the floor for the start of the "Virginia Reel." A newcomer wouldn't have known a blind girl was among the dancers whirling on the floor. Right hand allemandes, left elbow swings—wherever she turned, the other dancers knew to catch her hand or arm. She flew down the hall and back again.

Of the people in the hall that evening, only she and Val knew that the dance was once the favorite of England's Queen Elizabeth. Back when it had gone by the name "Sir Roger de Coverley." When the colonists renamed it the "Virginia Reel," they also danced it to fresh tunes springing from the New World like "Turkey in the Straw," "Uncle Penn," "Oh! Susanna," and "The Yellow Rose of Texas."

That history made sense to Loyce. Sure, the tunes they played tonight made her lonesome for Fate, but she wouldn't think of giving them up because of forlorn associations. In fact, in some way they were comforting. They transported her back to the many evenings when Fate had joined in playing twin fiddles with her.

After two more rousing tunes the dancers begged Val to slow the pace before they passed out along the floor. He picked up Loyce's fiddle and began playing the Irish tune "Star of the County Down" as a free waltz to close the evening.

"How about it, Miss Loyce? C.B. is putting Sam Junior to sleep, and I need a partner."

"I'd be happy to, Sam," Loyce said with a smile, as she held out her hand in the direction of his voice.

He smelled of fish and tar, and his steps were clumsy, but Loyce was happy to dance out the old year with her friend's good-hearted husband. The first verse of the melancholy waltz was ending when she felt a gasp of cold air and heard the door slam shut. Seconds later Sam's clumsy steps halted, and he opened the embrace that had held her to him.

"May I?" Fate said.

Before she knew what was happening, his arms were around her, his breath—still cold from the outdoors—on her face. Without even thinking, she melded against him and rested her head on his chest. They fell into perfect step.

"This is nice," he said, running the fingers of his right hand from the nape of her neck to the crown of her head, before tucking her head under his chin.

Loyce didn't know whether he meant her new haircut or the sensation of holding her against him, but it didn't matter. They had learned to waltz to the plaintive old tune when they were kids, Fate watching the grown-ups and telling Loyce what they should do to keep from stepping on each other's toes. They had been so close that it was second nature for her to anticipate the slightest inclination of his body in any direction and go there.

But tonight the old comfort surrendered to a new feeling. Her breath caught in her throat. Blood rushed to her cheeks. Is this what fainting felt like? Fate must have sensed her confusion. He held her even closer. She felt the solid strength beneath his clothes. She breathed in the scent of him. How she had missed that!

Loyce wanted nothing more than to press herself closer, closer. His breathing ruffled the fringe of her curls and sent a shiver down the length of her body. Again, he must have sensed something. She felt his head incline as if to look at her face. He stood stock still for the briefest moment, and then she felt his breath softly on her lips. Confusion flooded her senses.

He had hugged, patted, squeezed, and tickled her as long as she could remember. But Fate had never kissed her. Cousins don't kiss. Remembering they no longer shared that special intimacy, she stiffened in his arms. This is what he did with other girls, the ones he dallied with and left.

"What are you doing here, anyway?" Her voice broke the easy mood of the waltz. "It's not likely you're just passing through on New Year's Eve. Must be business, or you would be at some shindig in Baton Rouge or Lafayette."

"What's it matter to you?" His voice sounded more confident than she remembered. "Truth be told," he continued, smoothing his hand down her back to the slim waistband of her dress, "I just wanted to see out the old year with the people who mean the most to me."

He pulled her even closer. His embrace, like his voice, was also more confident, more in control. Loyce didn't have the upper hand. She didn't like the change.

"Hmmmph!" she said, straightening her shoulders and lifting her head from his chest.

"I know you, Fate Landry, and I take that to mean you must be hiding from someone to be out here in the swamp tonight. You don't just ignore us for months and then show up like nothing's happened." Her voice was rising and then broke off abruptly as they bumped into another couple. Loyce caught a hint of Roseanne's vetiver soap.

"Well, maybe it's past time for someone to start asking questions," Roseanne was saying. "Look at her over there pretending like nothing happened, just holding her head up proud as can be."

Just as Loyce realized Roseanne and her partner were stopped on the floor, she heard Adam's voice.

"Mrs. Barclay, all I'm saying is we've never had to bring the law in before, and there's a lot of people who like C.B. and Sam. Say they fit in real well around here."

"What's this about Sam and C.B.?" Fate stopped, and Loyce felt him turn away.

"Mrs. Barclay is bound and determined to bring the law out here to investigate whether C.B. tried to drown that young'un a month or so ago when he fell overboard," someone offered.

"She fell overboard too!" another voice chimed in. Loyce recognized Viola Persilver from over on Bayou Cozine.

"That's what she wants everyone to believe," retorted Roseanne.

"Mrs. Barclay, I'd be careful about accusations if I was you, considering your own situation!" Viola shot back.

"She was soaking wet when I brought Sam Junior to her!" Alcide Verret's booming voice joined in the chorus that was turning into for and against.

"Anyone would have the sense to make it look like she had fallen overboard too!" came a strident voice Loyce couldn't immediately place.

"Now hold on. Sam works for me, and I can say—" Fate started.

"You weren't even here, haven't been here for so long you don't deserve an opinion about anything that happens out here." Loyce raised her voice above the din and stepped out of his arms.

"I'm telling you, she looked like a woman who'd seen a ghost when I handed him up to her!" Alcide continued over the mayhem.

"Well, of course she did, after she thought she'd gotten rid of him and you come toting him back!"

"What do you mean by 'got rid of him'?" Sam's voice drowned out the others. "C.B. never hurt that baby, and anyone who says so will have to take it up with me!"

"Hurt Sam Junior?" No one had noticed that C.B., holding the bundled Sam Junior, had walked onto the floor. "I know where this started! Mrs. Barclay, you are a scheming, mean, dissatisfied, and rejected woman, jealous of me and mine. You ain't got a family of your own that wants you so you just have to take it out on someone."

Val had stopped playing and was placing Loyce's fiddle back in its case. He methodically put on his coat, picked up his accordion in one hand, the fiddle case in the other, and headed for the door. If conditions continued to escalate, he didn't want anything to happen to the instruments. He had played many a dance along the rivers that ended in brawls, sometimes with knives and guns coming into play. He strode quickly across the plank floor that just a minute ago had been bouncing to the feet of happy dancers. Now it was covered by the same people shouting and pushing to make their points as they took sides.

After stowing the fiddle and squeeze-box in his boat, Val went back inside. Loyce was standing uncertainly on the edge of the crowd. Fate was in the middle of the knot, waving his hands and trying to talk above Roseanne's voice.

"C'mon, *cher*, let's get you out of here," Val said. "Here's your wrap; the weather's still nasty out there."

"Not as nasty as it is in here," she declared.

They shuffled slowly through the edges of the crowd and across the threshold, Loyce draped in her cloak and feeling for the next step. Back in the boat, she sat quietly while he untied the line and tossed it on the bow. The rain had stopped falling, but the wind was still blowing drops from the trees. She shrugged deeper into the cloak and thought that 1908 was getting off to a rough start.

Loyce stayed in bed the next morning, listening to Fate chatting in the kitchen as if he had never been away. Adam would ask a question now and then. Roseanne's laughter drifted up, along with the fragrance of lost bread. Lost, that's what Loyce felt like—lost in her own home.

She was ashamed to go downstairs. Surely everyone had noticed her confusion in Fate's arms last night. How was she supposed to act around them today? Would they mention it? Or just exchange looks? As if she couldn't *feel* when someone was doing that to her!

And Fate, the cause of it all, blabbering away down there like nothing happened. That's what burned her cheeks the most. They flamed from her just thinking about the smug way he held her, like he owned the right! She flounced over in the bed, and the moss mattress crackled in response, but when she heard Fate's familiar tread coming up the stairs, she froze. She held her breath to keep even that from him. He paused. They both listened to the silence on the other's side of the door.

She continued listening as he left. Down the stairs, out the door, and along the plank walk. His stride was stronger and wider than before. Eighteen steps. He had outgrown her once and for all.

— 23 —

After the dismal end of the New Year's dance, winter bore down harder than usual on the far-flung community. The unaccustomed dissension among the residents gave the wind an extra bite. Raindrops were as sharp as frozen cypress needles. The gray days of January trailed one after the other, with nothing to break the gloom.

Even in a good year, late winter in the swamp is not for the faint of heart. Cheners knew that the rain would last until March, so they settled in for the siege, going outdoors only to bail rainwater from their boats, fetch firewood, or run fur traps. Laundry hung on lines throughout the houses and houseboats, disrupting the stove drafts and trapping smoke. Outside the dogs, cats, and barnyard animals huddled together under shelters.

Over on Graveyard Bayou, C.B. stayed close to home. She felt she couldn't go anywhere without spies keeping tabs on her and Sam Junior. Even on the deserted bayou, where she spent her days carrying firewood from the pile on the bank and stoking the little woodstove in the houseboat, she imagined that eyes followed her. Sometimes the feeling was so strong she would stand as still as a deer and gaze back into the woods from the bank, determined to spot the intruder.

Sam was spending longer hours and more days transporting fish now that Fate's business was growing. Not only had they worked out a regular schedule of pickups along the twenty-mile stretch of river between Bayou Chene and Atchafalaya Station, but they had also added paddlefish to their trade. The quality of paddlefish roe rivaled expensive caviar from Russia. As wealthy people along the East Coast discovered the homegrown delicacy, the prehistoric-looking, spoon-billed fish brought even higher prices than buffalo.

Barring mishaps, Sam was usually gone three days on the upriver run, stopping along the way to pick up fish. He would spend the night on Fate's boat at Atchafalaya Station before he could set off downriver toward home. The venture was bringing in more money than they ever dreamed of earning. However, there was no one for C.B. to share the good news with or even unburden her fears about being spied upon. All she had for company was the little one that more and more of her neighbors felt she had tried to drown.

When she did have to go in to the post office, eye contact with friends or strangers became increasingly uncomfortable. Roseanne had a ready audience all day and could use her position of authority to turn more people against the isolated young woman. Mutterings about "calling in the law" to investigate what happened that day in November seemed to follow C.B. like a bad smell.

As a result of the isolation and anxiety, for the first time in her life C.B. lost interest in her looks. Face powder in the flowered canister absorbed the damp air and turned rock hard. Winter sunshine glinted off her bare face. It also revealed the auburn roots of her hair. She didn't bother with the bleach nor the foul-smelling potions that produced the kink and frizz she so admired. An inch at a time grew out until there was more auburn than yellow. The locks were thicker than she remembered, hiding the pink of her scalp for the first time in years.

Some of the weight she had gained during pregnancy stayed with her, so she continued wearing the two jumpers Adam had passed along from Josie's trunk. Without the white face powder, her complexion lost its pale cast, and the red bumps that had plagued her faded away. The healthy complexion combined with the new roundness of her body and glossy hair transformed her from the crooked little canary that had arrived in Bayou Chene almost a year ago into a strong-limbed young woman who wouldn't be recognized by her friends in Natchez. Or even the people at the post office, if she dared show her face there. She found excuses to let Sam do more of their shopping on his way home from fish-buying trips, even if it meant she and Sam Junior did without some things.

As for Sam, he missed her merry chatter and flitting movements. These days she slogged as if walking in knee-deep mud. Instead of prattling about people she knew and opinions she had held dear for the past day or so, she kept her thoughts to herself. Even though she had usually talked about things that didn't matter to him, he longed for the sound of her voice.

What Sam did hear were the rumors. While he didn't believe them, his slow speech sabotaged any defense he would like to make in public. By the time Sam could put together a sentence, other people in the room or on the dock had moved the conversation along. He knew his halting speech made him seem slow-witted, and there was no ready way to correct the impression. So, under the circumstances it seemed best for him to plod along raising nets and picking up fish from those who wanted to profit from Fate's growing business.

Sam had always been most content alone out on the water. Even before he left St. Louis, he found comfort at the river's edge. He loved winter's soft gray water and leaden sky as much as summer's racing brown current and blue dome. He relished the smell of fish and driftwood. He could tell whether water lapping against his boat was caused by the wake of passing boats or the wind sweeping upstream.

The docks were a different world from the river itself. They were noisy—crowded with tools, cargo, and people. The other men would banter and trade insults, but Sam couldn't knit together thoughts and words fast enough to join in, especially now. He could only shut them out and put his back into the work of collecting fish, weighing them, and placing them into the bed of ice. Getting back out to the open water was always uppermost in his mind.

Back at the post office Loyce moved indoors to work on nets that she wouldn't sell until spring. This time of year she felt especially fortunate to live at the post office because of the customers coming and going. Some households along the outlying bayous wouldn't see anyone other than immediate family for weeks.

Val's company was the bright spot in the darkest winter days, but even he wasn't as merry as usual. She suspected he was suffering from the effects of being housebound. Perhaps now he understood her complaint of being a prisoner in the home she loved.

Fate stayed away, doing who knows what or where. No one in their small circle had heard from him since New Year's morning. She remembered feigning sleep until the rattle of his engine had faded into the chill, damp air. Why had she done that?

Had he come to her room only to wish her a happy New Year? Remind his little cousin to send word in time for him to play the music for her wedding? Fate had always insisted Val was sweet on her; surely he must know they were a couple, even though no one had said it out loud yet.

A closed door had never stopped Fate. In the old days he would have just barged in and sat on the side of the bed, probably stuffing a pillow over her face before she could defend herself. So, had something more been on his mind? Something to do with how she felt in his embrace? She would never know.

"Ooowwweee! Adam, you need to clean that stovepipe—it's smoky enough in here that I need Loyce to show me how to find anything!" Mary Ann bustled in the back door and broke into Loyce's reverie. The sound of the pony cart had been muffled by the rain drumming on the roof.

"Got my ladder ready, Mary Ann, but it won't stop raining long enough for me to get up there," Adam replied from where he was sorting mail by holding the letters up to the window light. Val looked up from the spread of dominoes on top of a wooden barrel between him and Loyce. "If you bring one of your roosters over here and tie a line to him, his flapping wings could go up and down the chimney, clean it out in no time, *enh?*"

"Now that sounds like a gimmick Fate would've come up with, 'specially if we put a likely young pullet on the top side," Mary Ann chortled in agreement. "Speaking of that sort of thing, either Drifter has been getting more than her share of biscuits, or she's expecting pups."

All eyes turned to the little dog lying next to Loyce's chair.

"Dang if you ain't right," Adam said. "Hadn't noticed how well kept she was looking. Well, I do remember seeing that bird dog belonging to the Larsons hanging 'round for a while. How far along do you reckon she is?"

Mary Ann's experienced eye ran over the sleek little belly. "Oh, by the looks of her, you got a few weeks to get her a basket fixed behind the woodstove. She's made herself such a name watching over Loyce, you'll have people standing in line for those pups."

"That'll be something to look forward to until spring comes." Adam added, "And it can't get here too soon for me."

"Looking forward to spring for robbing my bees," said Val. "Missing those regular paydays, me. Beside, feel good to get out, move around a bit, *enh?*"

"Well, that ain't no way to look at the situation, not atall!" Alcide Verret stumped in the front door, slapping water off his hat before jamming it back onto his white curls. "There's money to be made out there right now, gentlemen. All a fella's got to do is go out there and get it. Look at it as working for yourself, Val, not waiting for some captain to tell you what you're worth."

"What you talking about, Cide?" Val was curious. "What can a man do to make a dollar in this weather?"

"Why, I probably picked enough moss today to stuff four mattresses, six horse collars, and build a mud chimney with the leftovers," Alcide thundered on. "Wasn't nothing to it, just a pastime, nothing atall. Penny a pound once it's cured—that's good money."

"How about you take me with you next time?" Val asked. Money or not, the excursion would give him a chance to be outdoors using his muscles. Muscles that were beginning to squirm and twitch from the unaccustomed inactivity. He couldn't sleep. He was getting fat.

"Sure enough, we'll do that! How about starting tomorrow? Dot's been wanting to stay home and get some quilting done, so I could use another partner for a while. I'll leave home at daylight and stop by here to pick you up."

By the time Loyce came downstairs the next morning, Val was gone. He was so anxious to escape confinement, he had taken his breakfast to eat on the way. Adam told her he could hear their conversation drifting back through the mist. Val sounded like he was off on a big riverboat adventure instead of just going to pick moss with an old man.

It was three days before she heard Val's step on the plank walk again. She noticed that he wasn't whistling or humming, which usually let her know he was coming. She also noticed that his feet were dragging.

"You been gone so long, we was wondering if we needed to come looking for you," Adam spoke up from inside the kitchen, where he had just put a dried apple cobbler into the oven of the woodstove.

"Wish y'all had, *cher!*" Val stopped in front of Loyce and put his head down in greeting before he dropped into the nearest chair inside the door and heaved a sigh. She smelled wood smoke, green moss, and a slight whiff of cooking grease in his hair as she touched it in friendly acknowledgment.

"I'm tired to the bone, me, and ain't had no sleep in three

nights," he said. "I thought I worked when I was on the river, but I never done nothing like that!"

"What's so different?" Adam asked as he poured a cup of steaming coffee and handed it over.

"*Merci bien.*" Val took a grateful swallow and settled deeper in the chair, stretching his legs toward the stove.

"First we had to pole Cide's moss barge, the one with the high scaffold, way, way out in some bayou I don't even know the name of. If that old man had died on me, I'd never find my way back out. But it look like it was gonna be the other way around—that I was gonna die flat out and leave him to bring in my carcass. The moss was so thick back in there, it looked like curtains, just hanging everywheres. We took turns poling the skiff and picking the moss. Reaching way up with that pole, hooking it into a wad of moss and then twisting and pulling it down. Stomping it into as small a pile as we could and then reaching up for another one. Over and over all day. In no time at all my wrist, she was hurting from the twisting, my back, she was aching from the reaching and bending over. The only way I could keep moving was to think about freezing to death if I stopped."

"How did Cide manage?" asked Adam.

"Oh, *m'sieu!* He worked just as hard as I did, but he talked the whole time! Never heard him take a breath that I remember, *non*. And he'd go after li'l bunches of moss that didn't seem worth it."

"Well, it seemed like you'd be plenty tired enough. What happened at night that you didn't sleep?" Loyce asked.

"The first night wasn't so bad, if you don't count the bites. We stayed in a little slab shack Cide has in the woods. Lets anyone use it, but that night we was the only ones sleeping there. It was dry inside, and we made a fire. We threw some of the moss on the floor and just slept right on top. When it started warming up, them ticks and chiggers, they got to squirming, don't you know. After the cold settled in again before daylight, they stopped, that's for true, but I don't know which was worse, having my blood froze in my body or sucked out of it.

"Next day we run into some of them boys over by Canoeville. They started talking about this haunted houseboat where they was staying at. That Sinnet boy, Ursin, he just bought it from some man out on Deadman's Bayou. Been tied out there for about ten years or more, and he wanted it just for moss picking and running his nets in the spring. Well, Cide, he figured they was fooling with Ursin; you know the Sinnets got Chitimacha kinfolk, so they *real* superstitious. Cide up and says, 'Shore, we gonna go over there tonight, and I betcha there's nothing I can't figure out.'

"So, after another day of reaching and twisting and pulling down and stomping, I was so tired I figured it didn't matter if I bunked with the devil hisself. Fact is, the evening started off pretty good. We had shot us a couple a squirrels while drifting down to the houseboat, and Ursin, he had already caught some fish, even in this weather. Injuns can do that, you know. Wasn't long we had the squirrels cooking down pretty good and was getting ready to fry the fish when all hell done broke loose.

"That woodstove he started clanking and clattering like buckshot was dancing around in a iron skillet. Then the damn thing started shaking till I thought the stovepipe was coming right out the window. I was all set to head outside and get in Cide's boat when that stopped.

"The next thing we knowed, it sounded like rats—big ones—scampering all over under that floor. Now you know nothing can live under there, but it sounded like all kind of critters was just running this way and that. Poor Ursin, he was 'bout to jump overboard when it stop. Just like that. None of us could make out what it was all about, but it hadn't hurt nobody, and we was some tired out. So, we all just rolled up and went to sleep where we could find us a spot.

"Since it was Ursin's houseboat, he got one side of the bed. John Paul, another one of them Chitimacha relatives, got the other side. Rest of us made pallets 'round the floor since we had plenty moss. That's the best thing I can say about moss picking is you always got your bed with you, if you don't mind company. My head was so heavy I went to sleep 'most as soon as I hit the floor, me.

"Can't say how long I been sleeping when the next racket broke out. Seemed Ursin's shotgun had flew across the room all by itself and hit the back of the bed right above John Paul's head. Or at least that's all we could make out, after we lit a lamp to see what had made all that noise. There was the gun, lemme tell you, laying right on top of them two boys. Well, that was enough for me. I wasn't scared of no ghostses, but I didn't wanna get shot by no flying gun neither, so I set up against the wall for the rest of the night. Far as I know, there wasn't no more trouble, but my head hurt so bad the next day from not getting to sleep I couldn't hardly hold it up.

"We worked all that day, and me, I figured no matter what happen I can sleep tonight. Well, it started before we even lit the lamp! Heard the biggest racket you can imagine—a roaring and a thundering like a stampede of cattle outside in the damn bayou, but there was no place for a stampede even if there was some cattle. I knew there wasn't nothing 'cept woods and water out there, but I was on my way to open the door and see what it was all about anyway when this rooster—I mean a full-size rooster—flew through this knothole in the wall that was no bigger than a two-bit piece. He flew around the room two, maybe three times before he slipped right through the woodstove grate and up the chimney. Or I guess that's where he ended up. It happen so quick I can't say for shore if he ever came out on the outside.

"I told Cide, 'This was your idea; how about you sit up till daylight so's the rest of us can get some sleep.'"

"What'd he say?" Loyce asked.

"He just laugh, him! Say he already heard about that li'l houseboat for years, that no one owned it for very long 'cause of all the racket. Now that he done seen and heard it hisself, he could understand how come it changed hands so often. He said nobody had ever been hurt or kilt by whatever it was, just inconvenienced."

"Did he have a notion about why it happens?" asked Adam.

"Most anybody knows, 'cording to Cide, that it was used as a doctor's office out here during the war. Must have been a lot of soldiers from both sides died in it. Might even be the reason the place where it was tied up for so long is called Dead Man's Bayou. Cide's figuring that maybe them ghostses is still fighting the war."

"So, you saying this might be the end of your moss picking?" Adam queried.

"You bet, *cher!*" Val exclaimed. "Figure up all the time we already done put in and now we got to spend weeks curing it, watching it weigh less every day? It just don't seem to pay at a penny a pound, *enh?*"

— **24** —

Val's restlessness returned as soon as his body recovered from the moss-picking venture. He and Loyce played music to relieve the tedium of the shut-in days, but he had no new tunes to bring her. They were simply banging out the same old melodies that they had played with Fate, except now the fire was gone. That high-flying energy he used to feel when they were all together had vanished. He had felt it only once since moving to the Chene—the night Fate showed up at the New Year's dance. That was when Val realized the exhilaration had sparked between his two friends; he had only shared in their glow. Now Fate was gone, probably for good.

Val's misgivings about trying to settle at the Chene mounted alongside a growing dread of telling Loyce. What would her life be like if he left too? What would his life be like if he stayed? The boat whistles were already calling to him. St. Louis. New Orleans. Mexico. Never again would he stand on deck and watch those distant ports chuff into view or shrink in the *Golden Era's* wake.

Early March took a welcome turn toward spring, and Val could finally walk about the island checking on how well his bees had overwintered. The sunshine coaxed alligators, snakes, and turtles out to bask on logs and sandbars. Around the homes and houseboats chickens scratched for early grubs and sprouting grasses.

Hive inspections showed Val the bees were finding abundant forage, but it would still be weeks before he needed to add more frames. He fidgeted and paced. One day Alcide suggested that the impatient beekeeper could make some quick money at a timber camp.

"Why, Val! People are coming from all over tarnation to make money in these woods," Cide thundered. "You don't need to sit here and let 'em get ahead of you! It's just a pastime for anyone who can swing an axe. Nothing but a pastime, I tell you. I made plenty of money in the timber camps when I was young, and I'd do it again if I wasn't a married man."

Despite lingering misgivings from the moss-picking excursion, Val thought it over and joined the next crew boat that stopped for supplies.

Days passed, a week and then two. Loyce was embarrassed at the relief she felt during Val's absence. Until New Year's Eve she had been poised to plan a future with Val. Marrying would give her purpose, a life of her own. He had always cared for her, and she loved him dearly. She was just waiting for him to say the word, so she could say yes. Her alternative was to grow old on the post office porch.

Then Fate had busted into her life again. That's what always happened with Fate. The tumult of emotions, the heat charging through her veins during the waltz, shattered her future. She couldn't be Val's wife or anyone else's. She was imprisoned in a no-man's-land.

When the small steamer returned for more supplies, Val was aboard, gaunt and wizened.

"Ooohhh, *mais cher*," he groaned, inhaling deeply of Adam's chicken and dumplings in brown gravy. "I'm so hungry, me, I could eat the feathers you pulled off them roosters. We ain't had nothing but salt pork on biscuits for the longest time. They don't come in for groceries soon enough, and we run out of most everything but coffee, pork, flour, and lard. On Sundays somebody would take their half-day off to shoot a few squirrel, but just drop in that hot lard with no seasoning, they taste like squirrel cracklins.

"One of the worst things besides the food was the smell. All of us slept in one bunkhouse not much bigger than Cide's moss-picking shack. Built out of green slabs that shrunk all crooked when they dried. Big cracks in them suppose to let the air in and the smoke out, but mostly they just let the mosquitoes in. Wood bunks nailed to the wall with li'l flat moss mattresses covering the slats. We was all stacked in there like firewood. No good way to heat up more than a kettle full of water at a time, so bathing was just a dip in the cold river, where you wash yourself and your clothes all in one lick.

"And work! Same thing all day every day except for half a day on Sunday. Chop or saw from can't to can't. The only break was when somebody got hurt, and you hoped it wouldn't be you. The worse part for me was nobody want to talk, even when we wasn't sawing and chopping. Unfriendliest bunch you ever met. Most of them seem to come from somewhere else and didn't know each other or anybody who lives 'round here. A few came from lumberjacking them big woods up in Oregon. Others, they came from New York and places like that. Some of them didn't talk French or English, said they was Norwegian, but they could swing a axe or sharpen a saw like nobody's business, lemme tell you. Cut through wood like it was butter. From what I heard, they just stay out there long as they can stand it, and then one day they up and leave when they can't take it no more.

"Gotta admit the pay ain't bad, but it ain't no way to live. Maybe Fate needs some help? What's he got going on?"

As relieved as he was to have escaped the timber camp, Val wasn't ready to sit around the post office all day.

"We only hear of Fate when Sam's here between runs of the fish boat, and you know Sam's not much of a talker," Adam said good-naturedly. "More fishermen are signing up to send their fish north with him, so I expect he's doing all right, though. Now come on over here to the table and let me know if these dumplings will do for the paying customers."

Val put on a smile and picked up a plate. Loyce, sharing his disappointment, shifted in her chair.

A few days later Val scraped the last bit of bee glue from a honey frame and then leaned a backward arc, stretching his muscles in the opposite direction. Bees produced the resinlike propolis to seal small openings in the hive during winter hibernation. Cleaning the frames for the new season's nectar and pollen was the beekeeper's job. At least it was with these newfangled hive boxes that held movable frames of flat honeycomb foundation.

Val's grandfather had kept bees in short, hollow logs of swamp tupelo. Back then beekeepers would stand a log on end and drill a bee-sized hole in the bottom of it for an entry. A simple wooden cover kept out predators and rain. Sometimes called swamp gum trees, the tupelo produced a nectar that bees couldn't resist and wood that they liked to live in. While the swamp tupelo didn't produce the prized non-granulating honey of the dryland white tupelo—or bee gum tree—the quality was good enough to make the tree valuable to the honey industry. Some manufacturers, like Paul Viallon over in Bayou Goula, specialized in hives and frames made from Atchafalaya tupelo.

Val bought his hive boxes from Paul instead of building them himself because precise measurements were crucial in the modern beehives. Once assembled, the hives looked like wooden fruit boxes. He placed them on top of waist-high posts in case high water came over the bank. That extra height lifted them safely above any flood anyone could remember.

The morning was perfect for inspecting the colony and repairing the boxes. Warm, windless days of dappled sunlight had coaxed the bees out of winter hibernation. Val enjoyed watching them shoot out of the hives and then come lumbering back wearing thick yellow pantaloons of pollen. Wild honeysuckle was already vining up the hive supports. In a few weeks the colonies would be shaded under canopies of honeysuckle blooms.

In cottage gardens around the Chene bees were collecting nectar and pollen from flowering sweet peas and patches of winter greens that had grown beyond harvest into spires of yellow flowers. Peach and pear trees bloomed inside picket fences that protected them from wildlife. Along the bayou banks dewberries were blooming underfoot a month before the taller blackberries. Wild plum trees, early wildflowers under the tree canopy, even the grasses were offering up pollen and nectar to the foragers.

Val sighed with contentment as he tapped a small nail into place where an extra heavy frame of honey had pulled apart last season. What a luxury to have time to inspect the frame carefully before placing it back in the hive. This was what he needed after all! When he worked on the river, visits to the bees were quick and the hive maintenance was rushed. Sometimes he would come back from a trip to find that a bear or raccoon had torn into a hive, scattering parts all over the clearing. His bees would be long gone to find another home.

This would be his best season ever. He should make enough profit to invest in a few more hives for next year. *Mais oui!* He could make peace with this life, after all. First he had to make it official with Loyce and set a date. The newlyweds could have their own little houseboat by this winter, and Val would build the new frames while sitting next to his own woodstove.

He ran an expert thumb around the corners of the frame in his hand. He had built this one while sitting next to the *Golden Era's* big galley stove. Crew members always mingled with passengers in the galley, drinking coffee, talking about what they'd seen and done up and down the rivers. You never knew who'd be getting on at the next landing. And what a hodgepodge of tunes and musical instruments they brought along with them! Everything he knew about music had been picked up in that way.

He could join in with an Irish jig on any river in the country, and there was that fiddling style from Maine that sounded so like the Cajun fiddle Grandpère played. Three brothers from the Sabine River in Texas blew harmonicas with a twang he hadn't heard anywhere else. Dark-skinned Gypsies crossing their wagons and horses to the other side of the swamp drew haunting tunes from both fiddles and small accordions. The tunes would stay in his head long after the musicians had gone on their way. Val would master the melodies, eventually coming up with his own versions and passing them along to other travelers.

Val had never realized how much his traveling and music went hand in hand. In fact, that musical camaraderie was what he missed most about his past life. Now that Fate was gone so much, he and Loyce were the only musicians in the community. If he wasn't trying to stay dead, he could go down to the wharf when boats came in. Val tapped in another nail and then paused.

Did giving up his work on the river mean he couldn't visit in the galleys and along the decks? Visiting at the dock wouldn't be as interesting as actually traveling from river to river taking in the tastes and smells along with the tunes, but it would be more exciting than what he had now.

Well, maybe it was time to face Mama and tell her he was alive and settled down here. For the first time he wondered how she would take the news. Mad? *Oui, cher!* But maybe she get over it quick when she come meet Loyce, stay a few weeks, *enh?* They'd throw a big fais do-do for the wedding. Mama could get to know his new family. After that he could go out to the docks and play whenever a boat was in. *Mais oui,* that's what he'd do! Bayou Chene had kept his secret until its time had come. He would go straight away and ask Loyce to set a date.

Val pocketed his hive tools and strolled back down the woods path to the post office. The afternoon sun eased down behind the trees, and he picked up his pace, wondering what Adam was cooking for supper. Excited voices floated on the air through the dogtrot before he even reached the steps.

"Did you see her face when they said who they were looking for?"

"No, I didn't see anything. I just came along when I heard about it, and I wanted to see if it was true."

"Did they really take her away in handcuffs?"

"I heard they did, but then someone else said the deputies just escorted her out to their boat."

People were milling in the dogtrot and even beyond it out in the front yard. Boats and pirogues were tied all around the dock, even to the trees along the bank. It was the biggest crowd Val had ever seen in one place on the Chene. He squeezed into the gathering in the breezeway.

"Who? What's true? C.B. was arrested?" Val asked.

"No, but Roseanne was!"

— 25 —

The voices clamored from all directions, piling up on each other so that Val couldn't identify them.

"She was standing there looking so pleased with herself when that law boat tied up. Bet she was practicing how to tell them to find C.B.'s houseboat."

"That's right, but she went all white when they said they were looking for Roseanne Garnier Barclay!"

"Seems a Mr. *Charles* Barclay was reported missing when he never showed up where he was going, and his family said that he never came back home."

"They started questioning the crew on a steamboat that him and his wife was traveling on. Seems Mr. Barclay disappeared during the night, and the wife got off at the next dock—Bayou Chene!"

"They probably wouldn't have bothered coming out to the place where the wife got off except now, wouldn't you know, a body has turned up with papers that say he is Mr. Barclay himself—but no money—which makes 'em think he was robbed and pushed overboard somewhere by somebody."

"Now, since the wife—make that the *widow*—has been living out here in the swamp quiet as a mouse and not telling anyone about a missing husband—it's beginning to look more than a mite suspicious on her part."

Val worked his way through the crowd until he found Adam.

The postmaster was upstairs, sitting alone in Roseanne's room. He looked too big for the small rocking chair. One cheek rested in the palm of his right hand.

"She didn't do it, Val," he said, quietly. "I don't know what happened to her husband, but neither does she—I'm certain of that."

"They'll sort it out, Adam," Val said. "That's what the law does. Out here everybody knows everybody else and whatever goodness or badness is in them to do. No surprises. Anyone with something mean on his mind knows what would happen if he acted out that meanness. But most places ain't like that. That's where the law comes in to sort it out, just like you sort out the mail and find where it belongs even when someone shifts their houseboat over to another bayou in some cove way off."

Adam made no reply, and the only sounds upstairs came from the conversations thinning out below. As he often did in good times and bad, Adam was thinking of books—how thoroughly the legal system had failed the Count of Monte Cristo, sending an innocent man to a dungeon for almost two decades. Try as he might, Adam couldn't recall even one book where the justice system saved an accused widow from hanging. He had never felt so hopeless.

A day passed, then another. No word came from St. Martin Parish or Roseanne. Adam told himself it would all be straightened out soon and she would be back. Then he realized that even if she was cleared of the suspicion, there was no reason for her to come back to the Chene, the scene of her humiliation. She would probably return home to New Orleans. He would never see her again. So then he told himself she was just another person who had passed through Bayou Chene on the way to the rest of their lives. He tried not to think about the rest of *his* life without her in it. In his mind he kept rewriting her past and his future, trying to reconcile them in a way he could live with.

For the first time in years Mame stepped in for Adam. She took over the store and the post office with friendly efficiency. She commiserated with Loyce over the loss of another friend who probably would not be coming back. In Loyce's mind Roseanne had joined

Fate in that outer-land that was not the Chene. Boats came, and people left. Loyce stayed, would always stay, whether she wanted to or not. Mame couldn't change that fact, nor could she make the Chene the best place for a young blind woman to grow old.

Val and Mame didn't believe Roseanne was a murderer or a thief, but the rest of the community was divided on her guilt or innocence. Since she was a newcomer and they didn't know her husband at all, opinions on both sides were limp. The irony that Roseanne was arrested instead of C.B. was not lost on anyone.

An anxious week passed at the post office. Then the St. Martin Parish sheriff's boat tied up in front of the Bayou Chene Post Office for the second time in history. Roseanne sat ramrod straight on the seat next to a deputy. Adam strode to the dock, thanked the deputy, and escorted her back to the porch without a word spoken between them. It was only after they made it to the kitchen that she collapsed against him.

"Oh, it was Charles's clothes and wallet all right!" she sobbed out. "He's dead, Mr. Snellgrove! I didn't love him, but I wouldn't wish this on him or anyone else."

"Oh, my dear," he said, patting her back rhythmically like he used to do for Loyce when she couldn't sleep. "That's sad for sure, but there's comfort in knowing the truth, don't you think? Better than wondering why you haven't heard from him?"

"I suppose you're right. The body was so decomposed, they don't know how he died, and they may never find out who was responsible. Since there was no money in his wallet, they are assuming he was robbed. For now they seem convinced I didn't know anything about it, even though my behavior was not what one would expect of a bride on her honeymoon. They hope their questions will be answered once they track down all the crew members who were on the boat that trip. Someone who was out on deck that night might have heard something that they didn't realize as being important at the time."

She broke into another round of sobbing, until she was too exhausted to continue. Adam stroked strands of hair out of her tears and let her rest against him. Even in her grief, she felt solid and sturdy in his arms.

"Word will get out that you are no longer a suspect, Mrs. Barclay. I'll see to that."

"Be that as it may, Mr. Snellgrove, I'm ruined. I'll never have a life again. And suppose they never arrest anyone else? I will live the rest of my life under this cloud of suspicion. This scandal goes beyond any humiliation I ever feared."

"Well, maybe that's not all bad, Mrs. Barclay. Seems like you could be on the brink of a new life since the old one doesn't work anymore. Did you ever look at a situation that way before? You know that's what happened to one of my heroes—Robinson Crusoe. I know you've read the book, but did you know it was based on a man who really was shipwrecked and had to build a new life from scratch? I bet he's inspired a lot of people to make do with a bad situation. Sometimes—and I'm not one to say this applies to your situation, only you would know that—but sometimes it can be a relief to lose everything and start over."

She stepped away and looked up into his eyes.

"This is what has happened to C.B.," Roseanne's voice was deadly quiet as realization settled around her. "Even worse, *I* did this to her. No matter what happens in the future, she can never prove what happened that day. She will always be the woman who might have tried to drown her baby. Just like I will always be the widow who might have killed my husband. We are just alike, after all. C.B. always said that."

Her tears were dry now, and she went on.

"You know, it used to make me so angry when she tried to put me in her class. I suppose that's why I took such a hard stand on what happened to her that day. And truth be told, after it popped out of my mouth that first time, I realized I didn't even believe it! But it would have been humiliating to admit I might be wrong."

She wept afresh as if her heart had broken wide open. Adam stepped toward her again and held her close.

"Oh, Mr. Snellgrove, I'm guilty of more cruelty than what I've been accused of. At least I have *hope* of being exonerated someday, but since no one saw C.B.'s accident, she can never prove her innocence."

"Well, maybe this is your chance to start your new life on the right foot," Adam murmured into her hair. "No one would have more influence in lifting that cloud from C.B. than the person who put it there."

She didn't answer, but her eyes filled with tears again. Adam couldn't read the look she gave him before she turned away and trudged toward the stairs to her room. If he was ever going to say it, he knew it must be now.

"Roseanne."

It was the first time he had voiced her given name. One foot already on the stairs, she turned in surprise at the sound of it on his lips.

"I lost my own self years ago, when Josie died," he went on. "I somehow managed to get through by just putting one foot in front of the other, but I wouldn't call it living. It was more like just doing my duty. I had family and neighbors counting on me. Then you came walking out of the woods that evening and made me want to take up living again for myself. If you have any inclination to start a new life, I'd be proud to be part of it."

Suddenly she slumped down on the stair step as far as the whalebone around her middle would let her. The corset is holding her upright, thought Adam, like a broken flower stem Mame would splint with a twig.

And then she told him. The thing she had told one other person years ago. It came back in glimpses. Toddling behind the older cousins, trying to catch up. Being lifted into the air by the sharp-faced boy, his long legs propelling them both in pursuit of the cousins. Then the courtyard gate that opened to the garden shed. The leather-bound trunk where he stood her against the wall. Her tiny shoes wobbled on the leather strappings so that she slipped her feet wider apart to steady herself. His fingers probing, sliding her long white drawers down into a pool around her feet. Then his own pants open and a warm pressure between her legs. Stickiness. She pointed a small finger at the white stream and giggled.

There was no pain. Just the warm stickiness sliding between her tiny thighs and his fingers probing her the way her nanny would give her a bath except there was no soap, no cloth, just the wet slipperiness. The pain would come a few years later when she recalled the scene for her best friend, Marie, at the Sisters of Evangeline Convent School. How many times had it happened? Three, four, she was too young to count, so she didn't know.

Marie's eyes had bulged, and she had reared back like a startled pony.

"You can't ever, ever tell anyone about that!" she whispered. "You will go to hell if anyone finds out you are soiled. And you can't *ever* get married because your husband will know. He will tell on you, and you will go to hell!"

Soiled. It was the first time Roseanne thought about the curious experiences as something shameful. She was soiled.

"How will my husband know if I don't tell him?"

"I don't know for sure," Marie stammered in uncertainty. "But I've heard your husband can tell when you get married if you have been soiled, and then you will go to hell."

And so started Roseanne's attempts to become unsoiled. She washed her hands in the basin, not just for meals but several times a day, so often that her stepmother began accusing the servants of stealing the pale green bars of vetiver soaps. That was when she began haunting the linen closets and armoires for items, especially undergarments, in want of folding to her satisfaction. That was when her braids seemed to spring into disobedience, the ribbons defying her attempts to keep them identical in shape and spacing. The tiniest spot of rust from the clothesline would make her put a garment back in the laundry hamper to be washed again. She wouldn't leave the house in wet weather for fear of dirtying her shoes or her hems.

During the telling Adam had slipped onto the stair next to Roseanne. This time it wasn't just hearing loss that made him lean forward. He studied her face as she spoke. He could see the little girl before and after the incident. The teenager gliding among the nuns and their linen closets, looking to bring order back to her life. The horror of being forced into a marriage that she believed would condemn her not just to hell but to humiliation on earth. Her effort to avoid her groom's attentions and thus put off the revelation she had feared for so long. Her fear of being found out— soiled. For her entire life Roseanne had shied away from sensual pleasure lest she be found out.

Now Adam understood why C.B.'s forthright earthiness had repulsed her. It brought back that young man in the garden shed. Adam could also see how the perceptive, ambitious C.B. sensed Roseanne's abhorrence and resented it. The more Roseanne disapproved of her, the louder C.B. proclaimed their similarities, never guessing how far Roseanne would go in shoving her away, out of sight, even to prison.

Adam reached out and folded the weeping woman into his arms. The weight of her against his chest was a comfort to them both.

— 26 —

Roseanne slept deeply, dreamlessly, and awakened to the sound of the woodstove door clanging shut as Adam set about making a fire for coffee. That was the last bit of normalcy for the morning. It was to be a day with no precedent.

The first thing she noticed was her body. She was not curled tightly in a ball with the covers pulled up close. Her arms rested above her head and curved slightly on the pillow, palms up, fingers relaxed. Her legs stretched out, feet flopped outward. I feel like Drifter looks when she's sleeping with all four feet in the air, she chuckled. And when had she ever chuckled first thing in the morning?

The mirror reflected a smiling face as Roseanne stroked the brush through her hair. The entire length of it fell into waves where hairpins had crimped it in place the day before. No pins today! Maybe no pins ever again. She tied it loosely with a dark-red ribbon low on her neck.

Then she threw open the armoire. No stockings, too warm for stockings! And where were those little slippers? They were fine for skipping around the store all day. She loosened her corset strings and pulled her largest bodice over it. The first thing she would do after breakfast was order one of those brassieres and a larger bodice, but first she'd see if Adam had time to make lost bread for breakfast.

At the time Roseanne was waking to her new self, Sam was steering Fate's newest boat out of Jakes Bayou into the expanse of Lake Mongoulois, the widest point of the Atchafalaya River thereabouts. It was the most water he'd seen since leaving St. Louis. Today he was fishing his own nets and would run the catch up to Atchafalaya Station in time for the afternoon train.

The old skiff Sam had lost on his way down to the Chene served for those first experimental runs, but in no time at all Fate was agitating for a bigger boat to transport more fish, increasing the profit for each run. For transport these days they used an ark-like vessel with a larger engine, enough room on the deck for a drum of gasoline, a small cabin for shelter, and vast wells for storing ice and fish.

In addition to the big boat, Fate had recently come up with the flat-fronted bateau just for Sam to use for raising nets. It was no wider than the old push skiffs everyone rowed around the Chene, but it was long, almost twenty feet. Instead of sitting flat on its bottom, the front half was raked high so that the bow raised up out of the water, unless it was weighed down with nets or a load of fish. The sides were low, to make it easier to roll nets up and over them. It was equipped with a smaller engine and propeller than the transport boat, but it still sounded loud to Sam.

Noise didn't bother Fate. In fact, he liked nothing better than shouting over a fog of fumes and racket about the attributes of some new engine he was trying out. He still couldn't squat like other swampers, but he didn't stay still long enough to feel any discomfort. He scrambled around, checking the prop in the water, the fuel feed into the engine, the combustion pressure inside the engine jacket. Sam's head hurt just thinking about the noise and activity in Fate's life.

On that spring morning the Atchafalaya's banks were dotted with the pale green of new cypress needles. The river was gray and flat at dawn, but Sam knew it would be reflecting sparkles of sunlight just about the time he pulled the first net out of the water. The sun would feel good on his back because his front would be soaked. C.B. kept telling him to wear a slicker until he got better at raising nets.

Sam had watched Fate roll the dripping webbed hoops into his boat all day long without getting wet. But the same nets poured water down the front of Sam's pants and into his shoes. His sturdy brogans with brass grommets—the one proud possession he had to show from his work at the shoe factory—filled up with water. His feet squished as he wrestled a net from bow to stern. C.B. also told him to wear rubber boots like the other fishermen. She was probably right.

She believed he would get better at all this. That he could learn to tar nets without dripping it in his hair. That he could stage a box of a hundred fishhooks onto lines without dropping them in a tangled mess in the bottom of the boat. She told him this even as she cut chunks of tar out of his hair or helped him untangle another thicket of hooks and line. He wished he could believe in himself as much as she did. Or as much as he believed in *her*.

He knew Roseanne was wrong about her trying to drown Sam Junior. Sure, C.B. hadn't wanted a baby. And why would she believe *he* wanted one, especially a baby that wasn't even his? She admitted trying to buy those French pills the first time they went to the store in Bayou Chene. So, what would be the difference in taking those pills before he was born or drowning Sam Junior in the bayou a few months later? That's how Roseanne saw it.

What *was* the difference, anyway? That question was too big for Sam to ponder. What he did know was the way C.B. looked at Sam Junior of an evening, sitting on the deck. Like she'd just lifted the lid to the treasure chest old Lafitte was supposed to have hidden somewhere around Four Hundred Dollar Bayou. Roseanne didn't see her then. Still, Sam couldn't think of how to say that in her defense when the rumors chattered in the background on a dock or in the post office. It was a relief for him to forget about all that and just fish. The truth would just have to take care of itself.

Sam switched off the engine and listened to silence settle over the river. A net he had patched and tarred was telescoped and lying, small end up, on the bottom of the boat. The tarred line was coiled and waiting for him to stake it to the edge of the riverbed. He tied the line around a sharpened cypress stake, fitted his jugger pole over the stake, and shoved it deep into the muddy bottom near the bank.

Then he drifted down with the current, playing the line through his hands. *Shrp, shrp, shrp.* The hoops slipped off the bow and into the water, stiffening in the current, letting the water stand them up against the pull from the stake. The net was ready, waiting to fill up with buffalo, some in the twenty-pound range, before he came back to check it in a few days.

When Sam was satisfied with the set of the net, he cranked the engine and chugged upstream, looking for the bent willow that marked the next net in his run. He watched the willow slip just past the stern before tossing the three-pronged hook overboard. When he felt it thud against the river bottom, he started pulling, inching the weight along at just the right speed to grab the hoops or webbing of the net below. Sam had taken to this one task quickly, mapping the river bottom through his fingers. The sense of discovery thrilled him every time.

He was ready for the moment the line tightened and pulled the bateau back upstream a bit. Hand over hand, Sam pulled the boat and net together, watching for the first hoops to break the surface. This was what drew him. Fishing was like hunting treasure. You never knew what you would find in a net or on the end of a line. This morning it was buffalo with their blunt noses and broad backs covered with scales as big as Sam Junior's hand. He was ready for them. Ice filled his wells, and there was plenty of gasoline in the fuel tank.

Bracing his sturdy shoes wide apart on the wooden planks, he rolled the hoops over the gunnel and safely into the boat. Then with a mighty lift he collapsed the net on the bottom of the boat. The largest hoop rested flat on the plank flooring, with the smaller hoops telescoping into it. Picking up the tail line attached to the smallest hoop, Sam began to shake each hoop in turn. Eight large fish tumbled onto the bottom. He squatted on his heels and tossed the buffalo into the ice well. A catfish was tangled in the webbing. He reached in past his elbow to grasp it behind the barbs, untangling it and tossing it into its own compartment.

After washing the slime from his hands and arms, Sam cranked the engine and headed upstream to the next net. The morning was getting off to a reasonable start. He should have a good load by the time he was halfway to Atchafalaya Station and still make it to the depot in plenty of time. Day after tomorrow these fish would be on New York City dining tables.

Sam glanced upstream. Something out of place was drifting toward him. A dark-red upholstered chair bobbed in the current. It spun slowly, daylight sliding through curved armrests in rotation. The high back reared, silhouetted against the sky, and then dipped forward. Just an ordinary parlor chair but out here on the water—most likely, it signified disaster.

Sam sat down to watch it twirl lazily past his bateau. Nothing else seemed amiss on this side of the bend. The chair could have been thrown during a dispute over cards, portending nothing worse than a couple of passengers waking up to sore knuckles. But dread prickled across Sam's scalp. He cranked the motor and put-putted upstream.

Wreckage greeted him before he made it to the bend. Partially submerged bales of cotton wallowed in various stages of sinking. Barrels, broken and whole, wobbled past. Planks, slabs, whole rafts of wood lay scattered on the current as far as he could see. Then even more tragic than cotton bales and wood scraps came satchels, bottles, busted furniture—the implements of daily life that people had worked for and fussed over. Sam had no frame of reference for the carnage.

Whatever had happened—an explosion or a collision of boats in the night, maybe a wreck with one of the mammoth trees that had caved into the river—the cause didn't matter. Only survivors mattered now. Perhaps some were still swimming or floating on a piece of buoyant wreckage. Sam called out. No one answered. Nothing moved except to rock in the water.

Sam took a deep breath and started the engine. Methodically, he zigzagged to every shadow in the current and each pile of floating debris until there was no more wreckage visible upstream. He didn't find a single living soul, but he did recover eleven bodies, towing each one to a tree on the riverbank, securing it with heavy-duty line.

Then, out of reverence for the bodies he had found as well as the others that were already resting on the river bottom or headed downstream for someone else to discover, he shut off the engine. Seconds ticked by. Silence stretched out to the horizon. Still he sat, imagining their final moments, passengers and crew asleep in their beds or maybe even starting their day while he motored along the bayous to the big river. They were dead now. They were no more. Forever.

For the first time in his young life Sam pondered death. It was the only finality. He had *not* died on that sandbar months ago. C.B. and Sam Junior had *not* died that day in the water. Until death wrestled the strength from his own limbs, Sam could fight for those he loved. Whether it was keeping food on the table with his poor skills or rumors from the door with his halting speech. He might not be good at it now, but he would get better.

There was no urgency in his movements. These people were already dead. Steady as always, he started the engine and motored with the current back to the settlement. He would need help laying all these bodies to rest.

— 27 —

Loyce went to bed that night with the bayou outside her window crowded with unaccustomed traffic. She woke next morning to the sound of coffins being built. From upstream at York's lumber-yard the crack of hammers echoed from off the trees, ricocheting and colliding in midair. To her sensitive ears it was like so many woodpeckers trying to batter their way through a tin roof.

After milking the Jersey, Adam left for the cemetery to dig graves alongside the other men who weren't helping York build coffins. Roseanne walked down the path to the Bertrams' with clothes for the woman's body Mary Ann was tending. Prepara-tions were simple. Bodies were washed with rainwater, hair was combed, and burial clothes were found if their own garments were too badly torn for decency's sake. When appropriate clothes couldn't be found, the dead were wrapped in flour sacks ripped open to make shrouds.

The store and post office were closed until after the mass fu-neral, but no one would be inconvenienced since the entire com-munity was involved in preparing for the burials. Everyone except Loyce. She felt useless sitting on the porch in her best skirt and bodice—the worsted traveling suit that Roseanne had outgrown—waiting for someone to come from the cemetery to take her to the service.

Fate had returned to the community several days earlier to renegotiate prices and sign up new fishermen. Now that buffalo were slowing down for the season, prices would go up. The other men treated Fate as an equal now, even deferring to him whenever the talk turned to fishing as business instead of just for supper.

Whenever Fate stopped by the post office, Loyce couldn't think of anything to say to him. To cover her awkwardness, she sat up straighter and shook back her hair in animated conversation with anyone else who happened to be on the porch. She enjoyed feeling the waves lift from her face and settle back down, fringing her cheeks and jawline. She especially liked wearing the new close-fitting dresses and suits that Roseanne helped her choose from the catalog, and she wondered if Fate noticed how snugly they fit across her bosom. Even though she had never been able to see where he was looking, she had always been aware of what held his attention.

Now that connection was gone. Cut clean off. How different from the days when thoughts and feelings flowed as easily between them as water past the dock. Today she didn't even know whether he was helping build coffins at York's or digging graves at the cemetery.

"Morning, Loyce!" Alcide's voice, less jovial than usual, drifted up from the bayou. "A sad day, is it not?" The splash of his paddle accompanied the sound of his greeting.

"So it is. Who do you have?" Loyce asked.

"A pair of 'em. Dot's convinced these two are a mother and child, so we are putting them together. Whether it's so or not, they will be together from now on."

His voice faded around the bend as he headed on toward the cemetery.

And that's how it went through the morning; men and boys rowed from all directions toward the graveyard as the women pronounced each body sufficiently prepared. Each pirogue or skiff bore a body lying on its back with feet pointed toward the bow, hands crossed in front. Back at the homesteads, families changed into their Sunday clothes, climbed into their boats, and headed for the cemetery.

It was nearly noon, and the traffic had slowed considerably.

Loyce's stomach rumbled. She didn't know when someone would come for her.

"Come on, Drifter, let's see what we have to work with from yesterday," she said.

Loyce felt her way across the porch and followed the breeze-way into the kitchen. Drifter padding behind, her belly heavy with pups, didn't make it through before the screen door slammed. She yelped in surprise.

"Well, you just have to watch out for yourself," Loyce scolded in a soft voice as she bent down to rub the soft ears.

"You should know by now I can't watch out for you."

Loyce felt the slight breeze as Drifter waved her tail in forgiveness.

"Let's see, maybe I can make it up to you. We have a couple of baked sweet potatoes, some lost bread, and plenty of milk. That'll do me till supper, how about you?"

Drifter looked up hopefully, waiting for something extra to drop as Loyce peeled the sweet potatoes for them. Neither of them heard the boots on the porch, so the squeak of the screen door surprised them both.

"Val? Is that you already? I'll be right there." Loyce tilted her head toward the doorway.

Instead of an answer, she heard only Drifter's low growl followed by a thud, a yelp, and silence.

At the cemetery trees almost touched over the top of the narrow bayou, making a tunnel for the boats bearing the coffins. First came the solemn parade of little vessels bearing the bodies, most with a single passenger facing the sky. The majority of the dead were men of all ages and class, although station in life was hard to determine, since many were dressed in borrowed clothes. Two women were among them, and while it was unusual for a woman to travel alone, there was no way to know which of the bodies represented couples who had shared a life together before they were joined in death. One woman had a child lying in the crook of her arm. Two other children appeared to be siblings.

From intersecting bayous more boats joined the regatta of death. The dip and pull of the handmade paddles and oars left brief marks in the water, each one a signature of the man who carved it. The Cheners, who normally would be joking and talking, bent silently to their tasks.

One after the other the boats unloaded their burdens to men and boys on the bank. The soft thud of shovels, along with an occasional grunt or soft-spoken directions, broke the silence along the bank. Periodically, a wagon creaked down the path from York's bearing two or three coffins, which were unloaded near open graves. As bodies arrived, they were placed directly into coffins, which were then lowered into the ground to be covered with fragrant earth and leaf mold.

Even C.B. came out to help. Without meeting anyone's eye, she busied herself gathering small bouquets of honeysuckle for the graves where the unidentified children lay. When she had done all she could, she remained near the dead children and held Sam Junior tightly.

She stiffened and looked away when Roseanne arrived with York and Mary Ann Bertram. A moment later she was surprised to feel a hand on her arm. It was Roseanne's. No one else could hear what words were spoken, but it was clear that forgiveness had been asked and granted in the shadow of so much sorrow.

"Well, that's ten poor souls so far," murmured Mary Ann. "At least they have a resting-place. We'll never know how many had already sunk or gone downstream before Sam could catch them. How sad to think of people waiting for them at docks and not knowing something's happened."

"Once news gets around about the sinking and the steamer is identified, I suppose we'll be meeting some of their relatives," Roseanne added. "Adam is mailing all the personal papers that had addresses on them. They'll be a comfort to some, anyway. Look, I think this is the last one."

They turned to where Val and Sam met the final boat in the procession.

"Tie up to this little cypress; it'll hold till you unload," Val directed. "Here you go, Sam. Me, I'll get the other end."

Together they worked the corpse onto the bank. Within minutes it was laid out in the coffin and placed in the last open grave.

"What are we waiting for?" Mary Ann looked over the assembled crowd a few minutes later. "All the graves are covered, and the preacher's here."

"Adam sent Fate to get Loyce because his boat is faster," Roseanne said. "That was a while ago, so they should be here most anytime."

Mary Ann scanned the scene again, but there was no sign of Fate's boat coming down the bayou.

"Loyce! Loyce!" Fate's voice tore through the hushed crowd, not from the bayou but from the woods path.

Heads turned to the sound of his boots pounding the trail. A second later he broke into the clearing, glancing wildly around the crowd.

"She's gone!" he panted. "I thought maybe she decided to try to walk down here with Drifter, but I didn't see them along the path. There's no sign of them anywhere."

— 28 —

Drifter opened one eye. Pain radiated from the other one, which stayed shut and felt heavy. She inhaled a questioning sniff. A smell, like the snake on the plank walk but stronger, made the fur stiffen on her neck. She looked as far as she could see from where she was lying on the kitchen floor next to the stove. The room was empty. She listened. There was no rustle of dress and apron. No wooden rockers on the porch floor. She sniffed again. Loyce was gone, and all that remained was the faint scent of her almost overpowered by the snake smell.

Drifter drew her legs under her full belly and pushed up. Near the sweet potato that had fallen on the floor, her nose picked out the last pure spot of Loyce's scent and followed it toward the door where the danger smell blended with it. The combined scent led her off the porch, down the plank walk, and to the water's edge. She looked with her good eye, but if there was something to see, she missed it. Her nose was her true guide. She drew in rapid sharp breaths. There were willows that smelled like rain. The fishy water flowing past the dock. The rot of a lost shrimp net snagged under the logs.

Suddenly, there it was—a faint curl on the breeze. Drifter had not been in water since the day Fate had pulled her from it. In fact, she avoided the dock, boats, anything that brought water to mind. But at that moment she dove in without hesitation, heading toward the opposite bank and Loyce's scent. Her webbed paws paddled effortlessly, barely disturbing the current, which dragged her slightly downstream. When she reached the bank, her swollen body became heavy again, and she was breathing hard by the time she scrambled to the top. Not stopping to catch her breath, she snuffled the ground, the bushes, the air. There it was! Mixed again with the danger smell.

She paused for a heartbeat when she heard a familiar put-putting in the distance. Fate. The noisy human whose arrival always brought joy to Drifter and vexation to Loyce. Loyce!

Drifter turned away from the sound of Fate's motor and set to the trail again, single-mindedly forging ahead, sometimes catching hold of one or the other or both smells at once. Since she tracked by scent, not sight, a puddle or log across the path could throw her off. Then thorns and vines snatched her, blocked her way, and wound around her head, her feet. She backed up, pulled loose, or chewed her way through, always looping back to find the trail once more. The afternoon light in the thicket dimmed as evening came on, but it didn't matter because her nose held the trail, which was now mostly the danger smell.

Suddenly, there was a new pain, sharp like a thorn low on her stomach. She bit at it but caught nothing. She went on. Another pain, again nothing there. She slowed, her body getting heavier with every step, sinking on her short legs. The pains were coming faster, and she realized they were deep inside her. Exhausted, she collapsed, struggling to breathe.

Night fell, and despite the pull of the scent, she couldn't make her body move. Finally, a mighty wave of pain washed over her, followed by three more. Instincts set her tongue to licking the four little bundles. Only when they were clean and nursing did she groan and give in to sleep.

Loyce breathed shallowly, willing herself to stay conscious. Her efforts were hampered by a wad of cloth stuffed in her mouth.

She remembered being dragged along the walk to the dock, then picked up and dumped into a boat. Her heart pounded, but no matter how hard she tried, she couldn't pull in enough air and soon drifted into unconsciousness.

She didn't know how much time had passed when she woke to the gentle bump of land under the boat bottom. By then she was curled into a tight, protective bundle but had straightened her neck enough to breathe. There was a sucking sound of boots in mud as the small boat was pulled up an incline. Then, with a grunt, the man picked her up like a sack of cornmeal and threw her over his shoulder. Hanging upside down didn't disorient Loyce as much as it might a sighted person, but the posture hampered her breathing again and made blood rush to her head.

She was slipping out of consciousness again when his feet sounded on a plank walk. He kicked open a door, and fetid air closed around them like a sour blanket. She was dumped onto a cot. Loyce could feel the rope supports beneath a bare moss mattress. Years of sweat, soot, and unwashed maleness made her gag.

Fear. She could name it, even though she had never felt it before. Her sheltered life had kept it from touching her. Even the night of the snake on the plank walk, Drifter, Fate, and Adam had rushed to save her before she was even aware of the danger. Now there was no one to see, hear, or come to her aid.

Cold, prickly beads of sweat popped out of her skin. Blood thrummed in her temples, making it impossible to think. *This isn't happening, this isn't happening.* The useless words ran circles in her mind. She was not only blind but paralyzed by terror.

Slowly, her senses returned. First she heard rummaging, followed by the clink of a lamp globe. That meant it was dark enough for her to lift her chin and point her nose away from the stink of the bedding without her movement being detected. The longer she could feign being out, the more time she had to think.

How far was she from home? In what direction? Were there other people nearby? If so, would they come to her aid, or would they alert him if his prisoner tried to escape? Escape from where?

Who was he? How could she leave if she didn't even know where she was? Panic rippled through her at the realization. That's exactly what he had in mind!

Loyce willed control over her terror. *Pay attention!* That's what she was good at. She lay still and listened, thinking back through the day. It had been near noon when she went to the kitchen. It felt like several hours had passed since she was taken, so the day must be nearing its end. Yet even to her acute ears, no mothers called children to supper. No dogs barked greetings to returning fishermen. No cows lowed for their calves after milking. There was no clunk of boats against docks and houseboats. No sounds of human occupation except for the man's panting, as if breathing through his mouth.

He continued to rummage. She heard a fuel can rattle against a woodstove, then smelled the coal oil. Where does he buy supplies, she wondered. The stranger wasn't one of their customers, and his movements didn't sound like anyone she had ever heard described. More rummaging, then the thud of something heavy landing in a skillet was followed by the smell of rancid grease splashing on the stove.

Something sharp poked her between the shoulders. Her surprised yelp broke through the feigned unconsciousness.

"Gonna have some gator chunks ready in a minnit," her captor said, followed by more panting. "Might's well keep your strength up, since you gonna be here the rest of yo' natural life. My name's Pank, and I know you're Miz Loyce Snellgrove, blind girl from Bayou Chene. Blind girl that's gonna keep ol' Pank company for a good long time."

He started wheezing and repeated, "A good long time."

Loyce sat up on the side of the bed but said nothing. Listening seemed to be the better choice. First she had to calm her pounding heart so she could hear him.

"I figured it ought not make no never mind to you what a man looks like," he huffed. "And it ain't like you was ever going to see the sights, so to speak, or even be missed very much. But for me

215

you'll do jus' fine. I been needing me a pot washer and a ball licker, and you don't need to see to handle either one of them chores. Yo' daddy, he'll be jest as glad to be rid of you, probly, and Bayou Chene'll git along just fine with one less net maker. They won't even be looking for you long."

He wheezed off into a laugh and then continued.

"You ain't even my first choice. I had my eye on that little yeller-headed gal with them shiny dresses. I like me a woman what can dress. Used to watch her all the time, especially after she had that young'un and used to pull that titty out for the world to admire. I thought I had her that day she and that runt rocked overboard. Would have been so easy for me to let him drown and then fish her out. See, everbody woulda thought they both drowned and never woulda even wondered about not finding her body. Well, she fooled me first by somehow getting back up to the deck. I was considering whether to just go on over there and pull her into my boat before she knew what was happening, but then that old busybody had to show up with her baby."

More wheezing. Pondering his loss? Trying to catch his breath? Loyce couldn't tell.

"But you's better anyways since I'd had to keep an eye on that one all the time. She'd been more trouble than she's worth. Many's the time I heard that mouth going on and on whiles I was watching."

The reference to C.B. gave Loyce an idea. How many times had she laughed at C.B.'s outrageous stories of encounters with unsavory circumstances? The bluff, the brash talk that had helped her skirt danger and turn events to her advantage. Loyce sucked in air to steady herself and project her voice with authority.

"I might not be able to see what a man looks like, but how he smells is mighty important to a woman, particularly a blind woman. If you treat me like a coonhound, you'll have to watch where you put your hands 'cause you just might get bit. But if you treat me like a lady, I could make life mighty sweet for you."

She couldn't believe the words came out of her mouth! It sounded just like something C.B. would say.

"Whoohoo, look who's got a tongue in her head." Pank slapped a hand on something, maybe his thigh, and a wave of stench floated through the cabin. "Don't expect me to be jawing with you alla time, Miss Priss. I ain't used to it and don't truck with it."

"If you want some female company, you'll have to get used to it," she replied with more spirit than she felt. "That's part of the bargain between a man and a woman."

Bargain? Now that sounded more like Roseanne! She had even added a sniff, to accentuate her moral superiority over her listener.

"What bargain? I ain't making no bargain!" His retort dragged out on another wheeze. "You gonna do what I say, and no bargain into it."

Despite the threat, Loyce thought she detected a hint of interest in his voice. He liked being referred to as part of a pair. A man and a woman, him and her. She pushed down the sour taste in her throat and forged ahead. If she could just keep him talking! Maybe she could convince him to bring her home. Perhaps she could persuade him she would never be able to identify him. He might believe the lie.

"As for the romance you have in mind, you can bet your rank underwear that taking the time to procure my full cooperation will be to our mutual benefit. That means you'll court me like a lady. You'll bathe and wear clean clothes."

Now that sounded like something Roseanne would say in C.B.'s voice. The effect on Pank was not what she had hoped.

"Like hell I will!" he spluttered, and a crash that could have been a chair turning over drowned out the rest of the words.

He stumped across the room, and she counted the steps, four. The room was even smaller than she had estimated. She held her breath against the rotten tooth smell. He was either very short— not even as tall as she—or he was bending over. She couldn't say right then what difference it would make, but she wanted to find out.

As if to ward him off, her hand grasped the collar of her jacket, Roseanne's worsted one with the double row of military buttons. As she expected, he clamped a hand over her wrist. He was short, extraordinarily short. In fact, standing up, he seemed to be the same height as she was sitting on the side of the bed! He must be a dwarf? Or a midget? She had heard the words but had no frame of reference about the difference between them.

She could discern that he had the most powerful grip she had ever felt. Just like her senses of hearing, touch, and smell were highly developed, extraordinary muscle strength might compensate for his lack of stature. Was there a way this new information could work in her favor?

Loyce thrust out her chin. Despite the proximity of his reeking mouth, she sniffed once more for good measure and pushed on with Roseanne's haughtiness.

"I'm a young woman, and I can tell from your voice you are not an old man," she spoke, as if she already held the high hand. "We could be together a long time. You might well be right that neither of us could reasonably expect better in life. So, we might as well make the most of our lot. If you will meet me halfway, I'll make every effort to be a good woman for you. Make a list of what you expect from me, and I'll do the same."

Order. That's right—make order out of this chaos, she told herself. That's what Roseanne would do. If nothing else, it could buy her some time.

"What you mean, make a list? Even if I could write, who'd read my list? Not you for damn sure!" He broke off into laughter that turned into wheezing again.

Did he have a breathing problem that she could use to her advantage? She must keep him talking and moving around the cabin. It was the only way for her to learn anything.

"I guess you got me there, Mr. Pank," she admitted. "Unless it's in braille, I can't read a thing."

"What you mean by *braille*?"

"It's a way of writing using raised dots on paper. Just for blind people."

"Well, maybe you'll just have to show me how to do that, in case I need to make you a list!" he said. "And I ain't Mr. Pank. Just Pank. Pank Neeley."

"Neeley? O'Lamp Neeley's family?"

"She was my ma." Pank's voice rose over the sound of the sizzling where he was turning the chunks of alligator meat.

"You must be the one who disappeared years ago. You shot a woman."

"Wasn't my fault. I was aiming at that no-good man she was walking out with on a Sunday. They was just too far away, and I missed. There was talk about calling in the law for a trial and all, but I didn't stand for that. I just took off. Went to Texas for a while, but that place is too dry. Missed my swamp. Came back here a few years ago—can't rightly say how many. I keep up with the doings around the post office by peeking through the brush from the Indigo Island side. So swampy no one even *looks* that way—they so used to not seeing nothing there. I can keep up with pert near ever'thing. Like when you come back from that school. And when that pretty yeller-haired thing came along. I keep my eye out."

"What about your mama?" Loyce forged ahead, willing the conversation forward. "Don't you know she grieved for you until she died? And that you have a fine little nephew named Wuf? Wouldn't it be better just to show yourself and see what happens? So much time has passed—maybe no one would ever say anything, or if they did, the law might rule it was an accident?"

"Not s'long as Lurleen's family is still around there. I s'pose they are, huh?"

"Yes, but no one ever talks about it. That was so long ago." Loyce tried changing the subject from dead women, wishing now that she hadn't brought it up. She cast around for a cheerier topic.

"What about those alligator chunks you were bragging about? I was just fixing to eat when you yanked me out of my kitchen. Haven't had a bite since breakfast. What time is it, anyway?"

"Don't you worry about the time, Missy. Old Pank knows when it's time to eat and time to sleep, and I'll tell you when." He laughed like it was the funniest thing he had heard all year. "Here's you some of the gator chunks. Ain't what you used to, I know, 'cause I smell your daddy's cooking drifting over the water.

But it's good enough for old Pank, so it's good enough for Pank's woman, ain't that so, Missy?"

With that he shoved a tin plate against her chest. She raised her hands to take it, but it was no longer there. Pank fell into another wheezing bout of laughter.

"What's wrong with you, Miss Priss? Can't even catch a tin plate sitting in front of you? You gotta be quick to get ahead of old Pank."

Loyce knew anger would get her nowhere she wanted to be.

"You are a quick one, that's for sure. Now help me to a chair and table where I can eat properly."

"Ain't got no table, but this here chair'll give you somewhere to prop, and you can just eat in your lap like I do. Ain't missed a meal yet, table or no."

Loyce stretched out a hand in his direction, and this time he pulled her to her feet and steered her two steps, where her leg bumped into the chair. She felt along its ladder back and frayed bottom of cane. She settled gingerly and held her hands out again for the plate. He thrust the pan within her reach.

"There's some fried dough in there, too, in case you want to sop up some of the dripping."

Loyce felt around the lumps trying to distinguish dough from meat. Finally, deciding it didn't matter, she picked up one and brought it to her mouth. It was hot and greasy, too stringy to be the dough. The chunk of meat took a quantity of chewing before it was broken down enough to swallow, but it didn't taste as bad as she expected. Not so different from the breast of a worn-out old hen culled for dumplings. In fact, with proper seasoning and cooking, this plate of dough and meat could have been made into a decent pot of dumplings. She said as much.

"Gator dumplings! Who ever heard of such a thing?" Pank chortled. "I open me a can of tomatoes or beans now and then. That's as fancy as old Pank gets, so you might's well get used to it."

He seemed eager to stretch everything into talk. That was in her favor. Maybe she could entice some information he wouldn't normally give away to a prisoner.

"How do you live?" she asked in what she hoped was a normal conversational tone. "Surely someone knows where you are?"

"No way no one knows where I am. I got me one main trail off the 'Chafalaya that no one ever notices. Just pull my boat up there behind some buttonwood bushes and walk through the woods to my camp. Got me more little trails off the other bayous running along this boggy island. Each one of them trails got a little dugout pirogue tucked up there, looking just like a log to anyone who would see it. Sometimes I can paddle almost to my cabin down one or the other of them trails. Other times I got to walk and tote."

"But how do you live?" she persisted, lost in talk of trails she couldn't see, geography she couldn't imagine. That kind of information wouldn't help her.

"I kill me some gators, boil out the oil, and skin 'em out. Tan 'em, eat the meat. When I need other grub—like them tomatoes and beans—I take them hides and oil out to the river and tie up 'longside the next likely steamboat heading upstream. Go on board and find someone to trade with. Sometimes it's for money, sometimes for groceries and coal oil. No one ever asks who I am or where I come from.

"Most of 'em think I'm Injun under all this gator grease and soot. They say all kinds of things in front of me they wouldn't think of saying in front of a white man. Yessir. I'll just sit by their stove and make a cup of coffee last a hour or more on a cold night. You'd be surprised what all I hear from up and down the river. When I'm ready to go, it's all downstream to home."

"What do you mean, you hear stuff?"

It was evident now that Pank, indeed, was yearning for an audience. He probably didn't run across many people in a week, or a year, who listened to him. While Loyce wasn't interested in his gossip, she needed to keep him talking. She settled in to nod and murmur as long as necessary, buying time to plan her way out.

Pank's wheezing voice droned on as night sounds of the deep woods settled around the cabin. Of all the scandals he passed along, Loyce filed away only two stories to tell again if she got back home. When she got back home.

— 29 —

Drifter woke at dawn. A burning thirst fought for attention with her distress over Loyce and the needs of her pups. The pups had nursed during the night and were sleeping in a contented heap, but she couldn't leave them exposed even on such an isolated path. At the base of a large cypress tree she found a hollow cushioned with eons' worth of cypress needles. One by one she carefully moved the pups.

Once they were safely tucked in their new nest, she followed her nose to a pool where cypress knees stood like sentinels. After drinking, she circled wide to make her way back to the pups. That's when she caught Loyce's scent again.

Nose down, she snuffled along, picking up pace until the thickets opened into a small clearing. Almost lost in the shadows was what appeared to be a heap of driftwood and palmetto bushes. All traces of Loyce disappeared. Instead, Drifter recoiled from the stench of danger as thick as blood. The smell radiated from scaly hides nailed to posts framing the hut.

She was turning away when suddenly, on the foul air, she caught a slight whiff of Loyce. It was gone just as quickly as it came. Puzzled, Drifter whined softly, snuffled the ground beneath her paws, and lifted her nose again. Nothing.

Inside the shack fatigue had eventually won over fear, and Loyce had nodded off to the sound of Pank's voice. Time and again she had roused from fitful sleep wondering why she was cold and sitting straight up. When her plight surfaced from her dreams, she would run the events of the previous day through her mind again, finding no ready answers. Then she would nod off again.

Now she could feel the morning stirring before the night air lifted from the surrounding swamp. She heard the rustle of blankets and a blast of morning gas from the bed.

"Mr. Neeley, what provisions have you made for my conveniences?" she launched right into her case.

"Conveniences! What you mean by conveniences?" He mumbled, sounding as confused by her presence as she had been upon awakening.

"To relieve myself, Mr. Neeley. And to wash." She strove for the proper inflection Roseanne would have used. The tone that made her sound superior to her present company but also willing to bring him up to her standards.

"I just go on out there to the woods, never thought it inconvenient before." Pank sounded offended.

"Surely you don't expect a blind woman to go traipsing around in the swamp to relieve herself, do you?"

"You ain't going nowhere. I'll bring a lard can for your *conveniences*, as you say, and you can go dump it at the end of the walk."

"What about bathing? If I'm going to be here the rest of my life, I need a place to bathe."

"Tarnation, if you ain't wantin' one thing, it's another. You didn't have it all that fancy on the Chene—I know better'n that."

"The want of a washbasin is only civilized, Mr. Neeley," she said, hoping she hit somewhere between amiable and bossy.

It was clear by now that he craved conversation, especially bickering, but she didn't know how far to push arguing with him. At what point would he snap and lash out at her with a fist or a weapon? She had to pay attention more keenly than ever. Her life depended on it.

"And who's gonna tote in all that water for you to wash and then haul it back out again?" He was still enjoying the feisty exchange.

"I expect you will carry enough for the two of us, Mr. Neeley. *You* made the plans for fetching me way out here; it's up to you to see to the arrangements. Besides the water, I'll need soap, some towels, and a washing cloth. And what about a change of clothes? I can't wear this same dress for the rest of my life."

The silence told her this was new territory for her captor. She plunged on with her plan.

"If you really do like a woman who knows how to dress, you're gonna have to help me out."

"We'll see about that, Missy, once we get this thing under way. First we gotta take *off* what you got on."

Loyce reflexively touched the collar of Roseanne's traveling dress once more, as if she could protect herself.

"I can handle that part when the time comes, but right now I'm having my monthlies, and it wouldn't serve either one of us to act hastily. Even the Bible says a woman is unclean at this time. I'm pretty sure you risk your privates getting diseased, perhaps even falling off. We could use this time to get to know each other better—a courtship, if you will."

"One day, Missy," he said gruffly. "That's it. I have a boat to meet today."

With that he was gone down the plank walk.

Out in the woods Drifter's stomach growled. Hunger had driven her to abandon the faint trace of Loyce, but she was not experienced at hunting. Once her nose picked up the promising scent of a small creature. She followed the trail until it ended in a pool of water. Another track led her to the base of a live oak, where tender bits of twig dribbled down from the jaws of a chattering squirrel. The sun was high before she finally stumbled upon a nearsighted possum scurrying along to his lair. She clamped and shook until he was dead. Then she ate until there was nothing left but the skull and the tail.

Back at the nest her pups whined about their own hunger. They lifted their voices even higher when bushes rustled nearby. But instead of the soft muzzle they were expecting, heavy boots stopped short of stepping on them. A low grunt gave way to a wheeze. The footsteps retreated and then returned minutes later, inciting another chorus of whimpers. Then one by one, the pups were picked up and dropped into a sack.

Drifter knew something was wrong before she reached the nest. There were no sounds, and the danger smell was strong. Her steps slowed, she circled wide, finally peering through the thicket into the hollow. The nest was empty. She followed the smell of her pups combined with the stench along a path that appeared to be used often. A few minutes later she came to the big water, the one she and Sam had traveled. It was so wide she couldn't see what was on the other side. The scent of her pups ended here. So did the smell of danger.

Back at the cabin Loyce wasted no time. Even as Pank's steps faded, she was listening for new clues about her surroundings. Her body ached from sitting up through the chill night, but she padded to the door and swung it open as soon as he was out of earshot.

She felt around the doorframe but couldn't find a lock or bolt. It was the most telling detail she had gleaned so far, and it brought her a fresh wave of panic. Pank knew she couldn't go anywhere on her own. Apparently, she was buried so deep in the swamp no one would ever come close to finding her.

Her captor had left so abruptly that he didn't offer to make breakfast for her. Would it have been more gator chunks? She shivered at the prospect. Even though the foul lumps had gone down well enough at supper, during the night they bubbled back up her throat, first as a bilious cloud, then a sour liquid. With a churning stomach and aching bones, Loyce couldn't remember a morning when she had felt worse. Not the best time to be planning an escape from who knows where, she thought.

Taking a determined breath, she felt her way down the walk, sensitive fingers reading the rough wall of the cabin for anything that might help her escape. A few leathery hides crinkled under her hands. Nails in the posts. A rain barrel full of water. Nothing felt promising.

The fresh morning smells were obscured by the odor of rancid oil and drying hides. She had heard that Indians rendered alligators by burying the entire carcass and covering it with coals. She couldn't see to determine whether Pank used that process, but however he accomplished the gory separation, the smell gagged her. She sniffed a couple more times trying to break through the putrid air.

Then, finally, a whiff of something foreign—what was that? Coal oil? Gasoline! She felt along the cabin wall until she located the source—a large can, maybe three gallons. Her fingers felt around the spout until she could unscrew the lid. Sure enough it was gasoline. Pank hadn't mentioned a motorboat during his rambling discourse. The can was one of three, no four, standing against the cabin wall. It must have come from the same supplier who had delivered gasoline to the post office by mistake. The mistake that Loyce and Pank's nephew Wuf had helped set right.

She listened again to make sure she was alone. Then she hefted the can. Too heavy to carry into the cabin. She bent to drag it along the walk inches at a time. Once inside the doorway, she scooted one foot out in front to locate the can of coal oil that must be near the stove. Bump. There it was. Her fingers told her it was shaped the same as the one she'd brought inside, but was there a difference in color or something else that she couldn't discern? If so, would he spot the change? There was nothing she could do but try. The new can was full and heavy. The old one only half-full. Would he notice? Perhaps not, if she kept his attention on her.

She took time to note the direction of the spout and handle of the old can before moving it away from the stove. Summoning all her strength, she lugged the new, full can into its place. Then she felt her way back outside, dragging the coal oil container down the plank walk to the collection of cans. It took a moment to find the space where the gasoline had been. When she was satisfied the switch was as close as she could make it without being able to see, she had one more thing to do. Plan a route out.

Here she was stumped. There was only one plank walk. Just thirty-five steps brought her to its abrupt end. Surely there must be a path that continued on toward the river. She couldn't explore past the plank walk for fear of not finding her way back before her captor returned. That would raise his suspicions and perhaps make him look at everything, including the fuel cans, anew. She felt her way back to the cabin, feeling thwarted.

At that moment Drifter was cautiously sniffing her way back down the path that Loyce suspected was just past the wooden walk. The weary little dog had retraced the scent of her pups back into the woods all the way to the cypress tree, slowly approaching the river again, then again. Each time the breath of the big water gave up a whiff of her pups, nothing more. On this particular return trip she swerved back toward the cabin, where last night the evil smell had mingled with a hint of Loyce.

She snuffled the ground at the end of the walk once more, then deeper, sharper. There it was, the beloved scent! Not just wafting on air, as before, but solid at ground level. A footstep. Loyce had touched down there. Nose to the ground, the little dog ran in ever-widening circles, but every time she locked onto the most concentrated essence of Loyce, the oily stench overpowered her. It oozed from the walls and rose up from the ground around the cabin. Drifter's hair ridged up her back, and her tail quivered a stiff arc. She issued a low growl and circled the entire cabin again but couldn't penetrate the reeking barrier. Finally, she gave up and backed into the brush to wait.

Inside Loyce paced through the hours after making the switch. Feeling every object in the cabin, counting the steps to the door, four. Then mentally counting the steps to the end of the plank walk again. What was past the walk? She couldn't risk finding out now. That fuel can was her only hope.

It was late afternoon when his boots hit the plank walk again.

"Well, Miss Priss, I'm ready to claim my prize" were the words that greeted her. The smell of whiskey improved his breath but not his patience.

"First I'll need a bath, and I'll need privacy to get ready," Loyce said. "I'll bring in the water. You start the fire."

Pank couldn't contain his excitement as he watched her feel her way to the door. He clanged the stove lid and started rummaging the coals. Just as she bent to pick up the two buckets, he stopped still, and she realized her mistake.

"How do you know where the water barrel is?"

She couldn't see his face, but she felt him scrutinizing hers. What could he read there? She knew sighted people picked up cues that way, but she had never been able to decipher what those cues were, even if her life depended on it. Now it did!

She remained bent over the buckets and hoped the curtain of hair brushing her cheekbones covered any expression that would give her away.

"Oh, you didn't expect me to sit here in the cabin all day, did you?" She forced herself to trip the words out lightly, even though her knees were quaking under her skirt. "I felt along as far as the walk could take me, and I'll tell you right now, we're gonna need more plank walks! I'll also need a line to hang washing, and I want an outhouse like any proper household has. If you aim to have a woman of your own, Pank, it will bring changes. There's no two ways about it."

"All right! All right! Have it your way," he blustered. "We'll see to that later. Just go get that water now and be quick about it before I change my mind about that washing up."

She was out the door before he finished speaking. Making the most of her head start, she scouted with her foot toward the end of the plank walk, hoping he couldn't see that she went right past the rain barrel. The clank of the fuel can against the iron stove was loud, and Loyce knew that her life depended on something less than seconds. She dropped the buckets and stretched both hands in front of her, walking fast, faster than she had ever walked before, even in familiar surroundings.

By the time the explosion slammed her to the ground, Loyce had reached the limit of her previous explorations. Thirty-five steps. She lay stunned for precious moments while debris crashed up and then back down through the treetops. Flaming chunks hissed into water holes; others thumped into the mud inches from her face. She didn't know what lay in front, but she knew what was behind her—either a dead man in a flaming cabin with an untold number of fuel cans nearby or a live man who knew she had tried to kill him.

Scrambling to her feet, she poised to step into the unknown when something bumped her leg. The scream died in her throat when she realized there was something familiar about the touch. Another bump. She stretched one hand downward, and Drifter's tongue met her halfway. She didn't wonder how; she just trusted, stepping away from the barrier Drifter made with her body. Two steps, and there she was again, this time on the other side.

Heat told Loyce where she was in relation to the fire, but she'd have to depend on Drifter for the direction to take away from it. Step by step, the dog herded her away from the burning cabin. They went around trees, over logs.

Loyce felt the heat recede, but her terror intensified to the point she felt her heart would burst. Were those footsteps behind her? To the side now? Closing in from the brush? She couldn't tell whether the crashing sounds were of her own making or whether Pank was an arm length behind, reaching for her skirt tail. Thickets caught in her clothes, branches slapped her face, mud sucked at her feet and pulled off a shoe.

Suddenly, she cried out in pain, oblivious to the noise that would give her away. Something had bitten into the tender flesh of her calf and thrown her face first into the mud. Writhing in pain, her thrashing made it impossible to listen for clues. She tried to spring back up but then realized that no creature moved under her or held her down; pain simply radiated from her calf. She rolled over and felt the pull of a vicious briar. Relief flooded through her even as she strained to sit up and unwind the thorny bramble. In her haste and confusion she ripped its length deeper into her leg but finally yanked it free.

Drifter licked her face and urged her to her feet. Air burned back into her chest as she tried to stand, tripping over the long skirt, wobbling on the one shoe and bleeding leg. She was as unsteady as a toddler, but she never had to wonder about the direction. Every time she tried to take a wrong turn, the sturdy body pushed back against her.

Ever mindful of Loyce, Drifter was following the scent trail left by the bag of pups. It was faint, but she had traced it so many times she knew the way by heart. It led to where she and Sam had been together on the big water. Sometimes the scent disappeared completely, but now and then it wafted fresh in her nostrils, pulling her and Loyce in that direction.

Loyce was breathing hard when they broke into a small clearing. She could tell there was open space around her because of the slight currents of air. She waved her hands out to the side and above her head. No branches or tree trunks were within reach. They were standing in a grove of long-dead trees known as widowmakers. Lifeless trunks spiked into the sky, releasing twigs and dried branches over time. Eventually, each skeletal top would snap with no warning and plummet to the ground. Swampers knew them to be the most insidious danger in the woods. The slightest bump of a boat or even a wave of water could launch a dagger of splintered wood.

"Drifter?" She queried, knowing the little dog couldn't answer. "Is this the riverbank? Where are we?"

Loyce groped, unsure of where to turn. Arms outstretched, she tried to step but tripped over Drifter. As she tumbled, her hands broke her fall against a tree trunk. Unseen above them, a spire began to sway. Drifter pulled on the heavy skirt, urging Loyce onward.

— 30 —

Fate squinted across the gray expanse of Lake Chicot as he steered his bateau out of Little Bayou Chene. Sam, stripped down to his undershirt, crouched on the bow, waiting for Fate's word to drop the three-pronged hook again. Fate realized he was sweating inside his jacket. He had not even noticed when the morning chill had burned off to noon heat. Now he slipped off the garment without taking his eyes from the lake. Still focused on the water, he absentmindedly folded the jacket and slid it beneath him to cushion the wooden seat.

When the initial search of the island had failed to find Loyce and Drifter, every available boat in the community began dragging the bayou around the post office. They searched until dark. When daylight came again, the boats fanned farther afield. Adam and Val headed to the west side of the community, while Fate and Sam turned south, where the accumulated waters flowed into Lake Chicot. It was now late afternoon, and Loyce had been missing more than twenty-four hours. The expanse of Lake Chicot looked endless to their tired eyes. The engine put-putted steadfastly into the current.

Fate mopped his face with a sleeve. The cooling effect roused him enough to talk.

"She has to be somewhere, Sam." His voice was barely more than a whisper from fatigue and despair. "Why would she have gone to the bayou, anyway? Is it even possible she could be this far from home? But she's not anywhere on land, and we can't just sit, doing nothing like she'll show up on her own. And where is Drifter? Did someone take them? It just doesn't make sense."

Sam shook his head, concurring with Fate's puzzlement. Everyone had asked the same questions, but no answers came.

"Let's start here and work our way down," Fate said without conviction, pointing to a logjam that made an easy landmark.

Sam stood and dropped the hook again, playing out line until he felt the weight hit bottom. Fate took up the slack with the motor. They both watched as the line sifted through the water, both dreading the soft thud that meant the prongs had snagged something that was not wood or metal.

So far they had pulled up barrel hoops, buckets, and something that looked like part of a wagon wheel. The collection of relics was mute evidence that the wilderness eventually reclaimed itself from civilization. Time and again, Sam dropped the hook and let the line slide through his fingers, probing for evidence of the most recent loss.

It was futile to think they could find a body if there even *was* a body in the river channel, Fate thought, but he could no more give up than stop breathing. An hour passed. When Sam's thick shoulders ached from the throwing and pulling of the weight, he maneuvered the boat while Fate dragged the bottom. They worked their way slowly down the river channel through the lake.

Suddenly, Fate's eyes hardened. Sam saw his jaw clinch. His long arms inched along the line, willing whatever it had hooked to stay on the prongs. Slowly, ever so slowly, the line coiled on the bow. Both men stopped breathing as muddy fabric billowed into sight. Tears blurred Fate's vision, but he continued to hoist. When the cloth broke the surface, Sam looked away to give him privacy.

But instead of the wail of grief he expected, Sam heard, "What the hell?" He glanced back to see Fate pulling up the remains of a small trunk, clasps broken, one side missing, but straps intact. Ragged clothing still trapped inside the wreck waved like a sodden flag. The remaining wooden sides gave way with the weight of being hoisted. Fate reached down and slipped the strap from the hook, sending the bundle back to the bottom.

He was still shaking from the shock when a boom rumbled in the distance. The sound came from upstream far enough away that they might have imagined it, except that blue herons and snowy egrets lifted from the shallows in alarm. Sam jerked the crank cord before Fate had a chance to sit down. They both hunched to reduce wind resistance. *Chug, putt, chug, putt,* the boat was slower going upstream, but still they made better time than if they had been rowing. Ten minutes, then fifteen.

Surely they had traveled far enough to be in the vicinity of the noise. The disturbance may not have anything to do with Loyce, but nothing was too remote to overlook. Two pair of eyes scanned the bank where last year's leaves had thinned and this year's crop had not filled in, the sparseness allowing them to see deeper into the thicket than usual.

"There!" Fate pointed, and Sam turned the boat before seeing for himself the barely visible opening.

At any other time they would have dismissed it as a deer crossing so far away from the community. But now they saw the telltale ridges in mud where a light boat frequently slid into the water. Sam leaped out and charged down the path while Fate was still tying the bowline.

Both of them noticed a rough dugout pirogue stashed under buttonwood bushes ten yards up the bank. They didn't worry about noise as they tore through the nearly invisible path. They dodged trees and leapt over logs. Fate's long legs made up for Sam's head start, and he pulled ahead of his friend.

There she was! Hopping up and down, waving her arms as if conducting a choir, tilting her head in one direction and then another—listening, listening, as always. Her mouth was open, but the noise of their running combined with Drifter's barking drowned out whatever she was shouting. The maroon traveling dress was muddy on all sides and dripping wet. One shoe was missing. Mud covered one side of her face and matted her hair.

But she was upright and all in one piece. Fate had never seen anything so beautiful in his life. He scooped her into his arms with a joyful shout. She answered with just a whispered "Fate," but it was enough.

In the commotion that followed Sam had the presence of mind to fire three shots into the air, letting other searchers know she was found. A progression of shots dispatched the good news up and down the river. Boats closest to them began arriving. People clambered up the bank, shouted questions, then fanned out to search for the shack and Pank.

Loyce was propped against a live oak trunk, the remains of her skirt hiked up above her knee, where Fate was removing the last of the thorns. She winced as he jerked the final barb and cleaned the wounds with saliva, just as he had treated her scrapes when they were kids.

"I never thought I'd welcome the sound of that noisy boat," she murmured, still woozy with exertion and pain. "But today it was the sweetest music I ever heard."

"Good thing we got here when we did. You were waving at the woods and backing right toward the river," he admonished.

"Something big had crashed," she explained. "I thought it was Pank breaking through the bushes, and I just jumped, losing Drifter for a moment. I didn't know which way to run or whether he was about to take me down, but when I heard that rattling contraption, I knew I had to do something in hopes you would notice me. I took a chance to call out as well as waving. I guess it worked."

"Yeh, but you could still use some work on your aim," he grunted, lifting her upright and then swinging her into his arms like a child.

Assured that her injuries were not serious, Fate thought of nothing beyond taking Loyce home as quickly as possible. He carried her down to the bank and was settling her onto the bottom of his bateau when he heard Sam call Drifter. The little dog had not left Loyce's side during the commotion, but Fate had not even noticed her.

"Come on, Drifter, it's over," Sam cajoled from the water's edge. "You did good, girl. Now let's go home."

Instead of hopping in, Drifter danced and barked, running toward a willow snag leaning far out over the water. There she lay down and put her head on her paws, whining. Sam walked along the bank and squatted down in front of her.

"Hey, it's over now, come on, let's go home." Still she whined and looked out over the water. He followed her gaze but saw only the willow top waving with the current.

"What? Something there?"

She didn't move. Impatiently, Fate idled his engine, then seeing the standoff with both man and dog staring at the snag, he chugged the boat over to the trailing leaves. A burlap bag was cradled in the outermost branches hanging over the water. He stood up, steadying himself against a limb before lifting the bag. It wiggled and mewed.

"Well, I'll be damned," he chuckled. "Sam, did you notice that Drifter had her pups?"

— 31 —

Loyce raised up higher on the pillows. Fate roused at the same time. From across the room she heard his legs unwind and a chair shift under his weight. Other feet shuffled in the dogtrot below, on the porch, everywhere. Was everyone still here from last night? Or had they gone home and come back?

Last night had been *her* night. Finally. She had been the one to go away and come back with a story to tell. Not just *a* story but the biggest story in Bayou Chene history. Encircled by Fate's arm, anchored by Drifter and all four pups on her feet, Loyce had spun out her story like silken net from a golden shuttle. Four stories, in fact—hers, Pank's, and two more. She made them all proud, if she did say so herself.

She drew her listeners in right at the moment she was snatched from the kitchen. She took them captive with her through that long night. Then exploring the plank walk, followed by the desperate exchange of cans and her doubts about whether it would work. She built up to the explosion and the shock of Drifter bumping against her leg. At that point she went blank and had to take Fate's word for the events that followed. Well, Fate's word backed up by Sam's.

"What do mean 'backed up by Sam'?" he'd protested. "I most likely saved your life today—that dog's life for the second time— and you don't even give me credit for being able to tell it straight? You couldn't have wandered much longer in that swamp before you stepped on a snake or a gator decided to snatch a bite out of Drifter. And what if I hadn't noticed that burlap sack? What would have become of the puppies? I guess old Pank shortchanged the toss, and it caught in that snag instead of falling all the way to the water. How much longer till that branch gave way?"

"Fate Landry, when you earn yourself a reputation of knowing the truth from a stretch—maybe a year or two of it—a body might start taking your word without backup," she shot back.

"Quit fussing with him, Loyce, for once," Adam had begged. "And get on with the telling."

A chorus of voices and feet shuffling around the bed told her the audience agreed with Adam. Loyce picked up her precious thread again, this time unraveling the mystery of Pank's disappearance. There were gasps and more shuffling as she revealed he had spied through the years without letting on he was alive.

"Not even his old mother!" Alcide shook his head in disgust. "That poor soul would've given years of her own life to know her worthless cub was alive."

Other voices rose up then, recalling small livestock or tools that had gone missing over the years. York never had admitted to turning loose Mary Ann's hogs. Had Pank tried to steal one and let them all escape? Had he been creeping around their homes at night as well as watching from afar?

"Oh, but we weren't the only people he spied on!" Loyce reined her listeners back in. She had listened to enough skillfully spun stories to know you save the best for last.

Using no visual cues, she brought her audience to the banks of Graveyard Bayou on that warm November day. The rocking chair splashing into the water. The sound of the woman clawing her way up a fish trap. The watcher wheezing from his hiding place in the brush. Mud sucking around his boots as he pushed his pirogue from the bank. Alcide's shout dashing the hope in an evil heart.

The chorus swelled again.

"No!"

"Well, I'll be damned!"

"That's C.B.'s account word for word!"

"C.B., what do you say about that?"

"Did you ever feel you was being watched?"

Loyce felt heads swivel away from her to where C.B. and Sam were standing.

"Being watched? I live next to a graveyard!" C.B. retorted. "Everything feels out of sorts over there."

Sam was already flushed with being named one of the heroes of the day. This new revelation—proof of C.B.'s innocence to anyone who still suspected her—nearly felled him. He leaned against the wall for support. Not only had he helped rescue Loyce but, just as surely, his own wife. He didn't even hear the fourth and final story.

Loyce didn't notice the loss of one listener. She was taking the others out to the big river. The night air damp on their faces. A paddle wheeler chuffing upstream. A man hunched over a cup of coffee behind the stove. Low voices whisper about happenings on the river—words not spoken when the sun is shining or even when the moon is bright. Among the dark doings a man—a rich man who didn't know enough to stop cheating even after he had been warned. Well, he was stopped all right. When it was discovered that he was not traveling alone, a lifeboat had been jettisoned along with his body. A story not too far off from true was made up and his wife—not knowing she was a widow—dumped in shame at the next stop.

Roseanne gasped. It was her turn to lean, and Adam was right there to catch her. Some things have a habit of repeating themselves, he thought. But unlike that first time a year ago, she was breathing easily underneath a loose shirtwaist. And this time she was soft in the middle, warm against his arm. Adam smiled. He figured he was the only man in the building who knew what was on page 459 of the catalog.

— 32 —

"Well, I still hang onto the notion that empty skiff started it all,"
Fate said. "Bringing Drifter first, then the Stocketts following it."

Murmurs for and against flowed around the room. He held up
a hand for silence.

"But Val, you and Adam were right too. That letter started its
own ruckus. Set me free is what it did, as sure as it broke the hold
on Mame's mind. That letter told me there was a reason I couldn't
squat flat on the bow of a boat like all you duck-legged boys I grew
up with. It meant I could quit trying."

Loyce sensed the toss of his head, but she couldn't see the dark
hair—worn longer than most, the green eyes daring the listeners to doubt, and the smile that said he might be kidding after all.
Put it all together, and any riverboat shyster wanted that face. It
partly explained why everyone but Loyce wanted to believe in his
schemes, hoped for him to be right this time. She couldn't see the
things that drew other people to him, made them *want* to believe,
even when they were making fun of his blowhard ways.

Like now. His confession about the letter was met with good-
natured whoops and cries of "That's as gooda reason as any to
quit!" Then the listeners shushed themselves and leaned forward
to catch the rest of the story. Fate, used to an audience, didn't even
acknowledge the brief interruption.

"That's right, that letter set me free. It told me why a big load
of fish didn't make my heart sing like it does the rest of you knuck-

leheads. A big load meant twice as much work as a little load, and none of it brought in the kind of money I wanted to make. Wambly was the only person who understood. His ideas didn't always work, but they gave me some directions to think on."

"Didn't *always* work?" Loyce spluttered. "You name me one that has worked, and that'll be one more than I ever heard about."

"What about putting a motor in a boat and hauling fish in ice?" Fate shot back. "Seems to me that worked out pretty good for someone you thought wouldn't amount to much."

"I never said you wouldn't amount—" she started but was drowned out by hoots and laughter from around the room.

"This is *my* story," he said. "You're done with telling for now. But you're in it. In fact, you're smack in the middle of it. That's right. When Mame was setting us straight about that letter, I looked across the room and saw you standing in that dress—the one colored like a great blue heron just like your eyes. Of course you can't see it for yourself, so you'll have to take my word for it, even though that goes against your nature."

Loyce swatted in his direction, but he dodged and clasped her hand in both of his, kissing her wrist before taking up his tale again. His voice dropped from teasing to tender.

"Anyway, I was already thinking how wrong it was for you to be standing on the edge again. I wished I could make things different for you."

"You weren't!" Her voice rose up the scale to suspicion.

"I was too!" he protested. "You never believe I really want to help—you just blame me for anything you have a mind to. Always have. I'm used to it."

He broke into a full laugh now and pulled her close to his chest. It wasn't a new embrace, no different from what they'd seen him do through the years. But now everyone in the room recognized a tenderness they hadn't noticed before, and for the first time ever Loyce didn't slap at him. Instead, she relaxed into his arms. The crowd jostled to hear what turn his story would take next.

"I was still looking at you while Mame read her letter to us. It started sinking in on me that I came by my differences honestly—

not better or worse than anyone who wants to fish and mend nets and pick moss, just different.

"Like a flash of lightning, it hit me—I was free! I was free to follow my sights. I came from stock that looked across the world and took a chance in a new business. All I had to my credit was a butter churn and some other things that just missed their mark—not by much, though, and that was encouraging."

"Encouraging for what?" Loyce's voice was still skeptical. "All I remember is you disappeared without a by-your-leave!"

"Well, can't you give a man time to get used to a new direction?" Fate sounded out. "The whole world had just opened to me. What was I going to make of it? Oh, I thought about trying to find out if Grandpa Michaud was still alive and what he did when our war interrupted his plans. Maybe I didn't want to know if he went broke, so as not to start off my new life discouraged. Or maybe it just seemed like it would slow me down too much. So much has happened since then, I can't rightly remember.

"What I did know was no new ideas would be coming to me on their own. I headed up to Atchafalaya Station, where other folks were looking outward for their future. The air was fairly buzzing around there with everybody making plans and building stuff to be ready for that railroad crossing. There was already a general store and a bakery making money from the railroad workers. Then there was an icehouse, moss gin, a sawmill. Oh, just every kind of thing you might want to ship out of the swamp. Mr. Bernard already had more than five hundred beehives! He's aiming to put honey from Atchafalaya bees on tables all over the country.

"I talked to everyone, not just Wambly. Before you know it, I had that icehouse owner believing we really could ship fresh fish. I got Wambly to working on finding me an old engine that I could mount in Sam's skiff."

"That's when you came down here to show it off," Loyce broke in. "Why didn't you tell me I had some part in all these plans, if it's the truth?"

"I meant to—that was as much the reason I came as to talk to

Sam and Uncle Adam." Fate's voice took on the old defensive tone. "But you was too het up to listen! All you wanted to do was tell me how it wasn't going to work, so I just kept it to myself until I could prove you wrong. Good thing Sam doesn't suffer from the suspicions like you do, or I wouldn't have had a partner.

"Sure, there was some trials and some blind bayous and more trials to follow. I know you heard about some of them. But you ain't heard what it felt like when I saw that first load of Atchafalaya buffalo head out for New York City! Knowing that I was the one who pulled all that together. Let me tell you right now, I never felt so proud pulling a net load of those same buffalo out of the water. Now, I admit I like to wore out the plank walk in front of that telegraph office waiting to hear if my fish showed up still fresh or sitting in warm slime and smelling up the depot."

"Your notions do have a way of ending in a powerful stink," Loyce offered.

"Well, not this time," Fate went on. "They still had a bed of ice and were all sold the next day in New York. Problem was, the ice cost me so much I didn't make any money. The icehouse owner shipped his ice in from Lafayette—all he did was store it. It was clear and clean like water you drink. I didn't see any future in shipping fish that cost me more in ice than they brought in, so I stopped everything until I could figure it out. That's when I found out that people get mad if you take away something they got used to real quick even though it wasn't so long ago they didn't even know they wanted it.

"Those fish sellers in New York was wanting to pay me money. I was wanting to pass that money on along to Sam and the others, but that blame ice was going to ruin us all. Then I thought, why can't we make our own ice from river water? No one's gonna drink it. We just need to bed down the fish. It's the same water they spent their whole life swimming in.

"The icehouse man was willing to try it, but we had to find someone to put up the money for the equipment. Wambly knew some men in Baton Rouge willing to do that. Ooooh! Not men I want to spend a lot of time with, but they saw the promise in that idea. Once we took their money, though, I knew we couldn't miss the payback date or bad things was bound to happen."

"That must be the men I saw you talking with at the dock café in Baton Rouge," Val broke in. "I wouldn't want to run into them on a dark night, no."

"And that's just what would have happened if I didn't make that payback date," Fate said. "They woulda just knocked me in the head on a dark night and slipped me off a dock when no one was around to see the splash! For the next few months I was hopping. Trains left the station twice a day. If we missed one of those, it was a twelve-hour wait for the next one. Not a problem if you shipping moss, but fish and ice is different. If something broke at the ice plant, there was no putting off getting it fixed. I found out the fish dealers ordered more and paid sooner if I visited New York now and then to see what their end of it was like. I tell you, on some weeks it seemed like I needed to be three places at once.

"When I was getting so distracted that Dieu Cavalier nearly shot my head off because I forgot to pick up his ducks, I knew I had to make changes. First thing I did was turn my boat over to Sam to pick up and deliver the fish. That way I could stay around the ice plant to help keep it running smooth and catch a ride with the fish up to New York when I had to. That helped, but then I couldn't keep up with my post office box in Atchafalaya. Bills came in; money had to go out. Money came in and had to be accounted for.

"Just before I got wore to a frazzle, Wambly told me I ought to hire me some help—a bookkeeper. He said some classes at LSU was teaching people to do just that—keep accounts for business. That's how I found Rona, Rona Castille. I had my post office box changed to Baton Rouge so she could pick up my mail. She keeps my books in a corner of her husband's office. Once a month I take the train to Baton Rouge, and we go over what came in and what went out. It all makes sense when you see it laid out like that."

"I heard you were seeing someone named Rona, but we all just thought she was a new sweetheart!" Adam broke in. "What do you know about that!"

Loyce, trying to remember if she had ever said anything aloud about Rona Castille, didn't say a word. She took for granted that her own expression didn't give away emotions that sighted people could read, but she wasn't sure. In no time at all the talk took off again, but she heard less and less as the events of the past two days caught up with her and she nodded off to sleep, still anchored by Fate and Drifter.

— 33 —

Once again, the *Golden Era*'s whistle drifted into the post office on a soft breeze, accompanied by the familiar smells of fish, tar, and cypress trees. So like that day more than a year ago when a misplaced letter and a near-dead dog showed up. Loyce breathed it all in, storing it up in her memory just the way she stored away her wedding dress in the traveling trunk at her feet. She knew how it was when someone left the Chene. Despite the best intentions, they usually never made it back.

Of course, it sounded like she and Fate would be traveling more than most. His new job with the Lockwood-Ash Motor Company would take them initially to Michigan. Then they would travel to river towns all over the country, where Fate would demonstrate the advantages of a gasoline boat to fishermen. He also would set up retail branches for Lockwood-Ash, probably in existing machine shops, where mechanics could service the engines for customers.

Fate had already helped Mary Ann's father set up his shop to sell replacement parts and provide repairs right there in Plaquemine. York was now looking into starting a branch of the family business on the Chene, what with all the fishermen setting their sights on gasoline boats. Leave it to York to seize on an opportunity when it was in plain sight, Loyce thought.

It took someone with vision—someone like Fate—to get something new and exciting started. She had to admit this notion of his had worked out better than the others. And now wherever his work or his fancy took them, she would listen to music in every theater or concert hall along the way. Who could tell? She might even find ways to join in making that music.

"Do you have everything now?" Roseanne broke into her thoughts and began fussing over the new traveling trunk and a tapestry duffel bag. "What am I saying?" Roseanne stopped to laugh at herself. "You'll have so much more to choose from out there than you could ever get here!"

Out there. To Loyce the place that once stood for loss and longing now held shining promise. Wherever they lived *out there* she would have running water, an indoor bathroom, gas heat, sidewalks. *Out there* held solutions to the things that made life dangerous and confining for a blind woman at the Chene.

"Heck, now that Fate's showing off motors, you'll be shopping in cities up and down the rivers," said Adam. "It'll be like carrying that mail-order catalog wherever you go."

"But wherever she goes, she won't find anything prettier than this!" C.B. announced as she twirled through the back door in a new chartreuse skirt and bosom-hugging top. Her hair once again glowed with her favorite yellow dye. "Mrs. Barclay, you can accuse me of anything, anytime, if the apologies always include a new frock."

"C.B., you are the only person who could ever get me to order something that color." Roseanne shook her head in mock sorrow. "Take that as a compliment if you like."

"Well, maybe you should be thanking poor old Pank for that frock," chimed in Alcide. "He's the one who set the record straight for both of you. There's no telling what all he knew about the doings up and down the river, not just around here. The way he'd been spying for all those years—eight? ten maybe? But we'll never know because he took 'em to his grave."

Loyce shivered at the memory of the blast in her ears. She tried to put it out of her mind along with the unsavory stories Pank had related during his last night on earth. For Roseanne's benefit Loyce was glad she had paid attention to the story of Charles

Barclay's murder. And even though most people at the Chene had already moved beyond the rumors about C.B., Loyce was happy to be the one who cleared her friend's name beyond any doubt. As for Pank, his remains now rested in the graveyard where he had once spied on the yellow-haired object of his dreams.

"All of it might still be a secret if Drifter hadn't been watching out for me," Loyce added. "And I could have ended up as one more story about a mysterious disappearance."

At the sound of her name the little dog thumped her tail on the floor. The movement disturbed Jack, her remaining pup. He hiccupped and rolled over on his back, four white paws paddling the air. Adam and Roseanne had quickly claimed Jack because he looked most like Drifter. Sam, Alcide, and Mary Ann had snatched up the other three before anyone else had a chance to see them.

Fate looked up from where he was snapping the locks on his own bag and ruffled Drifter's ears. "The day she showed up, I told you she could be a help, Loyce; now you gotta admit I was right!" Before Loyce could counter a reply, he added, "Here comes Mary Ann, now. Everyone ready?"

They all trooped out to the pony cart, which Mary Ann had draped with ribbon and flowers for the sendoff. Fate hoisted Loyce up to the seat beside Mary Ann and then climbed into the back of the cart with their luggage. Adam and Roseanne linked arms to follow along the woods path to the dock. Mame and Alcide fell in step together. Sam, carrying Sam Junior, walked beside C.B. Drifter trotted in and out of the party with Jack running to keep up. Neighbors lined the path to join in the merriment, beating on pots and pans, blowing whistles and shouting good wishes.

When they rounded the bend to the dock, the *Golden Era* greeted them with three cheery blasts of her whistle. Valzine Broussard, working his way from deckhand back up to first mate, helped the newlyweds aboard. He and Loyce had never mentioned their mutual relief over the turn of events, just like they had never voiced the words between them that could have ruined three lives. Sometimes a long silence was best left undisturbed.

Drifter trotted behind Loyce across the gangplank. Roseanne

scooped Jack into her arms to keep him from following. Adam handed up the mailbag.

Only two letters were bearing the Bayou Chene postmark that day—June 21, 1908. One envelope, following its ill-fated predecessor forty-seven years to the day, was seeking Michaud Poussant in a French Pyrénées mountain village. It introduced his smart, ambitious grandson Lafayette Landry to anyone who still lived at that address. The other was to the George Garnier family of Eleonore Street, New Orleans, announcing the upcoming nuptials of Roseanne Garnier Barclay to Adam Snellgrove, Bayou Chene postmaster.

The *Golden Era* whistled farewell. The big paddles dipped and churned the water. Drifter ran in circles and barked as Loyce waved good-bye in the wrong direction. Fate tried to redirect her but got his hands slapped for his trouble.

SEPARATING FACT FROM FICTION

Facts

The **village of Bayou Chene** existed from ancient times, first as a home for the Chitimacha and other native people. Europeans discovered it in the 1600s, followed by Americans after the Louisiana Purchase. After the 1927 flood, as part of the channelization of the Atchafalaya River, the village was sealed off from the water that gave it life. By the mid-twentieth century most permanent residents had moved to settlements on the levees, taking with them the wealth of that community—their stories—to hand down to future generations.

In 1907 the **Bayou Chene Post Office** was located at the intersection of Jakes Bayou and Bloody Bayou. My great-grandfather Lewis C. B. Ashley was the postmaster at that time. His daughter, Josie, grew up in that hubbub. Josie's mother would not let her travel on the school boat to go to the upper grades, so after third grade Josie continued her education by sorting mail while standing on a packing crate to reach the counter. And of course, she learned to tell stories. Josephine Ashley married George Gilbert Voisin to become my Grandma Josephine Voisin.

Alcide Verret and **Calvin Voisin** are the only names of real people in the novel. I used Alcide's real name because I wanted to preserve this beloved old man as I knew him in 1970. Even though

Alcide would have been just a boy on the Chene in 1907. I've tried to capture his looks, his voice, his gallant flirtatiousness, and his expansive love of life for readers who did not have the pleasure of meeting him.

Calvin Voisin, child of Warren and Mame Voisin, never returned after walking down to bail the boats after a rain. His body was never found. Sudden and unexplained deaths or disappearances were not unusual in swamp communities, where so many dangers lurked. As with other people who died before we were born, young Calvin might slip from history as if he had never lived. I wanted to preserve the fact that he had lived and how he died. Calvin's baby brother, Warren Voisin Jr., honored the little boy by naming his own firstborn Calvin. That Calvin Voisin is my cousin and was my fellow adventurer in the memoir *Atchafalaya Houseboat*.

The confusing practice of **reusing given names** was very common at the Chene. Several generations of one family could have members with the same name. Adding to the confusion were women marrying into the family bringing their own common first names, like Mary Ann Bertram does in the story.

The **returned letter** is based on a real piece of undelivered mail bearing that blue Civil War–era postmark SOUTHERN LETTER UNPAID. In 2005 I had already determined that the post office would be the central feature in my novel, almost a character in its own right. I searched the term *Bayou Chene* online to see what research materials would surface. I found that a letter mailed from Bayou Chene was one of five remaining known pieces of mail bearing that blue stamp. A major auction house in New York was selling them as a bundle. The catalog description told the story of the blue stamp created by the Kentucky postmaster. Of the five letters the one mailed from Bayou Chene was pictured in the listing. I tacked a print of that letter over my desk. Every time I looked at it, I pondered what kind of trouble an undelivered letter could cause if it was returned to Bayou Chene forty-plus years after it had been mailed. I started with what I could make out from the faded date—June 21, 1861—and addressee in Hautes-Pyrénées, France.

I researched the history of the Pyrénées area and discovered that the economy, based on a dye made from a blue crustacean, lost out to the indigo plantations in the United States. Everything else about the letter, Mame, and Michaud is fiction.

Death by exploding fuel cans really did happen, at least once. Alcide Verret's first wife and two children died in such an explosion. No one knows for sure if the mistake was hers or that of the boat store that sold it to them.

Beekeeping was a viable occupation around the Chene, with at least one apiarian, Charles Henry Waterhouse, listed in the 1900 census. Paul Viallon of Bayou Goula was a pharmacist, apiarist, researcher, and writer for bee journals as well as a manufacturer of hive boxes and frames in the early 1900s. It makes sense that a beekeeper at Bayou Chene would have purchased supplies from Paul Viallon.

Fiction

Wambly Cracker's name, appearance, and personality came to me in a dream. I woke my husband, Preston, and said: "In case I forget, in the morning remind me of the name Wambly Cracker. He's going to be a character in my novel." I have no idea where that name came from; as far as I know, I had never heard it before my dream.

While **Adam, C.B., Fate, Loyce, Mary Ann, Roseanne, Sam, and York** came wholly out of my imagination, they represent the ways people came, settled, and eventually left the Chene community. They also represent the diverse socioeconomic and educational backgrounds of those hardy settlers.

Somewhere in Between

Loyce Snellgrove was inspired by my blind aunt, Lois Voisin, who was born after my family moved from the Chene in the 1920s. She cheerfully lived life as fully as her overprotective family would allow, and she served as the example of higher education in my family because she went all the way to the eighth grade at the Louisiana State School for the Blind in Baton Rouge. I've wondered what her life would have been like had she been born while the family still lived at the Chene, so I explored it for this book. I took the liberty of setting her free to a richer life than a blind woman could have enjoyed at the Chene.

All other first and last names were taken from the 1860–1900 census records around Bayou Chene. The names were chosen because I liked the sound or because they represented one of the ethnic cultures common to the area. The Chene was incredibly diverse, with settlers coming from all over this continent as well as right off the boats from the Old World. Other than the names of Alcide Verret and Calvin Voisin, any combination of first and last names belonging to actual persons was inadvertent.

For my fictional villain, **Pank Neeley**, I deliberately chose a name that didn't show up in census records so as not to embarrass any real families. There is a newspaper account of a Bayou Chener who used the defense that he didn't intend to shoot his girlfriend but, rather, was aiming at a rival beau who was walking with her.

Peter Bunch used to tell of seeing a **corpse with iron cooking pots** tied on each side when he was a boy. It was the first dead person he had ever seen. They never found out the man's identity. Mr. Bunch pointed out to me the burial place near his tar vat.

I heard from Alcide Verret and other people the story of a **woman whose rocking chair dumped her and the baby off the deck of the houseboat.** In some versions the baby survived, just as in my book. In other accounts it did not. Considering the number of houseboats and the fact that so many swampers, particularly women, never learned to swim, it's understandable that this particular tragedy could have befallen more than one family and with different outcomes.

Florence Chauvin told me a story of a Chener who went AWOL from a war and **lived in the woods, spying on his family for years,** lonesome but too afraid to come home. When Florence was a child, in the early 1900s, Indians found the man nearly dead from malnutrition and brought him back home. He lived out the rest of his life in a small houseboat. For little Florence, going to visit him was great entertainment because he was so mysterious.

ACKNOWLEDGMENTS

As a career nonfiction writer I was mystified by authors who could imagine characters and events that never existed. So, it was a cruel joke when Cairo Beauty, Fate, Loyce, and Val started swirling around in the air above my head, and I realized I wouldn't rest until I put them to paper.

One of my first discoveries was that a novel in progress is like a pregnant cat—no one makes eye contact when they see you coming with one. I was blessed with friends and professionals who not only invited me in but asked for a kitten.

Fellow nonfiction writer and connoisseur of fiction Laurie Cochrane asked repeatedly to read the earliest draft I was willing to turn loose. Her gentle nudges kept me working until I had something I thought might not be a complete waste of her time. She discovered potential in characters and plot that I couldn't see for myself, gifting me with a clearer vision for the book.

Greg Guirard gave voice to my half-Cajun character Val. Whenever I read Val, it's Greg's voice I hear. Calvin Voisin, whose own speech defines the vanishing cadence of Bayou Chene, listened to my Chene voices for authenticity. He also checked that I still knew how to describe setting out nets and cleaning catfish.

Shannon Whitfield, Georgia Luckett Champion, and John Mayne read from an outsider's point of view, catching phrases that would bewilder readers from the other forty-nine states.

Editor Margaret Lovecraft did such a thorough job of keeping me in line that now, whenever my husband or I run into fractured fiction, we admonish the page or screen with "Margaret wouldn't let you get away with that!"

Maria Hebert-Leiter, an early critic for the manuscript, was an inspiration. Maria's detailed commentary guided me in plumping my bare-bones manuscript into a more satisfying story. Copyeditor Elizabeth Gratch guided it through the final stage with skill, humor, and a clever eye for detail.

I relied on historians Jim Delahoussaye and C. Ray Brassieur for details about traditional boatbuilding and fish buying. Bayou Chene descendants and historians Bob Carline and Stella Carline Tanoos shared their anecdotes, newspaper clippings, maps, and lifetimes of research. Errors in facts such as dates, water depths, rake of bow, or the selling price of Spanish moss in 1907 belong to me, not the historians.

My husband, Preston, tiptoed the narrow, blurry line of being supportive but honest.